Michael,

No... I'm not *copying*
you..! I just saw this
book and thought you'd
appreciated a little fiction
to help escape some of
the day-to-day realities.

Love forever,
Demetria
Merry X-MAS

R L ' s   D R E A M

RL's Dream

BY WALTER MOSLEY

W. W. Norton & Company

New York / London

Copyright © 1995 by Walter Mosley
All rights reserved
Printed in the United States of America

The text of this book is composed in 10/13 Palatino
with the display set in Avenir Black and Giotto Bold.
Composition and manufacturing by the Haddon Craftsmen, Inc.
Book design by Michael Chesworth

Library of Congress Cataloging-in-Publication Data
Mosley, Walter.
RL's dream / by Walter Mosley.
p.   cm.
I. Title.
PS3563.O88456R5   1995
813'.54—dc20   95-8695
ISBN 0-393-03802-5

W. W. Norton & Company, Inc., 500 Fifth Avenue, New York, N.Y. 10110
W. W. Norton & Company Ltd., 10 Coptic Steet, London WC1A 1PU

3 4 5 6 7 8 9 0

For Leroy Mosley
(1916–1993)

RL wasn't no real man. A real man gits born, does what li'l he can, and then he dies. That's it! You could remember a real man and say how he lived an' how he died. But RL fooled you. He played the guitar when he shouldn't'a been able to, an' nobody knows how he died. Maybe it was the pneumonia, maybe a jealous man. Satan coulda come an' made him bark like a dog 'fore takin' him home.

But us po' fools lookin' fo' his story is lost 'fore we begin. 'Cause Robert Johnson wasn't never born an' couldn't die. He was Delta blue from the bottom of his soul. He was the blues; he is today. Ain't no start to his misery. An' death could not never ease his kinda pain.

Soupspoon Wise
Back Road to the Blues (1986)
Transcribed by Gerald Pickford

R L ' s D R E A M

Z E R O

Pain moved up the old man's hipbone like a plow breaking through hard sod. So much pain he could barely think. He shit himself on the long walk from the shelter toward home and fell in the street more than once. No one moved to help him—passersby steered a wide path to get away from the smell. Soupspoon Wise staggered up Bowery toward the East Village imagining being home again, away from the dormitory of disheveled men. Those gibbering and farting men calling out to people who weren't there.

Three blocks from the apartment he felt a crack come into the bone. A blood-black splinter that went so deep he cried out, "Oh, no!" His diaphragm trembled and the choked sobs came out in a broken whine. He went down on his left knee while trying to keep the right leg straight. He could have died on that frozen street, counting out the time between sighs—fingers drumming on his chest.

Music thrummed in his body; the rattles of death in the tortured song of his breathing. Soon he was moving his head to this rhythm; even the crackling pain in his hip pulsed in time. He got back to his feet and hobbled to the new music, reeling and rocking on a river of unsteady feet. Maybe he'd die before he got there. But he'd die singing and making music out of life the way real men did it a long time ago.

In the hot apartment the pipes still clanged and hissed steam even though it was spring. Soupspoon fell into the bed—soiling it. Even the feather mattress hurt him. Pain pulsed in his ears and leg until he longed to turn it off. His body shook with every heartbeat. He counted the beats until he forgot the pain and then, when the ache came back, he counted again. Soupspoon got to know his body weight so well that he could make minute shifts to keep the pain at bay. But he couldn't make it to the toilet and he couldn't sleep. Instead he conjured up a young man with short nappy hair and one dead eye. The young man didn't care about Soupspoon's plight but he didn't mind stopping awhile to visit. He wore homemade overalls and no shirt, and smirked like a fox with a belly full of chickens.

In the afternoon the old man crawled from the fouled mattress. In the kitchen he clung to the sink and sucked water from the tarnished spigot the way he'd done at the well when he was a boy in Cougar Bluff, Mississippi. Then he pulled a five-pound sack of flour from the cabinet, letting it fall heavily to the drainboard. While eating the raw powder he considered going into the hall and lying on the cold concrete out there until someone took pity and killed him— or saved him.

Leaning over the kitchen sink, using his arms to keep his weight, he felt less pain. He let the water run until it had the cold bite of a deep well in winter, holding his hands under the flow until they were numb.

There were rat turds on the sink.

"Po' rat gotta eat too. They's more than enough flour for the both of us."

When the doorknob jiggled he didn't notice. Even when the door came open he wasn't surprised. He turned, though, to see who it was. That's when he realized that his arms had gone numb and he fell hard to the kitchen floor.

O N E

"Tanya!" a heavyset colored girl yelled as she jumped into the subway car. "You bettah git yo' butt ovah here!"

She landed awkwardly, almost dropping her schoolbooks. Kiki eyed the fake rabbit fur and the lime-green hose that came up to the girl's tight brown miniskirt.

An electronic bell chimed and the doors began to close.

Somewhere outside two girls screamed, "LaToya!"

Kiki felt her stomach tighten and then the jagged stitch of pain down her left side. LaToya pushed her shoulders forward and her butt back against the door. The door stuttered on its rails and then slid open again. A sneer of grim satisfaction passed across LaToya's pear face.

Two more black girls came running in. One screaming, one laughing and bumping from behind. In the reflection of the window across the aisle Kiki saw the elderly white lady seated next to her take a shopping bag from the floor and hug it to her bony, blue-bloused chest.

At the far end of the car a small brown man, dressed all in charcoal colors, looked up.

"Release the door in back. Another train is right behind us," a woman's voice commanded from the loudspeaker. The bell sounded again and the doors slammed shut. The hum of the engine died and the train started off, first with a jerk and then into the smooth glide of steel on steel. Kiki's bruised stomach lurched along with the train.

The girls sat in a bunch across the aisle. They were all large. The two latecomers wore jeans and sat on either side of the girl with the big green legs. The one on Kiki's left had on a bulky brown sweater from which her stomach and breasts bulged sensually. Her hair was combed and tied back the way Kiki remembered Hattie's hair back home. The other girl's hair was a mess; all ironed and half braided. Her jacket was a boy's football coat; yellow and green with frayed cotton cuffs.

Nigger-bitches.

The voice seemed to whisper right at the back of Kiki's neck.

Nigger-bitches ain't worth a damn.

It was Katherine Loll, Kiki's redheaded aunt from Hogston. She was skinny and sour-faced and hated coloreds for taking the food right out of her mouth. ". . . and them nigger-bitches the worst ones. Filthy, rotten, and low," Katherine would say. That was when she could still talk, before the cancer took out her voice. The two years before she died, Aunt Katherine breathed out of a puckered hole in her throat.

Kiki hated Katherine. She hated the white trash attitudes. The names they used for Negroes and Jews; the jealousies and poverty. She hated how frizzy-haired Katherine smelled of beer and lard. But still the words went through her like electricity. A shudder of hatred for these girls.

"Dog," the unkempt one said, her mouth hanging open. All three were gaping at the smutty paperback book open flat in a notebook on the center girl's lap. The cheap paper was almost brown and the letters were so large it might have been an elementary school reader.

In the window Kiki saw the man in charcoal clothes get up and walk to within a few seats of the girls. He sat down delicately and stretched his neck, not to see what smut they were reading but to watch them reading it. His eyes devoured their young lips and breasts. His nostrils flared as if he were inhaling the breath of them.

Kiki wanted to get up and tell him to get away. But the thought of moving made her lay the palm of her hand against the soft flesh below her ribs—feeling for the dampness of blood.

When the brakes screeched the girls listed to the side; their eyes all remained glued to the page as the station filled the windows behind them. The girl in the sweater was grinning; the other two were wide-eyed in awe.

"Fifty-ninth Street, Bloomingdale's," the loudspeaker said.

The white couple came into the car looking at each other. ". . . with the wife. We're going down to St. Croix for a week," the chubby man, wearing a tan jacket made from some kind of synthetic blend, said. He looked like an eight-year-old that had been puffed up into man-size. The woman with him was young also, dressed in a fine maroon silk business suit. They didn't look around to see who was in the car. They didn't care about anything or anyone but him. He went on talking about his wife and his kids and his trip. She was smiling but it was that same smile of hatred that Katherine had for Negroes.

". . . we go every year. The kids love it. They got a park for kids right on the hotel grounds. . . ."

The doors slammed closed and the car went on.

"Dang," the sweater-breasted girl intoned. "Roger said Marie did that."

The sliding door banged open in the back of the car. The women all looked up. A Chinese man came by carrying a pile of hand-painted bamboo calendars over his left arm. He showed them first to the chubby man and maroon lady, then to the old woman and Kiki. There was a billowing yellow-and-red dragon, a tea garden with serving girls, and Hokusai's great wave. He didn't bother showing his wares to the girls or the little man.

The girls were crouched low over the book like kittens licking from a bowl. Above their heads Kiki could see the murky image of herself, no longer a girl in her twenties. Pale with crinkled red hair limp from days without washing. She traced the dark shadows under her eyes, thinking that she looked as if someone had beaten her.

"You're very pretty," the little man said in a slight Jamaican accent. He was talking to the girls.

"Mmmmmmmmmmmmm," the girl to the left hummed. LaToya slammed the book shut and shoved it back into her folder. Then they all leaned their heads together and laughed.

The train was moving fast, rocking from side to side as it rushed on. The old woman held a string of garnet rosary beads in her left hand. The maroon-silk woman lost her smile as she gazed up into the great moon face of the chubby man. And he talked and talked. Kiki watched his mouth move but all she could hear was the black girls' laughter. Laughter like hard fists. Kiki half-closed her eyes and held on to the rim of her seat through the storm of laughing fists in a haze of queasy pain.

One of the girls said something to the little man, but Kiki couldn't make it out. They laughed and rubbed shoulders. The man stared intently at the girl in the sweater, the one who had her hair like Hattie's. But she didn't look like Hattie. Hattie's skin was so dark that it was actually black. And all of her teeth had spaces between them. And even though Hattie was large her stomach never stuck out like that. And when she laughed it was a bass holler that tickled Kiki's neck from across the room.

A priest and a man in a gray suit got on together at the next station. When the train stopped again the conductor announced Fourteenth Street.

Kiki reached for the small cloth bag under the seat. The bag that the orderly had given her when she told him that she didn't have a suitcase.

It hurt to stand up. She could feel every stitch pull against torn skin.

The girls were ahead of her going out the door.

"Thank you," the little brown man said as they filed past him. When nobody answered he touched the last girl's arm.

"Thank you," he said again.

"What?" the girl in the football coat shouted. "What you want?"

"You should say thank you when you get a compliment," he said.

Maybe he was really hurt, Kiki thought.

"Come on, Clarice," her friends said.

Kiki could feel every step on the inside where the doctor said that the stitches would dissolve on their own. Some kind of plastic thread melting right up inside her.

The local train was waiting across the track. The girls were there, also the old lady with the shopping bag.

At Astor Place everybody got out. All of them, even the old lady, walked faster than Kiki. She watched them go, the girls laughing about what they had read and the lady struggling with her bag. Kiki had to take the stairs one at a time. Every step up jabbed into her. Sweat was trickling down her neck by the time she'd reached the top stair. There the frozen wind blew through her clothes, right down to her skinny frame.

Four hooded boys were standing at the corner. They were smoking cigarettes and bobbing their heads to the beat of loud hip-hop that blasted from a boom box set on the ground near them. They were young, twelve or thirteen. All wore tennis shoes, unlaced. Three of them had on jeans so loose that they threatened to fall off their skinny boy hips. The largest one wore satiny purple-and-pink-striped running pants. They were talking tough, making gestures like full-grown black men with little-boy grins. Kiki turned her back to them and went quickly through the crowds down to Broadway and around the block. She hated them too. Nausea rode on the wave of hatred. Kiki leaned against the store window at Astor and Broadway and threw up all the neatly cut carrots and green beans they'd fed her for lunch at the hospital. She went down on one knee and her side felt as if it had ripped open.

"Honey! Honey, what's wrong?" The cold fingers at the back of her neck felt good. Really good. Strong hands in her armpits and a feeling of weightlessness. The mature woman's face brought Kiki back to when she had the intestinal flu and Hattie took her home to care for her because her mother was too weak, and daddy never did know how to take care of little girls.

"Thanks, Hattie," Kiki said, more in a dream than on that cold March corner.

"What? Who did you call me?" The woman was short and pecan-colored. She had on a big red cotton hat and a zigzag quilted coat of many greens, blues, and yellows. Her bag was black patent leather, her shoes hospital white. "Look at what you done here. Here," she said, taking a large white handkerchief from her bag. "Clean the mess off your sweater." Then she began to wipe the cloth against Kiki's chest. Kiki leaned into the pelting blows, a girl again, so sad that she had thrown up.

"You okay, honey?"

The rush-hour crowd flowed around them. Some people would stop to stare a moment before moving on—like she was some kind of sideshow for them to snigger at.

"Yes, Hattie, m'okay."

"You sure?"

"Uh-huh." Kiki remembered another black face. The hard-faced little boy hating her so much that he seemed to hurt. He could hardly wait to do some harm.

"Thank you," Kiki said, not knowing whether she was going to throw up or cry. "Thank you, I'm okay now."

"You live near here?" the woman asked. "You need a taxi?"

"I'm real close, honey. Don't you mind," Kiki said. Her own words soothed her. The boy's face now far off, lurking somewhere in the crowds. His memory like the ache in her side: if she kept very still it remained at bay.

"Here." The woman pushed the handkerchief on Kiki. "You take care of yourself, honey. Take care."

Kiki watched her move away in the crowd. She pressed her bare cheek against the cold glass of the display window and watched the woman, dressed like a patchwork parachute, weave away. She could have almost gone to sleep there amid the droning motors and scuffling feet.

Even two blocks away she could see the yellow of the cold-fingered lady's coat.

The Astor Café was all glass and Formica. Kiki ate there every morning at seven-thirty before taking the subway down to Marshall & Pryde. It was crowded in the late afternoon. She held the hospital bag over the stain on her sweater and walked right to the ladies' room before anyone could say no.

They kept the heat up high in the rest rooms at the Astor. Sitting on the toilet, she wanted to sleep again. The heat and the running tap lulled her.

Kiki took off her sweater and got barefoot. She sat there letting the dry steam heat sink into her shoulders and feet. Then she unbuttoned her blouse, draping it over the pile of sweater and shoes. In the mirror she could follow the lines of freckles across her chest. She caressed her shoulders lightly with her fingers grazing the skin. She was happy, almost stupid with the heat.

The face in the mirror belonged to the same girl who lived in a shotgun shack next to Nigger Town in Hogston, Arkansas. That was before her daddy made it rich. They had a Plunkett water heater on the back porch. She'd go back there with Riley Mathias and Brewster Collins and lay up against the tank with a day blanket and oranges stolen from Aunt Katherine's basket. . . .

If her parents were out she'd give the boys kisses for nickels; but it cost a quarter if they wanted some tongue. If it was just Brewster, sometimes she wouldn't even collect, just let him owe her for someday when she was broke.

She closed her eyes, remembering one rainy day when Riley ran home because he didn't want to get wet. It was summer and still hot in spite of the rain. Kiki and Brewster didn't mind, though. They played in the rain until they were soaked to the bone and then they crawled up next to the water heater. She let him steal lip kisses and even stuck out her tongue now and then.

The gas jet through the grating was blowing blue flame. Their clothes made soft sucking sounds which Kiki associated with sex.

Katherine hacked on and off from the couch at the front of the house, but they didn't worry that she'd find them; Katherine was too sick by then to get around on her own.

"Bite me right here, Brewster." Kiki had pulled up her calf-length plaid skirt to reveal her skinny right thigh. "Bite me or I'll never be your friend again."

She closed her eyes so that all she knew was the clamping teeth on her skin.

"Harder . . . harder."

She put her hand on Brewster's head and patted it just like he was her dog.

"Harder, li'l boy," she said.

When the pain got to be too much she counted up to ten and then said, "Okay, stop! Right now! Stop it!" And she hit Brewster on his neck and on both sides of his head.

Later on she made him look at the dark bruise he'd caused. She put his fingers on the hot lump it made. Brewster's light blue eyes turned into lanterns of fear.

"If I ever show my daddy, you're dead, Brewster."

Loud knocking made her open her eyes on the emaciated image in the mirror.

"Are you okay, miss?" somebody asked through the door.

"Just a minute."

Kiki shoved the blouse and socks into the hospital bag and turned the light gray sweater inside out, tearing the tag from the back. Then she put the sweater back on, threw water in her face, and smiled her fierce tiger-smile into the water-stained mirror.

Randy was selling his magazines from a small folding table on St. Mark's Place. He had *Stroke* and *Vixens* splayed out in a double fan shape and a box full of back-issue X-Men and Spider-Man comic books on the side.

"Kiki! Where've you been? I called every day last week." Randy came around the table, pushing his long stringy dreadlocks back over his shoulder.

"I got stabbed," she said, putting her hand up to ward off his touch.

"What?"

"Goddamn little niggers all over this woman on Chrystie. You know? Prob'ly a schoolteacher. I don't know what she was, because she ran after they stuck me."

"What happened?" The concern on Randy's face accented his hybrid features. The broad nose and sad gray eyes. He had a long and angular face, like the Swedish actor Max von Sydow. His eggshell-brown skin and twiny dreadlocks marked him as a Negro, but Randy had a tight walk and way of talking that Kiki associated with northern whites.

He'd once taken her to a room over the Chinese laundry. She asked to see where he kept all the magazines and then they were on the little cot in the corner. She still couldn't inhale the odor of old magazines without thinking of that peculiar bony weight on her chest and the shock of Randy's small black cock buried in thickly coiled pubic hair.

"You surprised?" he'd asked with a wide grin.

"Yeah," Kiki said as she grabbed the thing and squeezed it.

"Uh . . . big, huh?"

"Ain't so big really, but it sure is black."

Even now, on the cold streets, she remembered how sweet he was. The memory bringing that jagged ripping feeling inside.

"They were messing with her," Kiki said. "And I came up, you know, to help her. I mean, they were just kids. But this one boy, this one boy . . ." *The boys were all over the schoolteacher, pushing at her and grabbing at her bag. The fool was playing scared, and those boys, those boys were on her like flies on shit. They were little boys. Some of them seven or eight and not one over ten. But there were lots of them. Nine maybe. Then the teacher started to scream. Kiki tried to protect her from the little attackers, but there was this hard-faced little boy. He hated Kiki. He screamed and it would have been funny if she hadn't seen the knife. He swung once and Kiki slapped his face in return, but weakly, and then he did it again and again. She was on her knees. Somebody was screaming.*

"Kiki! Kiki!" Randy shouted. He was shaking her. "What's wrong, honey? Oh shit. You're bleeding."

Kiki looked down to see the spots of blood that had stained the inside of her sweater.

"I was on my knees," she said to some point beyond Randy's eyes. "But I stood up to him. He mighta killed me, but I wasn't scared." She shook her head slowly—denying the pain of any blow that she'd ever been dealt. "I'm not really bleedin'. They got these tubes comin' out to drain it. It's not too bad."

When Kiki realized that Randy was holding her she pulled away.

"I gotta go home, I'm really dead," she said.

"Hold up a minute, sugar," Randy said, not letting her go. "Hey! Man-well, Man-well."

A small Puerto Rican man selling art books a few feet down turned to look.

"Watch my stuff for half an hour?"

The pock-faced little man nodded.

"I don't need your help." Kiki heard her father's voice in hers— slurred and lopsided like when he'd been at the Thunderbird and they were all locked in for the night.

She tried to pull away, but Randy just held on and began to walk. They went down St. Mark's. Past the bookstore window and dozens of young women and men who sported pink spiked hairdos and safety-pinned flesh, many with peekaboo tattoos under torn clothes that exposed every possible color of skin. Past the outside game machines and the boys who played them. The wind kicked up and Kiki felt cold everywhere except her side. That was hot and cramped.

"I don't need you to help me, Randy," she said, but she leaned against him when he put his arm around her and she didn't struggle when he took her bag.

He smelled of patchouli oil and sweat, of old magazines.

"I just wanna take you home, honey. That's all."

"You ain't gettin' any with the way I been butchered, so you might as well give it up."

"You've been saying that for months anyway. If that's what I was after I wouldn't even say boo."

"It hurts, honey," Kiki said as she watched St. Mark's pass by through his swinging dreadlocks.

"We'll be there soon, Kiki."

And they walked down to the park with its fires and shanty tents. All the people living through the cold snap in the New York spring. Down to Sixth Street and over toward the Beldin, past Avenue C.

T W O

Soupspoon Wise sat out on the sidewalk in a dilapidated chair, a blanket wrapped tightly around his shoulders. He was staring up at the facade of the Beldin Arms. The bronze letters had been pried off and stolen years before. You could barely make out the words in the cracked, discolored granite arch.

The arch protected an oak door that had been painted green in '64, and again in '78. The panels on either side of the door were beveled glass when Soupspoon first moved in. The fancy glass had been busted out and replaced with plain glass. The plain glass had been busted out and replaced with pine plank. The graffiti boys put down every curse word they learned in school on those planks.

A large colored man came out of the doorway carrying Soupspoon's folding chairs and a drawer from his rosewood dresser. He dropped them on the curb, then turned to go back into the building. Another man came out, a white man, carrying the rest of the drawers from the dresser that Soupspoon got when he and Mavis broke up. The white man threw the drawers down, spilling old clothes and bone dominoes out into the greasy, gritty street.

In one of the drawers Soupspoon saw his mouth harp. There was a box of pencils and a bunch of monogrammed handkerchiefs he'd had made when he was a regular on Thursday nights at the

Savoy in Chicago. He had sixteen pairs of shoes back then. Each pair a different color to match the suits and sport jackets he wore. They weren't good shoes. If he wore any one pair for over three weeks running, the soft soles would wear through. But nothing lasted long in the gaudy-colored nightlife of the blues. You looked good and died young, that was the way to play it, because an old bluesman was no better than an old dog.

He wanted to play on that harp, but he couldn't reach it. He couldn't even think of standing after being dragged out to the curb like some old broken-down piece of furniture. And anyway, he didn't have the lip to play a harp anymore; couldn't even bend his fingers on a cold day in late March when they put old men out to die.

"How much for the guitar?" The white man stood there with an open guitar case in his arms. Soupspoon's red-enameled twelve-string Gibson lay in the black cardboard case like a king laid out in a poor man's coffin.

"Fuck you!" Soupspoon shouted, but he sounded like a dog who'd had his voice box cut out.

"What?"

"Goddamn fuck," Soupspoon wheezed. He pushed himself up by the tattered gold arms of the chair. "I could whip yo' ass. Now put my guitar down!"

When Soupspoon got to his feet the pain exploded in his hip. He fell to the sidewalk, emitting a hoarse cry that put fear on the white man's face.

"What's happenin' out here, Tony?" The colored man had an armful of Soupspoon's old suits. The clothes he played music in. The suit he was married in.

"Please, no," Soupspoon rasped.

"He just fell, Nate. I didn't do it, I swear I didn't."

"Here you go." Nate dropped the suits and lifted Soupspoon as if he weighed no more than the pile of old clothes.

Nate put the old man back in his chair. He pulled the blankets around his shoulders to cover the smell.

"People from Social Services comin' to get you, Mr. Wise. Don't worry, they'll be here soon."

"My things," Soupspoon said as clearly as he could.

"I don't know," Nate said. "Mr. Grumbacher said we gotta empty the place. You had notice. You had three months. They'll be here."

"My things," Soupspoon said again. He felt sorry for his poor guitar and for this colored man who didn't even know how to act with his elders.

"Com'on, Nate." Tony put his hand on the big black man's shoulder, and Nate turned away.

When the men were gone, Soupspoon pulled the blanket close. A few people looked down from the hollow windows above. Mrs. Manetti had argued with the men when they moved him outside. But he knew she wouldn't help him. He thought about all the poor folks huddled up in the apartments; about how scared they were. They were scared to open their doors.

Them two men could go from 'partment to 'partment an' th'ow out ev'ry one. An' ain't not nobody gonna lift a hand t'stop'em. We was poor in the Delta, but we wasn't never that poor.

The slow creaking of metal wheels sounded down the street. It was the old woman again. She wore a dark green trash bag, cut like a poncho, over many sweaters and blankets, and pushed a shopping cart piled high with junk. As she went by the growing pile of Soupspoon's belongings, she slowed. Her face was black and streaked, but she was a white woman.

"Get away from here! Go on! Git off!"

The woman took a step closer, and Soupspoon pushed himself up again; the pain made him see glitter in the darkening sky. But that scared her for a minute. She backed off across the street and stayed there—waiting.

Like a big greasy rat waitin' for Death to come on. Come on, Death. Come on.

Nate and Tony came out of the front door carrying the sofa; the woman moved a little further down the street. They dropped the old couch down and stood a moment to catch their breath.

"Please don't do this to me," Soupspoon begged. "It ain't right."

"What's he sayin', Nate?" Tony asked.

"He just mumblin', man. Must be hard bein' put out like that."

"What in the hell is this?" a redheaded girl cried. She seemed to pop right out from nowhere, pushing her chest forward as she stalked up to the men.

"What the fuck you think you're doin'?" She went right up to Nate, her pale face no higher than his chest.

"Who are you?" Soupspoon could hear the big Negro's fear. Big old coward when it came to white folks; even a scrawny little white girl scared him.

"Are you okay, sir?" Kiki asked Soupspoon.

He recognized her. The skinny redheaded girl from upstairs somewhere. She left every morning with matching shoes and dress, and went out every night in jeans and no bra. She used to say hi if he was sitting on his old box out in front of the doors. She was from Arkansas. Something like that.

"My things," he whispered. She frowned at him and shook her head as if she hadn't understood his words.

"Mr. Grumbacher called Social Services," Tony said. "They're coming to get him."

"The goddamn sun's going down!" Kiki yelled. "You can't leave him out here at night! This is an old man! An old man!"

"Kiki." A skinny boy was behind her, his hand on her shoulder.

"Get away from me, Randy."

"But, honey, remember your side."

"Listen," the big black coward said. "We got a job to do. He ain't paid a thing in eighteen months and the eviction has gone through . . ."

The redheaded girl swung a blue cloth bag suddenly. There was a dull thud and Nate went down in a crouch holding his head and cursing. Soupspoon hadn't seen anything like it since he saw Bonita Smith knock a St. Charles Parish, Louisiana, sheriff into the street for calling her son a pickaninny.

"Fuck you!" The redhead swung her bag at the white man and the black one in turns. Both men and the Rasta-boy tried to get away from her wild attack.

Soupspoon watched the white girl, really she was a woman past thirty, swinging her bag with one hand and holding her side with the other. Everything seemed slow to him though. The world was winding down like a child's mechanical toy.

"What the hell?" Tony yelled. He grabbed Randy and balled up his fist. He threw a punch too, but it got tangled up in the gangly boy's arms.

"What's the problem over there?" a loudspeaker barked.

The police were already out of their car when Soupspoon turned around to see them.

White boys, neither one of them over twenty-five.

Nate jumped up and ran at the redhead, but the cops were on him before he could get to her.

"Bitch hit me in the head! Look at how I'm bleedin' here!"

He held out a hand with some blood on it. Soupspoon shook his head, embarrassed by the blowhard.

"All right now," one of the cop-boys said. This one had a deep voice and milky skin. He held a billy stick out in front of his chest with both hands.

"Just spit," Soupspoon said. "That's all ya need for them." Nobody understood him, though.

"Okay, everybody calm down." The second cop was fat. He had soft womanly eyes with long lashes, but his skin was bad.

"Bastard!" the girl shouted. "You put an old man out 'cause he's sick! You motherfucker!"

Soupspoon could hear the south in her voice. Trashy south. White man's south.

"All right, that's enough now," the cop with the billy stick said. "Just calm down."

"Sir?" the fat cop asked Soupspoon. "Are you okay, sir?"

Soupspoon just stared at him. He was thinking about another policeman, a long time ago.

"Sir?"

"Luther's sick, officer," the redheaded girl said. "I've been in the hospital and I just got out today and when I got here I found these men doing . . ."

"Naw, naw, officer. That ain't right," Nate said. "This here man's name is Wise, Atwater Wise. He was evicted. Social Services come an' took him to the shelter on Bowery. An' when we come here to clean up today he was back there. We got a job, man . . ."

The policemen both stared at Soupspoon.

"He's my godfather, officer. From down Hogston," the redhead said.

Soupspoon looked at her again. Maybe she was crazy. Drunk maybe, or insane.

"Aw, man, com'on," Nate said. "She don't even know him."

"He's my godfather," she said flatly. "Now pick up his things and take them upstairs, apartment forty-three."

The fat cop turned to the Rasta-boy. "Is that right?"

The boy nodded, not looking the cop in the face.

"What's his name then?"

"I only ever called him Pop, officer. That's all. But he's Kiki's godfather all right. He's the one who told her about this place."

"Shit," the white moving man said.

"Watch your mouth." That was the deep-voiced, soft-skinned policeman. The fat kid came over and they talked a minute.

Soupspoon watched the two children as they settled his fate. He'd learned a long time ago that if you couldn't throw the dice yourself, then somebody else would throw them for you.

"You got someplace to take him?" the fat cop asked Tony.

"Somebody supposed t'be here, officer. The city got somebody to get him."

Soupspoon remembered how they came to talk to him, the Social Services people and the police. Rat-faced Grumbacher was saying how he had lost five thousand dollars. Five thousand dollars! After Soupspoon had paid his rent on time for twenty-seven years!

The Social Services people promised to bring his things, but they never did. And even the few little things he brought with him were stolen from under his cot. His comb and razor, his ring from right off his finger.

"I don't see anybody here," the fat cop said.

"They're comin'," Nate said.

"You can't leave him out in this cold. Do what the girl wants," the policeman said.

"But, man . . ."

"Listen," the baby-faced cop said, trying to be like a reasonable adult. "If you leave him out here and he dies, then we have to come after you for manslaughter. Maybe worse."

The moving men looked at each other. Both of them sighed.

They left the furniture in the street. The redhead said that the apartment was too small for dressers and sofas and that she had an extra bed for "Luther." They put all his clothes and small things in the dresser drawers. Tony took the drawers while Nate carried Soupspoon. He came through the apartment door breathing hard and frowning at the smell. He put Soupspoon on a floral-patterned stuffed chair that was set in front of a window.

Pain ground through Soupspoon's hip from being jostled so much.

Down in the street he could see the filthy white woman going through the couch, looking for lost change between the cushions.

Rats ain't got me yet.

"Smell'im?" Nate twisted his nose at Soupspoon. "That's what you got into. His whole place smelled like a toilet and a old dead man."

"Get out of my house." She wouldn't even look at the men.

Randy held the door.

"Mr. Grumbacher is gonna hear about this," Tony said. "This apartment is signed up for one. He's gonna come back here and kick you out too."

"I want you out of my house," was her reply.

After they'd slammed out of the room she slumped onto the

couch and put her hand against her side. Then she looked at the hand as if maybe she expected to see something.

"You okay, Kiki?" the boy asked.

"Yeah," she said, looking at Soupspoon. "I'm fine."

It was a shabby room. There was a TV with a coat hanger for an antenna on a bench at the foot of a big purple bed. A couch and stove, a bathtub on corroded enameled feet and a sink. A table and two chairs stood in the middle of the studio pretending to be a dining room. There was Soupspoon's chair at the window and a shelf full of books next to it.

He pulled the blankets tight.

Outside the sun had just set. Soupspoon could still feel the chill in his feet. His eyes closed with the fading light. Even the loud hurt in his leg couldn't rouse him.

There was a harvested cornfield. The stalks were broken and bare. It was twilight in November. It was cold and spiky and he wanted a pair of shoes so bad that he'd been crying. He was crying on the ground. He did that for a long time, until he forgot why.

He looked up and felt the chill of a cool breeze across the tears on his face. The chill was bracing and he wanted to laugh but didn't.

Far away through all the broken tilted stalks he saw a rabbit. A big gray bunny with red eyes. They stared at each other until Soupspoon noticed that the sun was up and it was spring. The field had been sown and new corn sprouted all around him.

"Sir?"

The window was black with night. People moved around in the lighted rooms across the street.

The redhead had on jeans and a T-shirt. He could see her small, masculine nipples against the thin cotton.

"I ain't no Luther," he said. "Name's Soupspoon."

"What?" She leaned forward, holding the scarlet hair back from a pale, freckled ear.

He pulled the blankets tighter and said, "I ain't no Luther. Name's Soupspoon."

"Soupspoon?" She stared right into his eyes, frowning. "That's your name, hon?"

He nodded and wondered what was wrong with this girl. She didn't move away even though he smelled from shit.

"You been sick, darlin'?"

"My th'oat an' my hip. Cain't hardly stand up."

"Here," she said. She pulled the blankets back and began to unbutton his sweater.

"What you doin'? Stop that."

"What did you say, honey?" She stopped unbuttoning and leaned her head over again.

"I said, what you doin?"

"I ran a bath. If we can take off your clothes I'll carry you over. Maybe it will help your hip."

"I ain't no baby."

She went back to undressing him. The smell didn't seem to bother her. She pulled his sweater and shirt off from the back and got him to put up his feet to get off the pants and soiled underpants. When she took off his socks she said, "You got these sores because you don't get up and walk around. Now come on." She turned her back to him and hunkered down. "Get up on my back and I'll carry you over there."

The failing man rode her horseback across the room. He wrapped his skinny arms around her neck and gritted his teeth. He was panting by the time she lowered him into the water. When she turned around he saw that there were tears in her eyes. She went down on her knees and moaned as if something had broken inside her body.

"You hurtin', sugah?" he asked, reaching out to touch the pale cheek.

"Lie back now, Soupspoon," she said. She breathed deeply and stood up.

Soupspoon nodded in the hot tub while Kiki took his pants and underwear and poured ammonia over them in the sink. Then she took a sponge from a high hook and squatted down next to the tub.

She was gentle where the skin of his buttocks had chafed. She washed his chest and arms and down between his legs. All the time she hummed a sad sweet tune. Soupspoon didn't know the song, but he heard the long-drawn country notes in it.

"Where's that boy?" he asked.

Kiki brought her ear to his lips, and he repeated the question.

"Randy's gone, Soup. He has a store down on St. Mark's."

"And what's your name?"

"Kiki."

"Why you take me in here, Kiki?"

She moved her head back and looked him in the eye for a moment. Her eyes were the kind of green that you saw sometimes in the waters of the Gulf of Mexico.

"Don't you remember?" she asked.

Soupspoon stared at the woman, too tired and sick to try.

"It was on that real nice day after Christmas. We were coming home and you were sitting next to the door on that old box," she said, prompting him.

Soupspoon shook his head slowly.

"I was really sad. Something . . . something happened to my friend where we worked and she was staying with me. I guess we both looked pretty sad, because you called out and said, 'Don't worry, ladies, you're young—you'll be okay.'

"You didn't even know us, but that made us both happy. We went upstairs and laughed and now Abby's just fine in Boston—just like you said."

When Soupspoon started to talk again, Kiki moved close to hear him.

"You go through all'a that downstairs just 'cause of a few words? You crazy, girl?"

"Yeah," she said. "I guess you could say that. So crazy that I don't think somebody should just stand by if something is happening and they know it's wrong."

She stopped a moment, the last word half-gagged in her throat. Soupspoon watched her eyes as they shifted from friendly to hard and clear.

"I just got back from the hospital. A boy stabbed me. Little bastard tried to kill me, but he couldn't do it. I wouldn't die. All this time I been afraid and now I see that I don't have to be. You don't have to be scared, because you're going to die when you're meant to—not when somebody else thinks so.

"When I saw you out there in the street I knew that they couldn't hurt you—because they couldn't hurt me. It was like I was meant to be there. Like I was meant to save you."

Her breath trembled behind a rage.

She pulled a straight-back oak chair up next to the tub, sat, and rubbed his chest again. She washed his body while Soupspoon looked at her face. He never thought that he'd be this comfortable again.

After the bath she helped him into the chair and dried him off. Then she put a terry-cloth robe around his shoulders and helped him to a chair at the table in the center of the room.

"I'll make you some tea for your throat," she said.

Kiki took a bottle of Jack Daniel's sour mash from the cabinet for her tea.

They drank and she ate pork and beans. Soupspoon couldn't talk for his sore throat. Kiki didn't talk either. She just sat looking at him, taking him in in a way that almost scared the bluesman.

"You should eat your food, Mr. Wise."

Soupspoon put his hand to his stomach and shook his head, no.

"When did you eat last? Yesterday?"

No.

"The day before?"

Soupspoon hunched his shoulders.

After a while a knock came at the door. The two looked up at each other. The knock came again.

THREE

The woman at the door wore a cheap cranberry jacket and a skirt of the same color. There was a grease spot on the hem and a weak red stain the size of a fried egg on her white cotton blouse. She had hard brown eyes on a young face that was too round for a white woman's, Kiki thought. The leather satchel that hung from her shoulder was overflowing with papers in manila folders. It was so heavy that the young woman favored that side. Her brown hair was braided tightly across the top of her head, and the twist to her lips said that she didn't want to be there.

The stranger stared at her, expecting common courtesy, but Kiki didn't say a word.

After a while Soupspoon coughed at the back of the room.

"Is that Mr. Wise?" the woman asked.

"Who are you?" Kiki replied.

"Tatum," the woman said stiffly. "Miss Tatum from Social Services."

Kiki counted the painful pulses in her side, hoping that Miss Tatum would leave.

"Is Mr. Wise in there?" Miss Tatum asked in a loud voice. Maybe she thought Kiki had tied the old man up; was selling him off for body parts.

"What's it to you who's in my house?"

"I'm from Social Services."

"So? I'm from Arkansas. Does that mean I could go and bother you at your table?"

"I'm here to pick up Mr. Wise. I'm supposed to help him get to the Bryant Shelter."

"That was a long time ago, honey. Back when the sun was still up and they had that poor man down in the street. That was hours ago. The man you wanted would've froze up and died waitin' for you."

"I thank you for taking him in, Miss . . . ?"

Kiki stayed quiet and held the doorknob for support.

". . . I know a lot of people wouldn't have taken him in. I appreciate your, um, concern."

"Soupspoon's with me now," Kiki said. "We don't need you."

"I'm sorry, but I will have to check that for myself." Miss Tatum looked over Kiki's shoulder, trying to see into the room.

"Tell me something?" Kiki asked.

The social worker's lips twisted so that she could barely ask, "What?"

"What would you do with him now, even if he wanted to go with you?"

"I'd take him to the shelter tonight and the hospital tomorrow. Mr. Wise is a sick man."

"You waited until he couldn't even talk to decide he's sick?"

"There are a lot of people at the shelter, Miss, um. . . . Sometimes it takes a little longer than we'd like."

"Well, he's with me now."

"If you don't let me speak to Mr. Wise, I will have to get the police."

"You can come in, but that's all. Just ask him if he wants to stay and then get your butt away from us."

Soupspoon was tilted over to the left side in his chair. He gaped at the women. His face, handsome at one time, was shrunken with deep furrows where his cheeks sagged and caved in from lost molars. His lower eyelids hung open, exposing their glistening red membranes.

"Mr. Wise?" Miss Tatum said.

Soupspoon's mouth opened and closed as he nodded.

"I've come to take you back home to the shelter."

The jaw swung loosely on its hinges when he shook his head.

"I don't know if you understand me, Mr. Wise. I've come to take you back to the shelter."

The loose jaw answered back. Then the sick man leaned forward, looking as if he might topple sideways out of the chair, and made a sound that was unintelligible and obviously painful to his throat.

"I can't understand you, sir!" Miss Tatum shouted. "Can't you speak up?"

Soupspoon sat back, a look of frustration on his emaciated face. The bags of his eyelids filled with tears.

"Can't you see that he's hoarse?" Kiki said. "Can't you see that you got to get up next to him?"

By example she went over to Soupspoon and bent over.

"I . . . can't . . . live . . . in . . . no . . . shelter," he rasped. His lips brushed against Kiki's ear.

Kiki blushed and felt a twinge in her side.

"He said that he's staying here with me."

"I don't believe it."

"He said that he likes it here and that I'm his girlfriend now and that you better get your Yankee butt outta this house."

"I will not leave without knowing that it's his decision to stay," she declared. And then to Soupspoon, a little loud, "There's already a hospital bed assigned for you, Mr. Wise. I can take you there tomorrow."

"If you want to hear what he has to say, then go put your ear to his mouth so you could understand him," Kiki said.

"That's ridiculous."

Kiki wanted to slap her face but that would have torn stitches and she needed to be healthy. She needed to be strong.

Soupspoon lifted his hand three inches from the table, beckoning Miss Tatum.

"What?" she asked, not moving.

He waved her to him again.

She took slow steps around the table. When she was in reach he took her hand.

"Oh."

He pulled her hand until he could grab her lower arm. He pulled that until he could reach her biceps.

It looked to Kiki like a drowning man trying to pull himself out of the drink.

From her shoulder he reached her neck, and she said "Oh" again but still she allowed him to pull her head to his mouth.

"Please . . . please . . ." he said.

"What?" Miss Tatum was trying to pull away but Soupspoon had her with both hands and he was holding on for his life.

"Don't take me from outta here . . . I'll die . . . please leave me here," he said. Then he lost all strength and let her go, falling back into his chair.

"Oh! Oh!" Miss Tatum pulled away as quick as she could. She went right for the door, stopping only to pick up her bag on the way.

"A senior agent will be sent," she said while looking around the floor for something, anything, she might have dropped. "An agent will be notified."

She left without getting Kiki's name. But that didn't matter, Kiki knew, because they knew where she lived.

An agent never came. Miss Tatum took her report back to her office the next morning. It was flagged with a red paper clip and filed in a cabinet labeled *Open Files*. An agent was even assigned. But there was some confusion and he went to Soupspoon's old apartment on the first floor. When he found the apartment empty he marked Soupspoon's open file *Deceased*.

FOUR

e awoke to the smell of whiskey
over lemongrass; remembering
the small bare breasts of the
redhead, Kiki, and how she came to bed in just underpants—a big
hospital bandage on her left side.

"How are ya, honey?" Her speech was slurred from the sour
mash.

He could barely nod.

"Motherfuckin' bastards." She propped herself up on one
elbow and looked down on him. "They don't give two shits 'bout
what happens to us. They don't care."

When she bounced around to get her place on the pillow, Soupspoon could feel his bones jostling.

"You hurt, Soupspoon? Don't worry, I'm not gonna jump
around anymore. I'm not gonna let anything happen to you. Tomorrow I'm gonna get Randy, I mean Ran-*dall*"—she pronounced the
name in a southern impression of an English accent—"and we're
gonna get you to a doctor."

Soupspoon saw the girl's ghost hovering halfway next to her
like an afterimage on a snowy TV. He wanted to go to sleep; he
wanted to die with no pain. But instead he beckoned Kiki to his lips.

She butted his head leaning forward in the bouncy bed.

"What?"

"That your boyfriend?"

Kiki's grin was toothy, half-wise.

"Why?" She leaned back toward him—a child playing games in bed after the lights are turned out.

" 'Cause I don't wanna be layin' up in his girlfriend's bed."

Putting her cheek to his and whispering into his ear, she said, "Don't worry, baby. I fuck him sometimes, but Randy don't own me."

The whole of his life Soupspoon had been around hard-drinking, hard-talking women, but he never got used to it.

"Anyway," Kiki said, "he's not like you. He's just a wannabe; wannabe white. He says he's South American and *Caucasian* North African, that means a light-skinned Arab."

Kiki leaned over to reach across Soupspoon, her pea-sized nipple poking at his eye. When she heaved back she had the whiskey bottle and swigged at it from the neck.

"When he comes up here I tell him that I wanna see his hard black dick." She sucked her tongue in a way she must have thought sexy. "You should see all the changes he goes through. You should see him."

The young woman was all of a sudden sad. She swigged down another drink and leaned across to put the bottle back.

"He goes down there to Pace University to be a stockbroker. Wants to play polo with the peckerwoods down there. He told me he wants me to be his wife so we could hang out at some fuckin' country clubs where they got fish eggs an' fuckin' Nazi polka music. . . . He thinks he's somethin' just 'cause he wannabe. But he ain't no more than these wild nigger boys roamin' up and down, up an' down." For a moment the girl was lost in thought. "Like dogs."

When he sighed, Soupspoon didn't know if it was from the pain in his leg or from the pain he felt from that girl.

"What's wrong, honey?"

"Hip."

"Your hip?"

"Mm. Yeah," he whispered.

"Is it better on your back?"

Soupspoon nodded but he didn't know.

"Is it your right side? Here, let's get you up on your left side and then you could lean back against me."

Kiki moved him gently and molded her body right behind his. He could feel her alcoholic heat work its way down into his bones. It felt good.

"That's okay, baby," she whispered. "Don't you worry. Nothin's gonna happen to you. I'm here. Shh, I'm here."

Soupspoon let himself lay back against the hot girl. He listened to her words and felt her light touch on his ear and forehead.

And he felt okay for the first time in a very long time. The closeness shaking loose the loneliness that had been his life for years.

Now he was alone in the big purple bed. His head full of dreams about catfish frying and juke joint dancing and women laughing open-mouthed while he played his red guitar. Only it didn't feel like a dream. It felt real. More real than this strange bed.

The scent of sour mash was in the air. There, on the dresser next to the bed, was the half-empty fifth of Jack Daniel's.

Crackling pain moved around in his leg.

If I could sit up then I won't die this mornin', he said to himself.

It felt as if there was a clawing lion digging in from behind, into his heart and head, but Soupspoon sat up. By bending over double and holding on to the side of the bed he could stand. Taking baby steps, he made it to the far end and rested.

A tune came into his head.

> *If the blues was walkin' shoes, momma*
> *and hands was feet*
> *I'd do a handstand for ya, darlin'*
> *walkin' right down on Hogan Street.*

The five steps to the chair and table left Soupspoon on his knees. He made it into the chair, trying to remember the chord he played behind that song. It wasn't in his mind but he was sure that his fingers remembered.

Through the window he could see three pigeons on the clothesline that stretched across the street. Two together and one apart. He smiled at them and rapped his knuckles on the tabletop—one-two, one.

A ruckus erupted in the hall and the door flung open. Soupspoon expected to see Nate and Tony again, but it was the girl. Kiki came in breathing hard, pushing an ancient wooden wheelchair. It must have been fifty years old. All cherry wood except for the cracked wicker back and seat. The back was high and the wheels were surrounded by thick rubber strips. There was a big lever brake on it and big flat armrests like on a reclining chair.

"Mrs. Manetti loaned it to us." She had a brilliant smile for him. "What do you want for breakfast, Soup?"

He smiled and hunched his shoulders for her.

He was amazed again. All the years he lived as a poor man among poor people and it always happened like this. You might know somebody for twenty years and never know their first name or what their feet looked like. But then one day something happens and somebody you never even thought of is there in your life closer than family. You know their smell and their temper.

That's how it was with Robert Johnson.

You looked up one day and there he was singing and acting crazy. He told you about far-off places in the world and played music that was stranger yet. He made songs that were deep down in you—and then you looked up again and he was gone. He took something of yours that you didn't even know you had; something your mother and your father never knew about. And taking it away he left you with something missing—and that something was better than anything else that ever you had.

Kiki fried canned spaghetti in leftover bacon fat and made sandwiches from it with dark toast. Soupspoon drank mint tea. He watched her down a shot of whiskey.

"What you lookin' at?" The girl's voice was hard. "You don't know what I've been through. This is the only thing keeping me together right now."

She stared into his eyes until Soupspoon lowered his gaze.

He'd been stared down by angry women before.

Hard lovin' comes wit' hard knuckles, his Uncle Fitzhew used to say.

Kiki lightened up after that. She didn't mind helping Soupspoon with his toilet. She helped him on with his wedding suit and put him in the chair. Randy came soon after, and together they lowered him step by step to the bottom floor.

Soupspoon looked around at the gray-green walls of painted plaster and at the cracked granite floors. There was a sixty-watt lightbulb at each narrow landing. But even in the dim light he could make out the dirty corners.

Almost thirty years in that building and he'd never been above the first floor. The walls echoed from Kiki and Randy groaning. He had the feeling of being a child; carried about and wheeled around.

"You okay, Mr. Wise?" Randy asked.

Soupspoon nodded and smiled in the gawky boy's face.

Arab my butt.

On the first floor they went past Soupspoon's apartment door. It was open on the empty living room. The floor was bare and unswept; even the shades had been taken off the windows. Twenty-eight years it had been his home and now it wasn't anything. He couldn't remember how his things fit in there.

There was already graffiti across the wall slapped on with emerald-green paint:

CB2 ROO XLM
BOARDWISE FUK

Soupspoon didn't know the language but he knew what it meant. It said that he could never live in his own house again.

Outside a dog was lifting his leg against the big yellow sofa. The cushions were gone, somebody's bed now. The bed was still there, so filthy that Soupspoon hoped they'd pass by quickly so that no one would make fun of him. The rosewood dresser was half the way down the block, shattered.

Kiki put a blanket around him and they went to Avenue A and up by Tompkins Square Park.

Soupspoon watched his breath form into frost on the blanket.

They cut west when they got to Twelfth Street. Long barren walls and an occasional drug dealer was all there was.

"I told you that I tried calling you, didn't I, Kiki?" Randy said at the beginning of the block.

"Uh-huh."

"But then I remembered that you always unplug the phone, so I called your job too."

"Yeah? What'd they say?"

"That you quit."

"What?"

"Have you called them?"

"Not yet."

"But why do you think they say you quit?"

"I don't know," Kiki answered. "I didn't wanna call'em when I was flat on my butt in the hospital bed."

"Why not?"

"I don't know. I just didn't."

"But suppose they fired you?"

"What can I do about that? I didn't call. I can't go back and change that now."

"But you should have called them. You should have."

Kiki stopped suddenly. The big wooden chair lurched so that Soupspoon had to bite his lip to keep from crying out. She turned with the chair to face her sometime boyfriend.

"Get away from here, Randy," Kiki said in a voice so hushed that Soupspoon could hardly hear.

"Aw com'on, honey."

"Get your ass away from me."

"I gave up my spot to help you today. I skipped classes for this."

Soupspoon could hear the cold hatred in the girl's breathing. Her ragged silence carried on the cold air.

"Damn!" Randy said after half a minute.

Soupspoon watched him walk back the way they had come.

Then Kiki yanked the chair around and they were moving again.

They went for blocks without her saying a word. Past the big yellow video store and the Korean market and florist. At Broadway was a large bookstore that specialized in "monster books" and toys.

They moved quickly down the street after that, Kiki bouncing the chair on its hard rubber wheels up and down the curbs. Soupspoon closed his eyes. A large spike was being driven into the bone, cracking it wide open. He wanted to yell, but his throat was closed. He wanted to run, but he could barely hold on to the chair. . . .

"What?" Kiki shouted. *"What?"*

Soupspoon opened his eyes and saw that they had stopped moving. He had turned halfway around in the chair and grabbed Kiki by the arm. The hot spike ran down his right leg. She looked like a demon with her eyes opened wide and her brows deeply furrowed. He could hear the bone-cracking gale of hate. *"What?"*

But when Kiki saw his face he knew that she saw his suffering. She stroked his forehead and turned him around and got down on her knees next to the chair. She fussed with the blankets, pulling them up around his neck again, and then she kissed him over his right eye.

From then on they rode slowly and Kiki went out of her way to find the special ramps they built for people in wheelchairs. They went across University and Fifth and Sixth. Finally they reached Seventh Avenue and turned left. Kiki wheeled Soupspoon up a wide ramp and through two wide glass doors that were held open by a black man dressed all in white.

The sudden heat made Soupspoon sleepy. His eyes felt scratchy and he started to nod. He had the feeling of motion, though, and he could hear voices. Kiki's voice, petulant and on the way to getting loud. Another woman was talking too.

"I'm sorry but you'll have to wait."

Then something about a doctor. But it was the smell of rubbing alcohol that told him he was in a hospital. He was so tired that he fell asleep listening to them argue and bicker. The choppy voices worked their way down into Soupspoon's sleepy mind, taking him back to earlier arguments.

Ruby and Inez sit out on the front porch arguing about politics and recipes and what so-and-so said at the store last Thursday.

His parents and brother were already dead. Influenza tore through their small shack, leaving a five-year-old boy just barely alive. He staggered away from that death too, like he had from the shelter. And he was saved then also. Because if Ruby and Inez hadn't taken him in he would have starved or gone insane from loneliness.

Ruby wore a blue cotton dress that had rough yellow flowers printed on it; Inez wore pants like a man and she smoked a corncob pipe. Inez kept a praying mantis around the house to eat pesky bugs. The big green walking stick could often be seen riding on Inez's shoulder or striding down her arm. When he was a boy little Atwater thought that walking sticks were the souls of saints that protected them all from harm.

Ruby and Inez were his only family, but he wasn't blood to them. They weren't blood to each other. But just good friends that lived together and that took care of him because they needed a child to order around.

Soupspoon felt a sharp jolt in his hip that opened his eyes. He saw a little blond boy, less than two, sitting on the floor with a red-and-blue ball between his legs. He was looking at that ball like God gazing at the world. Soupspoon imagined rivers and trees sprouting under that scrutiny. A whole world of buffalo and dinosaurs, flowers as big as your head and cold water deep and clean.

Asleep again, with lion claws digging into his hip. The darkness of half-sleep became bright sun shining through the plate glass. The baby yowled and Soupspoon roused to look at him again. A pinched-faced white woman was holding him in her lap. Next to her sat a dark man, probably Latin. His left arm was wrapped in a shirt deeply stained with blood. He was nodding off too. The baby struggled to get free. He was looking at that ball like it was his last chance. And Soupspoon wanted to get it for him. He wanted to get up out of his chair and go get that ball. He wanted to cry like that baby.

"Mr. Wise?"

A young man, younger even than the cops from yesterday. He was dressed in doctor white, not orderly white. He was short and smiling. Behind him Kiki looked worried.

"Can you talk, Mr. Wise? Can you make words?"

Soupspoon shook his head, hunched his shoulders, and smiled.

"Well, your friend here here says that you've had a pretty tough time of it." The doctor turned to Kiki and said, "Why don't you bring him along?"

They went through double swinging doors into a hall where nurses and doctors went from patient to patient, between aisles of sick people loitering in their beds. It was a long hall filled with flat tables that were separated by raspy plastic curtains. At the far end of the hall was a wide door that burst open suddenly. Four men carrying two stretchers rushed in, followed by more men. When they rushed past Soupspoon, he saw the bloodied face of one of the patients. He could tell by the angle of the eye and the loose lips that the man was already dead. He tried to see the other one, but they moved too fast for him.

"A-M-P thirty-one," a paramedic barked out. Then they were gone. With his voice the way it was, Soupspoon couldn't even whisper a prayer.

"You should always say a prayer when you see a dead body," Uncle Fitzhew used to say. "You know they souls be all confused when they die. Yo' li'l words might set'em straight fo'heaven."

Soupspoon always respected the tall gravedigger "uncle." He was no more blood than Inez or Ruby, but he came by once in a while to drink wine and play dominoes for nickels. He had the biggest thing in Cougar Bluff, everybody knew it. White men used to ask him would he take a dollar to show it off, but he wouldn't, "not for no white man."

"Open wide, Mr. Wise," the doctor said. He poked a popsicle stick down his throat and felt his neck. Then he pulled Soupspoon's eye wide and shone a light into it. He took something and shoved it in his ear while looking at a red-lit panel. Numbers jumped around until they stopped at 102.5.

The doctor and Kiki helped him off with his jacket and shirt, shoes and socks. The doctor listened to his chest and felt his skin. He looked at his fingers and toes and at the sores along his ankles. Then he sat in a metal chair at Soupspoon's side.

"My name is Mussar, Mr. Wise. Alan Mussar. I'm a resident here." The young doctor smiled with his mouth, but his eyes looked sad. Soupspoon wondered how a man could work in a place where they dragged in dead people every day.

"Are you a relative?"

"A friend of, of his daughter's, doctor. We just found him at the shelter yesterday. They hadn't talked in a long time and she didn't know what he'd come to. She had to go to work and I brought him over. Is he real sick?"

"Well, there's infection in his throat and he's got a fever. His glands are okay. But we need X-rays for the hip." The doctor stopped a moment and looked closely at Kiki.

"Does his daughter have health insurance?"

"Sure she does. She works for the city, they have full family coverage."

"Do you have her card?"

"No, but I could go get it. I mean, by tomorrow I could."

The doctor took a prescription pad from the shelf behind him and jotted something down, and then he took another piece of paper and wrote a short note, which he signed along with his phone number.

"Take this," he said, handing her both pieces of paper. "And fill it at a pharmacy. Bring your friend to the University Hospital. Make sure you have his insurance cards. They won't admit him in this hospital unless you can prove that he can pay."

"Thank you, doctor," Kiki drawled. "She'll get him there tomorrow morning."

"He's got a bad infection in his throat," the doctor said. "Warm liquids, salt gargle, and this prescription four times a day. And," he said, taking a handful of small aluminum packets from a drawer, "give him these for any pain he might feel."

"Yes, doctor," Kiki said, taking the dozen or so packages.

Soupspoon wondered why the doctor didn't talk to him. He was the sick man.

Outside Kiki was singing. It was late afternoon and warmer than the morning or the day before. They stopped at a deli and got chocolate chip cookies and apple juice. Kiki kept saying, "We did it. We did it, Soupspoon Wise."

FIVE

hat night, when Soupspoon took his blanket and stretched out on the couch, Kiki came over and sat down next to him.

"You don't have to sleep over here, daddy. There's still room in the bed for you."

"No," he said. His voice was weak but still strong enough that she didn't have to put her ear in his mouth to hear it. "It ain't right."

"I don't mind. And I don't know if that couch isn't too hard for your hips."

"A man ought to be able to sleep by hisself, girl."

"You scared of me, Soupspoon?"

"It ain't like that, Kiki. I really 'preciate it, what you done and all. But I hurt an' I need t'sleep alone."

"Please," she said, sounding as if she meant it. "Please come to bed with me."

"Why?"

"I . . . I don't know. I'm just lonely, I guess."

"I'm not your boyfriend. I'm twice your age, more. An' I'm sick. You don't even know me."

Kiki jerked her hands back and forth and picked at a loose thread in the seam of her jeans. Soupspoon could see the fear in those hands.

"My hip hurts, honey," he whispered. "I got to sleep by myself.

But if you get scared you can come on over an' visit. Okay? I'll be right here if you get scared."

Kiki smiled like a child. "Okay. But maybe you should have the bed."

"No no no no no," was all he said to that idea.

Kiki made sure to give the old man his antibiotics after the meal. She washed him again and helped him go to the bathroom.

Kiki lay in her bed a long time before sleep came. That night, like every night, she would almost fall off to sleep, she would be on the edge, and then the image of a man's pale lips arose, and the smell of the dank basement under the new house. For just an instant she was a teenaged girl again—trying to hold down her skirts, trying to stay off her stomach.

She'd start awake again. A dozen times it happened.

Some nights she didn't get to sleep at all; the nights she didn't drink. Kiki's father was in her mind every night of her life, except in the hospital when she was on their drugs.

She thought about him every night and hated him every morning.

It took five shots of JD before she drifted off that night.

And when she finally got there it wasn't worth the trip.

During the night she had nightmares about a small boy who was carved from black stone and who carried a black iron knife. While the boy stalked her, Kiki could hear Soupspoon moving and murmuring in his sleep. It was almost as if he moaned in sympathy with her own fears as the stone boy kept coming; kept coming with no emotion in his sharp-angled onyx face, the knife held out in front of him like a black flame. He weighed ten thousand pounds and moved slowly, but Kiki was so scared that she could hardly move. She'd fall down and have trouble getting back to her feet. He'd advance a step and she'd fall again. And every time she fell it seemed that Soupspoon groaned or spoke aloud, "Oh, God!"

Late in the night she heard a heavy thud and sat up straight, afraid that the boy had taken his first deadly step inside her room.

She crawled to the edge of the bed, cramped at her side from the stiff stitched wound. She looked at the door and saw that it was closed tight. She waited for another knock, but none came. Nothing came but the hot feeling of the wound and the stale aftertaste of Jack Daniel's on the back hump of her tongue. Sleep crept back into her eyes and she looked away from the door to the empty couch.

Empty, she thought, and felt loneliness, dark sleep with no purpose except darkness. Empty. Empty?

And then Soupspoon was back in her mind. Soupspoon with his voice like snake's breath and fat, black, sagging cock. His skinny thighs. His sour breath filled the room with the smell that Katherine Loll gave off before she died in their house. The good house on Knox Street that was built from cedar and pine and reinforced with brick brought all the way from Georgia. The house with two magnolia trees in the front yard. Their smell sweet and tangy like citrus but not quite. And all the sleepy bees buzzing so dull that she could sleep out there not even worrying about them. The sweet magnolia scent wiping out completely the smell of poultices and Katherine's breath.

Inside the dream of the girl-child dreaming, her father hollered about how much it cost to keep Katherine alive and Momma, in her high-necked gray cotton dress, shushed him and begged him to be quiet.

"But how the hell do you expect me to pay for it? She's just gonna die and then how do you expect me to get my money back?"

Somewhere Katherine was wheezing. Daddy never meant to kick her out, he only wanted to make her feel she wasn't wanted. He only wanted to see Momma begging and to hear the old hag wheeze upstairs. That harsh ragged breath you had after you'd run so long that you could just fall down dead like the first man to run a marathon.

Kiki could still hear Katherine breathing after the dream had passed. She was still asleep, or almost so, but the breathing continued. Harsh and painful with a small hurting wheeze behind it. But it wasn't Katherine.

Kiki opened her eyes again. The couch was empty. The weak streetlight through the imitation lace curtains fell across it, making it look like a dimly lit stage where the action was about to happen.

Not knowing why, Kiki got up and went to the couch.

The old man lying on the floor didn't surprise her. She wasn't quite sure who he was at first. Those dark glistening eyes and still darker skin. The ragged breath and that smell.

"Fell," he whispered.

"You have to go?"

She helped him into the toilet, helped fish his thing out of the folds of his boxer shorts, held him steady from behind while he stood at the cracked commode. They stood for minutes, Soupspoon doddering and holding his penis. He stared straight down into the lined brown bowl and waited until the sluggish sprinkle began. She could see the spurts of droplets beyond his slim legs. When he was done she felt his body move as he shook himself.

"Take two of these and your hip will stop paining you. And then we'll get you to a doctor tomorrow."

"But how we gonna pay?"

"Don't worry, I know how to handle it."

She gave him water to swallow the pills with and helped him back to the couch.

They both slept after that.

In the morning she dragged the chair downstairs and then took the steps, one stair at a time, with Soupspoon. The Percocets dulled the pain and the antibiotics turned his whisper breath into a surpris ingly musical tenor. She went with him to University Hospital and left him with a Bahamian nurse and the note from Dr. Mussar.

"I'll bring the card this afternoon," Kiki told the long-lashed woman through a glass wall.

"We need proof of insurance before we can admit a patient, Mrs. Wise," the nurse said simply. She made no move to buzz the door, to let them into the office.

"I can have it this afternoon." Kiki spoke earnestly, looking directly into the woman's large almond eyes. "He was up all night in pain. All I thought about was getting him in here. Dr. Mussar said it was okay. I mean, I do work, you know."

The nurse's finger hovered above the brass button on the desk. The long red fingernail had a tiny star of gold etched into it.

"Well . . ."

"I'll be here by five forty-five."

Marshall & Pryde Health, Accident, and Whole Life Insurance had the twenty-third to twenty-ninth floors of Number Two Broadway. The entrance to the building was crowned with a large mosaic depicting red Indians and yellow Spanish soldiers meeting on a gold-tiled beach before a blazing crimson-and-ocher sun.

The bank of elevators for those floors was cordoned off by a thick velvet rope stretched across the entranceway. A red-faced guard stood leaning against a podium and staring off into space. Somewhere a small radio played an old-time big-band tune.

"You have to sign in, miss," he said when Kiki came up. "It's after nine."

He said the same thing to her every morning. Brian Coulane, vice president in charge of staff operations, had instituted the policy over two years before. If employees felt that they were being monitored, they would come in to work on time. All latecomers had to sign in. Sarah Fields, Coulane's secretary, had told Kiki and the other girls on floor twenty-seven that she got the sheets at the end of the week.

"Do you make a report?" Brenda Jones had asked.

"No, honey, I just throw 'em away. I got enough mess in that office that I don't need no more trouble."

Everybody had laughed, but no one came in late after that. Nobody but Kiki.

The only time Kiki ever came in on time was when she had a crush on Sheldon Meyers, her boss. She'd come in early so he could drop by her desk and talk for a while before the day's work began. He had a little potbelly and his hairline was receding, but his smile was kind and he never said anything rotten behind people's backs.

Sheldon would lean against her desk and talk about all the world events he had studied in the *New York Times* on the shuttle van ride from Jersey City to the World Trade Center. He talked about famines and wars while on the verge of tears. Whenever Israel would retaliate against the PLO, bombing one of their settlement camps in Jordan, Sheldon had a pinched look.

"When children die it's a sin," he'd say as if he'd been the one to give the go-ahead for the slaughter.

"Don't you ever wonder if it's all real?" Kiki once asked.

"What did you say?" Sheldon's lips were large and wrinkled like those of some black men she had known.

"Nothing. I mean, we never hear any bombs or see a million starving bodies or anything. We just get on the bus or the train and come to work and go home. It's kinda like stuff on the news is just another TV show. Something somebody made up."

"You mean," he said, "that there's more to life. That if I really cared about all this I'd be out there doing something about it."

Kiki let her hand slide across the desk until her fingertips pressed under Sheldon's thigh.

"I mean," she said, "that we feel bad for all those people because they don't have a chance to enjoy life. You got to enjoy life."

They sat there, barely touching, for minutes before Sheldon broke away and went into his office.

But then he came in one morning and told Sarah (he didn't even have the nerve to tell Kiki) that he was engaged to some woman that nobody in the office had ever even heard of. A Jewish woman who Sarah said was from New Jersey and who didn't eat shellfish and who had to cut off all her hair after the wedding. But when Kiki saw a picture of her with their first child she could tell that it wasn't any wig that she was wearing.

Her name was Sury, but Kiki always asked Sheldon, "How's Sorry doing?" It hurt him, she could tell, but he wasn't the kind of man to say anything or even correct her. He was a coward actually, and Kiki was ashamed at herself for ever liking him and coming in at eight-thirty and bringing him coffee, even paying for it with her own money sometimes.

After that she never came in before nine-fifteen and sometimes not until nine forty-five. She dressed in sharp business suits but under the jacket she often wore a spaghetti-strapped silk blouse that tended to fall open at the breast. She'd bend over Sheldon's desk so that he couldn't miss the curve of her small breasts in the half-cup bras. The coward would have to look up sometime, and then he'd have to see what he gave up for that skinny Jew girl.

Kiki didn't have anything against Jews, not really. But she knew that Sheldon talked to her before work in the morning because he wanted a date. He wanted to have some fun, but when it came to something serious he went back to the fold. No Christian girl for Mom and Dad.

So she'd lean over and flash her tits, sometimes she'd let her nipple stick out. She never came in early to work again.

A woman was seated behind Kiki's desk. A woman the size of a refrigerator. Moles, not freckles, festooned her pasty pale fat face. She had a jelly doughnut, a Styrofoam cup of coffee, and a cigarette, burning in an ashtray, set before her. There were crumbs and ashes and burnt-out matches scattered across the blotter.

Rawna McPherson. There was even a name plate for this temp! She must have brought it with her. One of those people who come for a week-long visit and bring their pets.

"Yes?" the refrigerator said.

Kiki just stared.

"Can I help you?"

"This is my desk."

"Excuse me?"

"Excuse you? You're a pig. How do you expect me to excuse this shit on my desk?"

"Oh." When Rawna McPherson raised her head her jowls hung down the sides of her neck like curtains bunched open to expose a stage. She must've weighed three hundred pounds. "You're Waters. Oh no, you got it wrong. They fired you and hired me to take your place."

How long had it been? She'd been taken to the hospital on Tuesday, the Tuesday before last. She worked that day and got stabbed that night. And this was Thursday, so that was, that was . . . There was no mail from Sheldon. Nobody came down to the house. . . .

"You're supposed to go down to personnel. They have your check—hey!"

Kiki had forgotten about Rawna and the mess on her desk. She went straight for the closed door behind the secretary. Rawna didn't try to push herself up from the chair. She just turned her head and said, "Stop!" in a voice that was used to being obeyed.

Kiki slammed the office door open and then slammed it shut behind her. Sheldon had been lying back in his chair, putting bottled tears in his eyes; his ducts didn't make enough tears. He dropped the little bottle and lurched forward, squinting through the drops.

"Oh God!"

"What the hell do you mean by firin' me? You think I'm just some piece'a-shit temp that you don't even have to talk to? Huh?"

Sheldon looked up at her. His shoulders were so small that no off-the-rack suit fit him right, but nobody in his family had ever had a suit tailored except for funerals or weddings.

"I'm waiting. Who the hell do you think you are, anyway?"

"Mr. Meyers? Mr. Meyers!" Rawna barked over the intercom.

Even little-necked Sheldon had some pride, some backbone. He used that little bit and stood up shakily. Kiki admired his spunk, but she was still mad that she'd ever shown him anything.

"Your, um, your check is . . . is down at personnel, Miss . . . Waters. We don't run the kind of ship here . . ."

Suddenly Kiki understood. She could see that he was forced into this terrible position by the others, the people around the office who laughed at him. It was probably Marilyn Walsh from down the hall in the auto division. She was always laughing at Sheldon, always sneering and cutting him off when he was trying to make his point. She'd done it, turned poor Sheldon into this gibbering thing.

Kiki had dressed well that morning; burgundy pants suit with a cream blouse and a shoestring tie. When she unbuttoned the jacket, Sheldon fell back into his chair.

"Wh-what?"

She said, "I was stabbed and unconscious and in the hospital, Mr. Meyers." She tore open the blouse from the bottom, popping fake nacre buttons all over. Then she ripped off the bandages. The jagged line of holes went down toward the pelvis, so Kiki pulled down her pants a little. She never wore underpants with trousers, except with her period, so a line of orange pubic hair blossomed out around her pale thumb. The stitched slits were puckered, still moist with blood and healing flesh. Each one had a flat white rubber tube sticking out, dripping pus and fluid from the internal wounds.

She held the blouse up and the pants down and Mr. Sheldon Meyers couldn't take his eyes away. He swallowed like some fool in trouble in a bad comedy, his pudgy lips hanging open. When Kiki saw that she had him, she pulled the pants up and shoved the shirt-tails back in. She was just buttoning the jacket when Rawna McPherson came rumbling through the door.

She wasn't only fat, she was tall and lardy in the arms and legs. Her skin was pocked with hard cellulite. She was fat everywhere except her hands, which were small and delicate. If Kiki's mother had liked a woman like this she would've said, "Oh, Rawna, yes, Lord, she has beautiful hands."

But Kiki didn't like her. She thought that her rainbow-patterned dress might have been a tablecloth last night. Her makeup hid acne that put Kiki's wounds to shame.

"Mr. Meyers?" Rawna asked. "Are you okay?"

Sheldon was gasping like a fish. His eyes were wide and he breathed through his mouth.

"Yuh." He nodded and went on gasping.

"I told Miss Waters to go down to personnel, sir. But she . . ."

"That's okay, Rawna." Sheldon fixed his red power tie but it didn't need it.

Rawna was looking at a button on the floor and at Kiki fixing her jacket.

"Uh," Sheldon uttered. "Kiki's, uh, back here now. She, she has, um, well, there was an accident. Um, so sh-she wi-will be back at her desk."

"What?" Rawna asked.

"Don't worry, Rawna, we'll keep you. But it's just that we didn't know, and now, and now we do."

For the first hour Kiki scrubbed her desk. Loose food attracted cockroaches and vermin. Wall Street was built on ancient basements that were filled with rats. There was once a woman who was attacked by a swarm of rats driven from their subterranean home by a demolition blast. They ran right up on top of her, right up under her dress. When Kiki saw her carried away to the ambulance she was screaming and blood was coming from bites on her cheeks and lips.

Brenda and Sarah and Rudolfo came to find out what had happened.

"When you never answered your phone, girl," Brenda said to Kiki, "we thought that you had left. I knew you were looking for a job a while ago."

"I wouldn't leave without tellin' you, honey. I might not tell them, but I'd tell my friends."

When they heard that Kiki had been stabbed, they were all excited, wanted to know every detail. But they were really in awe when Kiki told them how she'd kept her job.

"You really opened your shirt?" Brenda asked, her eyes wide with bawdy wonder.

"And pulled down my pants so he could see some pussy too."

Rudolfo, whose real name was Henry, did a dance around Kiki's desk when she said that. He kicked his legs up high like a cheerleading majorette and crooned, "Ooooooooooo!"

"How could you do that?" simple Sarah from Great Kills asked. She loved her friends but considered herself different from all Kiki's and Brenda's wildness. Sarah had a husband who traded commodities on the Floor and two children who went to elementary school on Staten Island.

"He would have fired me if I didn't show him something. And I can't lose my job right now. I got responsibilities."

"He wanted to fire you?" Brenda shouted loud enough for Sheldon to hear in his office. "You could sue him for that. Him and this company too."

By eleven, Kiki's friends had to get back to work on the other side of the building. Over there the windows looked out over the Statue of Liberty and Ellis Island.

By noon it was as if Kiki had never been gone. She searched around her top drawer for the box of single-edged razors. They were still there, at the back. She got the yellow pass from a hook on the wall behind her desk and took the elevator to the twenty-ninth floor; the computer floor. The elevator opened into a small frigid room where she was faced by a large sliding glass window and a locked beige door. Through the window Kiki could see a chubby Asian man sipping at a straw from a large plastic Big Gulp cup. His sneakered feet were up on the table in front of him. His eyes were almost shut. He wore a woolen sweater decorated with yellow and brown skiers that seemed to be negotiating his large belly.

"Hey, Kiki," he said.

"Hey, Motie."

"You wanna come in?"

She nodded and Motie reached under the table. A buzzer sounded and she pushed open the heavy metal door. Inside the air was even colder. Air conditioning to cool off the millions of dollars in machines either leased or bought from IBM. The electric hum in the air was accented by a hucka-hucka sound of large paper machines that the operators called bursters. Behind Motie Kiki could see row after row of squat boxes, each one about the size of a washing machine. Disk drives. She needed to get into one of them.

"What you want?" Motie asked. He hadn't gotten up. If he was still drinking scotch from the plastic cup, Kiki wondered that he was still awake.

"Fez around?" she asked.

"What you want with that motorhead fool?" Motie's parents

were Korean but he had been brought up on the streets of Newark. He was a homebody; raised on Motor City and weaned on brown sugar.

Fez, the big-bellied white-shoed giant, was also from Newark. But he was from the white side of town.

"I need him to do somethin' for me."

"What?" Motie sat half the way up in his chair. "I could do it too."

"No, uh-uh, Motie." She liked Motie and Bernard and DJ. She didn't want to get them into trouble.

But Fez . . . Fez had raped Abigail Greenspan in the service elevator at the Christmas party last year. Everybody was drunk and Abby liked to flirt, but Kiki saw the bruises, torn skin, and teeth marks on Abby. Fez had told her to come with him down to the storeroom and then used his key to stop the elevator. He tore off her clothes and hurt her until she did all the things he wanted. When he was through they went back up to the party and Abby broke down crying in Kiki's arms.

Kiki stayed with Abby for three days; until the poor broken girl got packed and went back to Boston, to her father and stepmother back home.

Kiki was sick for a month after Abby was raped. She looked for a new job all of January, but no place would pay near the salary that she made as Sheldon's executive assistant at Marshall & Pryde. She avoided the computer room for a long time, and when she did go back she stayed far away from Fez.

In the janitor's hopper room, where Kiki had taken Abby to wash out the bites on her arms and legs, Abby cried, "What am I going to do, Kiki?"

Kiki answered, "I'm going to take you to my place and when you can travel I'm going to put you on a bus for home."

"Shouldn't I go to the police?"

"No," Kiki said in a small voice. "Better not. Just better get outta here. You know Fez is crazy and he'll do something. Believe me, I could tell. You better just get away."

"He's down in his office," Motie said. "Prob'ly playin' with his-self."

All the operators who weren't white hated Fez. He called them names behind their backs; often loud enough for them to hear. But he was the big boss on the day shift, and he let all kinds of things go on. They had a daily number right there in the computer room and a running bar from the tape archives. If Fez didn't like you, you got fired. Nobody wanted to fight him; he was big and rough, and had that kind of crazy look in his eye that let you know he wasn't afraid to go too far.

Everyone was afraid of Fez. And he was the head of computer operations. Kiki was the computer room expert of her floor. She got her knowledge by hanging out with her operator friends. They'd go out for lunch together and smoke reefer and drink beers. She liked the operators because they weren't stuck up like the men and women who ran the insurance floor.

The reason Marshall & Pryde paid her so well was that she knew computers and got along with the operators. She could get a computer job done twice as fast as anybody else. But Kiki tried to do her business with Fez over the phone. When she had to go to the computer room she talked to Motie or one of his friends.

Kiki was so frightened by Fez that sometimes she would leave a job undone rather than go to him.

But that changed in the hospital.

She was still scared, but now she wondered, what good was being scared going to do? Abigail was afraid. Did that stop anything? Kiki was afraid. That never stopped her father, it didn't stop those boys.

Now, even though she was still a little scared, Kiki wanted to stand up to Fez.

"Yeah?" he called after Kiki had knocked on the glass door.

She slid the door open and walked in.

Fez was a gentleman. He stood up, all six foot four of him, and came around his desk to say hi. He wore polyester dark green pants with white shoes and a white sport coat. He couldn't have buttoned that jacket over his stomach. His shirt was a tight orange skin of satin. He never wore a tie. Nobody wore a tie in the computer room. They were proud of being *back office.* They laughed at the programmers and office managers downstairs.

Fez moved to kiss Kiki on the cheek. She allowed the kiss as the currency of their transaction. She could smell the Old Spice and see the razor nicks on his damp face.

"What can I do for you, honey? Kiki, right?"

"Uh-huh."

"Sit down." He licked his lips. Kiki had never liked Fez, even before Abby, because he had skinny lips.

"I got a problem, Fez. . . ."

"That's why we're up here."

"I fucked up."

Fez's beady green eyes could have been electric.

"Like how?" he asked.

"I entered some special accounts for Mr. Merwyn and I did it wrong."

Fez smiled and went back to his chair. He sat down in front of his terminal and said, "Shoot."

"I gotta do it myself, Fez."

"Why?"

"Because . . . because Merwyn gave me his personal ID and I can't tell anybody what it is."

"So you want me to sign on and let you do what you want? You think I'm nuts?"

From her tote bag Kiki brought out two bottles. The first was a fifth of Chivas Regal and the next was a quart of Courvoisier XO.

"Please," she begged.

Fez's eyes got hungry, just like she knew they would.

"Okay," he said. He got up and gestured toward his chair.

Before Kiki was seated, Fez was at the door shouting, "Roger! Roger! Look what we got for the store."

The store was the bar that ran from the tape library, or tape archives as they were called. All day long you could go out to the archives and pick up some scratch tapes and a Dixie cup filled with whiskey. Nobody could come into the computer area except the vice presidents, and they didn't care what happened as long as the complex computer runs went through without trouble.

The moment Fez was out of the door, Kiki started hitting keys. F12 for insurance systems. F12 again for policy files. F7 for entry data. Bright green characters flashed across the black screen. Kiki held her breath a minute, wondering if Fez's log-on had the priority to update the insurance database. If it didn't the screen would freeze and the database manager would be flagged at his terminal on the twenty-fifth floor.

"Yeah." Fez was right outside the door. "Kiki brought it. Right, honey?"

Kiki looked up from the screen. If the program rejected Fez's log-on the terminal would make a loud beep.

Kiki put her left hand in her pocket and pinched the razor between her fingers. She could take out an eye before he could hurt her too much. A cold joy that made Kiki shiver went across her forehead.

"That's right." She smiled at him and the brown-suited jerk Roger who stood behind.

Kiki hit the F3 key to initiate a new entry. F2 for health insurance. This screen offered for entry a list of blank information lines on the insured.

"Okay now." Fez was patting Roger on the shoulder. The slump-shouldered, big-nosed man was at the door, wiping his lips as if maybe he had drooled with gratitude for the liquor.

"Thanks, Kiki," he called through the door.

Kiki let go of the razor and pulled a small piece of notepaper from her pocket. She took a deep breath and ran her fingers across those keys as fast as she could manage.

Atwater and Tanya Wise lived at 784 Carmine Street, apartment 430. It was a post office box that Kiki kept under an old roommate's name—Rachel Fraumeister. She used the box so that no one would know where she was. That way they could never tell her father how to reach out after her.

Atwater and Tanya had paid their first year's installment in cash six months before to a private agent, but somehow the paperwork was lost. But now they were entered, with ages appropriately different and all the information she could make up.

Fez was in the office now about to look over Kiki's shoulder.

"Could you get me a cigarette from my bag, Fez?"

BORN: 01/12/21, 07/30/59

"You can't smoke in here."

"Com'on, Fez. Who's gonna see?"

POLICY EFFECT DATE: 03/01/87
POLICY COVERAGE DOLLARS: 1,000,000
REVIEW STATUS : COMPLETE
MAIL DATE: *IMMEDIATE*

"You don't have any cigarettes in here," Fez said.

"In the side pocket."

REVIEW AGENT: SHELDON MEYERS (Route to operations, Central 617)

Kiki hit the enter key, and a string of characters, in red lights instead of green, appeared at the top of the screen. AJ3119-A22x.

"What's that you got up on the screen?" Fez was right there with her, was reaching toward the keyboard.

"Just the policy I had to . . ." Kiki put her hand out—"Here, let me scroll up to the top"—and hit the F10 key—transmit and send. Immediately the screen went blank.

"Oh, no! Oh shit!" she yelled. "Fuck! Now I really messed it up. Why the hell did you have to ask me anything?"

Fez's face lit up. He patted Kiki's shoulder and said, "Oh, that's too bad, honey. You know I'd need more than a bottle of booze to open the database for a hex dump. A lot more."

"You did that on purpose. You motherfucker."

AJ3119-A22x, AJ3119-A22x.

She got up and pushed his hand away. "I wouldn't ask you for a thing, even if my job depended on it."

"You'll be back." Fez smiled and put his hands behind his back. "I always wondered if you were a natural redhead."

AJ3119-A22x.

Kiki ran from the office. She ran down the hall to the exit door. Motie was still in his chair, still sipping at his scotch. "Kiki."

"Motie, could you do me a favor?"

"Sure. Do I gotta get up?"

"I need a policy that should be coming off the laser soon. It's going to oh-six-seventeen."

Motie took a pencil from his pants pocket. He tried to scribble with it on the desk top, but the lead had broken off. He used his dirty thumbnail to pick the wood away from the broken point until enough lead was exposed.

"Yeah?"

"AJ3119-A22x," Kiki said, sighing as she watched Motie write the number on the top of his desk.

"When did it get issued?"

"I don't know. Mary should have sent it while I was up here."

"Okay, I'll call Phibbs. He'll bring it as soon as its printed. You want it to go to the checkers?"

"No. It's routed to Mr. Meyers. Have him bring it there," Kiki said, and then, "This is special, so I might need you to route it to him for a few months."

"I need to put that past McMartin, Kiki. He's got to okay special processing."

"Come on, Motie. Don't be like that. I fucked up on this and the agent complained. If I don't get it right, I'll be in trouble. It's already going to the general box. All you have to do is pick it up when I call. How would they know it's you?"

Motie was a good kid.

"Okay," he said. "I'll see."

Kiki did a turn in the air and yelled, "All right!" in the elevator down. She swung her fist at Fez's imaginary gut and felt a stitch give way deep inside.

That afternoon Kiki called the medical center and gave them Soupspoon's new medical information. Before the day was over she had made appointments with a bone specialist, an oncologist, and a dentist for her charge. She'd left work early and bought him a woolen blanket and a side table with her credit card.

That night they had smoked ham hocks from an Italian deli and chocolate–chocolate chip ice cream for dinner.

Soupspoon had to take three pain pills before the pain finally subsided.

"How'm I gonna pay for these here doctors you got me goin' to, girl?"

"With those insurance papers you signed."

"I ain't got no in-surance. Shit. I be lucky to get some Medic-aid."

"But it's like I said, I made an application at the place where I work. That's better than being on the county, hon. All kindsa stuff the government won't pay for."

"But how could I get in-surance just like that?"

"You just do," Kiki answered. "Why don't you lie down and try to rest now? We could talk about it later."

Soupspoon knew there was something wrong with the documents that she had him sign, but he was tired. Something was wrong with every breath that he drew. That's why he was thinking about the blues again. That's why he was lying there on that angry girl's sofa. He couldn't change it. So he let Kiki spread the blanket over him and closed his eyes. The medicine had turned the pain in his leg from fire to cold stone. If he turned just right on the couch he barely felt the nugget of hurt.

He didn't fall asleep but he closed his eyes and listened to Kiki move around the apartment. Later on he heard a knock at the door and then whispers.

"Shh! He's asleep," Kiki said.

"How long's he gonna be here?" It was the skinny boy, Randy. The bedsprings sighed.

"I don't know. Until he's better. The doctor said that he might be real sick."

"That doesn't mean you have to take care of him."

"So if you were so sick that you couldn't wipe your own butt I should just let you lie out in the street?"

"But you know me, Kiki."

"But suppose I wasn't there?"

It was quiet for a while after that. Soupspoon drifted, wondering about what the police could do to him now that he was so sick. He heard the wet crackle of kissing and then, "Uh-uh, no, honey. You got to go, Randy."

"Come on, Kiki, I won't do anything. I'll just hold you."

"I'm sick too, honey. Just wait awhile, till we both get better."

Soupspoon heard the door open and close. Then the silence of the room seemed to hover above him. His neck felt the tickle of skin so close that it almost touched and then a moist kiss on his cheek.

S I X

nez used to kiss him at night when she thought he was asleep. She'd come to his corner of the big room after he'd been in bed for a while. First she'd strike a match on a piece of sandpaper that was tacked up on the wall. Then she'd puff on the pipe in little gasps until Atwater could smell the sweet smoke of her cured tobacco.

Inez came very close but he kept his eyes shut, not even making a peep, because *li'l boys s'posed t'be 'sleep when it gets dark outside—an' thas all they is to it.* But he wasn't asleep. He was wide awake in his cot, fooling Inez; and that made him want to laugh and dance. But he couldn't make a sound while she was still there.

Inez hovered over him. He could feel it like you could feel the harvest moon when it was over the frail sharecroppers' huts in the Delta. And like that moon she brought sweet smells and slight breezes that tickled his skin the way Kiki did over sixty years later up on the fourth floor.

The child had ants in his hands and feet. He wanted to laugh out loud and caper to let Inez know that he was fooling her. He couldn't keep it in, but if he moved, Inez would get mad. Inez got mad when children couldn't control themselves. She wasn't like Ruby. Ruby was rounder and darker and she smiled almost all the time. Inez was sweet-smelling but Ruby smelled like bread.

Ruby didn't get mad even when Atwater kicked over the

bucket of cleaned and peeled turnips, or when he threw that rock and broke Ruby's grandmother's colored window (which Ruby's mother had given her from the deathbed). Ruby never got mad. She'd just let her eyes get real big and say, "Atwater! How did we let that happen?" and then they'd get together and work hard to clean up the mess before Inez could find out.

But it was Inez who came out to check on Atwater at night after the alcohol lanterns were turned down. It was always Inez. And Atwater was always scared that he wouldn't be able to control himself and would make a peep and then Inez would be mad and he'd have bad dreams.

But, just when he knew he had to let go, Inez would take a deep draw on her pipe and blow a sweet wave of smoke over him. The ants became long dewy blades of cool grass between his fingers and toes. The moon gave way to blue sky and Atwater was rising and falling like one of the great box kites that Fitzhew made for the windy days of fall.

Atwater Wise came out of the sky and hit the ground running. Faster than the dive-bombing bumblebees and with nobody to tell him when to come in. There was chest-high yellow grass to run through and a hundred different odors of earth. There was the blood from his ankle, once, from a sharp rock hidden in the moss of Millwater Pond. There were the hilly nests of fire ants that would swarm over grasshoppers and tired dragonflies.

Cold water was good. Blood, scabbing over and sluggish, was good. Even the fire-orange specks on the shiny green eye of the dragonfly were good.

The wind through the stiff yellow grass wheezed like an old woman. Hidden in there were all kinds of birds that were named for their colors and sizes and personalities. They sang and warbled and croaked.

Crows came from the devil but they couldn't catch him. They called his name in crow words but the little boy just laughed.

His dreams were full of colors and smells and music. There,

under the blanket of Inez's sweet smoke, he ran and played while she sat back—too old to have fun anymore.

And then the kiss. Warm and moist. It was only when she thought that he was asleep that Inez kissed Atwater. The loud groan of a timber and the snick of the door told the boy that Inez had gone back to the big bed with Ruby. He could open his eyes, but now he was too tired to move.

The young boy fell asleep but the old man came awake. Tears saved up from over half a century came for the death of that poor dragonfly. The red bird, the gray fat warbler—lost. Soupspoon had tears over the great herons and the train that ran right through town carrying the big bales of cotton down to the Mississippi River.

He remembered the one-eyed cat that came to the window to look into the house; looking for Inez's praying mantis like Death searching for that one soul who slipped away behind some trees and was overlooked, half forgotten.

Soupspoon remembered days and days down by the river with his little boyfriends—fishing, rafting, swimming among the catfish and carp.

He remembered the cotton fields and all the men and women lumbering off to work from the plantation barracks. Hollers and calls came from the fields even before the sun was up. But it was silence he heard at the end of the day.

I'm way past tired to almost dead, Job Hockfoot would say. But by midnight on Saturday he was dancing full out.

A Negro didn't own too much back then, but he had the ears to hear music and the hands and mouth to make it. Washboards, washtubs, and homemade guitars. Mouth harps from the dime store and songs from deep down in the well. . . .

"No, daddy," Kiki cried. Her voice was small and helpless.

Soupspoon wondered if it was her nightmare that woke him.

He sat up to look. The blankets were all kicked off her bed. Her naked behind was thrust up in the air because she was hunched over the pillow and some sheet.

"No."

A white woman; skinny butt stuck out at me like a ripe peach on a low branch. There was nobody left to tell. Nobody left to understand how strange it was, how scary it was. Nobody to laugh and ask, "An' then what you did?"

An' then I died, Soupspoon said to himself. There was nobody there to hear him. And even if there was—so what?

That was the blues.

He was eleven years old the first time he heard the blues. The year was 1932. It was on a Saturday and Atwater had been hanging around at a barn party. He got to stay late because Inez forgot to send him home.

It was Phil Wortham playing on a homemade four-string guitar with Tiny Hill working a squeeze-box. It wasn't like anything that Atwater had ever heard. The music made him want to move, and the words, the words were like the talk people talked every day, but he listened closer and he heard things that he never heard before.

Your heart breaking or your well running dry. Things like cake batter at the bottom of the bowl and the mist clinging to the road on summer mornings.

The music made Atwater want to dance, so he knew that it had to be good.

A good friend of the boy's—an older man named Bannon—had been killed only a week earlier. Atwater hadn't shed a tear.

People died in the Delta; they died all the time. Atwater hadn't cried, but a dark feeling came over him. He didn't know what it was until he heard Phil and Tiny play at the barn party. He didn't know that he had the blues.

That music had changed him. From then on at night, after Ruby and Inez had gone to bed, he'd go out the window and make it down to the Milky Way.

The Milky Way was a beat-up old chicken barn that had been

coated with tar and dotted with yellow splotches of paint that were supposed to be stars. It was a lopsided ugly building in the daylight. But at night, when you came through Captaw Creek and around the old elm, it looked like something magic; like, Atwater thought, a hill house of God.

He was too young to go into a juke joint, but he made up his mind to try on his birthday.

And so on a summer's evening, when the sun was still out, Atwater told Ruby that he and Petey Simms were going to set nets for crayfish down at the creek. But really they meant to take the quarter that Fitzhew had given Atwater for his birthday and get two glasses of whiskey from Oja, the midget owner of the Milky Way.

Petey made it as far as the old elm—where he stopped and gawked as Atwater walked on ahead.

"Wha' wrong wichyou, Petey Simms?" Atwater asked when he turned to see that he was alone.

Petey just shook his head. He was a long-necked heavy-eyed youngster who everybody but Atwater called Turtle.

Atwater followed Petey's gaze to two women who were standing out in front of the juke. They were big women wearing loose dresses that flowed in the breezes, flaring up now and then to expose their legs. They had very big legs. Petey was looking at those women (especially, Atwater knew, at those legs) and shaking his head.

Atwater was scared too but he thought that they'd be safe as long as they stuck together.

"Come on," he said. "They ain't gonna bite you."

He said it loudly to shame his friend, but he didn't expect the women to hear.

"Hey you," one of them shouted.

Petey took off like a scared hare. Shoop! He was gone.

"Hey, boy!" the voice called out again. "You!"

One of them was coming toward him. She had a kind of rolling motion in her thighs as she walked. She waved for him to come to her while her friend stayed back near the juke, shading her eyes to see.

"Me?"

"Come here!" the woman shouted—none too kindly. She was tall and heavy-chested with hair that was combed straight back from her head.

"Come here!"

Atwater's bare feet obeyed, but he didn't want to walk down there.

"Hurry up, boy! I ain't got all night!" The big woman was smiling, one meaty fist on her hip.

"Yes, ma'am?" Atwater said when he stood before the woman.

"Elma," she said. Her smile revealed that one of her upper front teeth was gone. Another one had been broken in half. "Elma Ponce is my name. What's yours?"

"A-A-Atty . . ."

"A-A-Atty," Elma mocked the poor boy. "What you doin' out here, A-A-Atty? Yo' momma know you here?"

"Elma, what you messin' wit' this baby for?" The other woman had come up to them.

They seemed like women then, but now, on Kiki's couch, Soupspoon remembered them as teenagers—maybe eighteen. But they were women to Atty Wise. They wore the same cut of loose dress. Elma's dress was blue while her friend's was a washed-out orange.

"Jus' playin' wit'im, Theresa." Elma took Atwater by the arm. "What you doin' here, Atty?" The sweetness in her voice was not lost on him.

"My birfday," he whispered.

"What? Talk up."

"My birfday today."

Elma showed her snaggle teeth again. "Yo' birfday? An' you come down to Milky Way to get a kiss?"

"N-no . . ." Atwater said. He could feel himself shaking but couldn't stop.

"You scarin' the poor boy, Elma," Theresa laughed. "Let him be."

"I come to get a drink on my birfday day," Atwater said. He

said it fast to keep Elma from getting mad. He didn't want to see her mad. "I come t'get a drink wit' my birfday quatah."

"You got a quatah?" Theresa asked. She was black-skinned and good-looking the way a handsome man looks good.

"Uh-huh. Yes, ma'am."

Elma, still holding the boy by his arm, pulled Atwater toward the door of the Milky Way. "Come on," was all she said.

The dark blue front door had a big drippy yellow circle painted in the middle. That circle was supposed to be the moon.

Elma pushed the door open, dragging Atty in behind her. Theresa followed up the rear, holding on to his pants.

Elma went up to the bar and shouted, "Oja! Bring a pint bottle ovah here!" She pointed across the dark room to a row of makeshift booths hammered together against the far wall.

"The hell I will," small fat Oja replied. He climbed up on his stool to face her. "Where you gonna come up wit' money for a pint an' not ten minutes ago you couldn't even buy no beer?"

Theresa pinched Atty's butt and giggled in his ear.

He was thankful for her closeness, because the Milky Way on the inside scared him to death. The floor was black and sticky, covered with crushed peanut shells. It smelt of sweat and sour beer. The ceiling was uneven and low; at some points a full-grown man wouldn't have been able to stand up straight.

And it was hot.

"I cain't pay for it," Elma hooted. "But my boyfriend here could."

Elma yanked Atty's arm, pulling him away from Theresa and up next to her.

"Well? Pay the man, Atty," she said. "You want yo' birfday toast, don't ya?"

Atwater took the quarter from the pocket of his cutoff trousers and handed it to Elma.

"Not to me. Give it to the barman an' tell'im what you want. That's what you do when you a man."

Oja had a mashed-in black face with a long cigar stuck out between his battered lips. He was too small to work in the cotton fields, so he had to go into business for himself.

"Well?" the bartender asked.

Atty pressed his quarter into the pudgy little hand.

"Yo' a'ntees know you down here, boy?" Oja asked once the coin was in his pocket.

"Yes sir."

"You sure?" Oja had this thing he did with his eyes. He'd open one very wide and close the other until it was just a glistening slit.

"Put that eye back in yo' head, nigger," Elma warned. "He done told you that they know an' he done give you his money too. So pull down that pint. The *deep* brown stuff too."

After they collected their whiskey and tin cup, Elma pushed Atty until she had him dammed up between her and the wall in the booth. Theresa sat on the other side. She held his hand from across the table. After tasting the first drink, Elma leaned up against him, rubbing his chest and holding the cup to his lips.

"Drink, Atty. Thas it. Take some more, baby. This here will make you into a man."

His tongue and throat burned. The fumes from that homemade brew made his eyes tear and his breath come short. But what Atty felt most was Elma rubbing and pinching his chest.

"We gonna grow some hair right ovah here tonight," she whispered.

Theresa's smile was bright against black skin.

They all drank. Atwater held his breath as he watched the cup go from Theresa's lips to Elma's mouth and then to him. Their hands were all over him and they laughed more and more with the liquor.

Elma was almost on top of him. She let her arm rest in his lap.

"I think A-A-Atty like me, Theresa," she said.

Theresa reached over and grabbed Atwater by the back of his neck. She pulled on him until they were kissing across the table.

"You better let up from him, bitch," Elma said in a serious tone. "I'm the one found'im. He mine tonight."

When they weren't fighting or feeling on Atty the women talked trash. Atty learned that they lived on Peale's Slope: a little shantytown where most Negroes slept under propped-up shelters with no walls or right outside on the ground if the weather was good. Elma stayed with her old uncle up there in a small cabin. Theresa had lived with them since her boyfriend had left her.

Atwater wanted to know everything about these women. He could repeat every word of what they said, but he didn't understand it all. For years after that night he'd remember things they said and suddenly, because of something that would happen, he'd realize what they meant.

As evening came on, people began to fill up the bar. It got noisier and smokier but Atwater hardly noticed. Theresa and Elma were enough for him. When Elma would lean close he looked down between her breasts and she'd give him her shattered smile and say, "Atty? What you lookin' at?"

"How you girls doin'?" A slender man slid in on the bench next to Theresa, but he was looking Elma in the eye.

"Who you askin'?" Elma replied. She took Atty's hand and held it tight.

"You, baby. Who else I'ma be talkin' to?"

"All I know, nigger, is that you was s'posed t'be here nine days ago."

"Nigger?" The man had a baby face, but when he smiled he looked evil. Elma's hand tightened under that smile, and Atwater's heart began to race.

"I don't know what you smilin' at. Atty here took me out for a drink, so he my boyfriend tonight." Elma's voice had lost all of its play.

The fine young face turned toward Atty. He smiled again without showing his teeth.

"Cody," Theresa asked, "what you doin' here?"

"I said I was comin'," he said.

"That was more'n a week ago."

"I had sumpin' to do, woman. I got here as soon as I could."

"What you had to do?" Elma asked.

"I don't see what's it to you. You done already got another boy-friend." Cody smiled and reached down beside him. He brought out of his overalls a full quart bottle of store-bought Old Crow whiskey. "I planned to say I was sorry wit' this here, but I guess I got to find me another girlfriend.

"You still wit' John, Theresa?"

The handsome black woman's mouth came open and she shook her head to say that she was not.

"Theresa!" Elma shouted.

"I ain't did nuthin'," Theresa screamed. She licked her lips and avoided Cody's smiling eyes. "He jus' axed an' I told'im."

"You ain't gonna go messin' 'round right under my nose," Elma said. She was crushing Atwater's hand.

"Come on, girls," Cody said. "Don't let's fight. They's whiskey for all of us. Right, Atty?"

"I-I think I had enough," the boy answered. The room was hot but his forehead felt like ice. "I got . . . I gots to go home."

Cody reached down into his pants again and came out with a long homemade knife. The blade was from a five-inch metal saw that had been shaped and sharpened by a grinding stone. It was black and jagged but Atwater could see that it was still sharp. The haft was wadded cork wound tightly around with fly-green fishing twine.

Cody put the knife down next to the bottle and said, "You not refusin' my hospitality now is ya, man?"

"Cody . . ."

"Shet yo' mouf, Theresa. Ain't nobody axed you. If this man here is man enough take my woman then he man enough t'drink wit' me."

Elma sat stock-still. She let go of Atty's hand. That was the scariest moment for Atwater, because he knew that if Elma was scared then he didn't have a chance.

"I drink it," Atty said.

While he was still smiling, Cody poured the tin cup full to the brim and then pushed it in front of Atwater.

"Cody, he cain't drink all that," Theresa said. "He ain't no man."

Cody raised his hand and Theresa flinched back so hard that she banged her head on the wall.

Atwater picked up the cup and started sipping. Fifty and more years gone by and he was still amazed that he had the strength to drink as much as he did.

Cody put a finger to the boy's throat to make sure that he was swallowing.

When Atty finally put the cup down, Cody smiled and said, "That's only half."

The room changed after Atwater drank. Most of what he heard was just noise but he could hear some talk, even from across the room, very clearly. Colors became stronger and the yellow paint on the walls really did look to be stars.

Elma was saying something but he couldn't make it out.

"I gotta go," Atwater said.

"See?" Elma pointed at him. "You done made the boy sick."

She moved quickly to get up off the bench and let Atwater out. He slid over with no problem, but standing up was a whole new experience. One leg gave way and then the other. He struck the table with his chin, but the feeling was more sweet than it was painful. He was afraid of falling to the sticky floor, but Cody caught him before he tumbled all the way.

The evil baby face came up close to his and said, "You go out an' do yo' business an' then come on back, ya hear?"

The boy thought about nodding—maybe he did.

" 'Cause if you ain't back in two minutes I'ma come out there an' cut you bad."

Then Cody pushed Atwater toward the door. It was a crooked path to get there; bouncing off one body and then into somebody else. It was like a playful child's dance with everyone laughing and pushing. He didn't mind the horseplay though, because, even in that small room, he was too drunk to find the door by himself.

There was the moon again. About three-quarters floating in a thick black eye. The night clouds were golden shoulders for that cyclops. The air was chill and for deep breathing, not like the hell smoke of the Milky Way.

While Atwater relieved himself he laughed because it felt so good. Then he started walking. The leaves crackled and the stream sounded like baby bells. Every footfall was a bass drum going off.

He was lost but that didn't matter. He had a long talk with his murdered friend and said goodbye.

He scraped and scuffed himself and finally fell face forward in the cold stream. The water sobered him for a moment and he sat on a big rock and wondered where he was.

Once he heard somebody call his name. At first he thought that it was Inez out looking for him. He almost called out but then he worried that it might be Cody. So he kept quiet and played dead.

The next morning he awoke in Alyce Griggs's barn, just about a quarter mile from his house. A white hen was clucking and dancing around his feet.

"What you doin' in here, boy?"

When Atwater lifted his eyes to see the woman he felt sharp pain throughout his head and jaw.

"Sorry, Miss Griggs," he said to the elderly white woman. "I got drunk at Milky Way an' I landed here in yo' barn."

"That's the devil in you, Atty," the scrawny white woman warned. "You know that, don't ya?"

"Yes, ma'am," he said, and meant it.

"Go on now. I hope Inez hides you good."

He never did get a beating for that night. When Atwater came through the door he was staggering from fever. The chill and the whiskey had made him sick. For three weeks Ruby and Inez took turns sitting over him, covering his forehead with damp towels and feeding him foul home remedies one after the other.

His lungs filled up and his dreams walked around the house with a life of their own. He choked and coughed and finally accepted that he was going to die. He made his goodbyes to Ruby and Inez so bravely that even stone-faced Inez cried.

When Atwater got out of bed again he knew that he was a man.

"Daddy?" Kiki was sitting up in the bed.

"You okay?" Soupspoon asked.

Fully naked, she got up from the bed and came over to the couch. She sat spread-legged before him and held out her hands for him to hold.

It wasn't sex on her part. It was a frightened girl, no older than Atty at the Milky Way, holding out her hands to be saved.

"What's wrong?"

"I don't know. I'm scared," she said all at once. "I'm scared of ... of ..."

"What?"

Kiki told him about her dreams of a stone boy stalking her with his knife.

"It's okay, honey," Soupspoon said when she was through. "He ain't gonna get in here."

"That's not all," she said, avoiding his eyes.

"What else is it?"

"I can't tell you yet. I ... I have to wait."

"Okay," he said, trying to catch her eye without ogling her orange-brown crotch. "I'll be here when you ready."

"What's wrong?" Kiki asked. "Why you look away from me?"

"I don't know. It's just that you're a nice girl. You should cover up in front of a old man like me."

"You shy?" She smirked while trying to get him to meet her gaze.

"Naw, I ain't shy. I seen it all. But I like you an' I feel like I don't wanna get the wrong idea."

Kiki's face went smooth when he said that. Her eyes became perfect circles with tears beaded up on the lashes. She leaned forward as if she meant to hug Soupspoon but then she got up and went to the bed and rummaged around on the floor. She came up with a ratty brown robe and wrapped herself in it.

She held out her arms as she came back to the couch.

"Can I hug you, Mr. Wise?"

"Sure."

"I won't let anything happen to you," she whispered into the embrace.

Soupspoon was thinking about little Atty wandering through the wilderness over stones white as skulls.

SEVEN

"The tests show that the tumors in your pelvis and lung are cancerous," Dr. MacDuff said.

Soupspoon felt bad for the poor woman. Here she had three little ones and a husband to take care of and he was causing her sorrow that a young mother should never feel. Babies could taste it in their mothers' milk; hear it in the way they talked.

"That's okay, honey," he said. He reached out to take her hand. At first the young doctor tried to pull back but then she relented.

"Don't worry 'bout'a old man like me, darlin'. I done had almost seventy years in this world. I seen more than mosta your presidents an' kings. You gotta worry 'bout them chirren you got."

Dr. MacDuff tried to say something but choked, her white cheeks turning pink.

"I . . ." she stammered.

Soupspoon thought that maybe if he could have cried she would have felt better.

"Here you are being nice to me and I'm the one who should be consoling you," she said. "Will Tanya be here soon?"

"Yeah, she's comin'. But you better let me talk to her 'bout this. You know Kiki got her a short ole fuse."

"Kiki?"

"That's, uh, that's my nickname for'er. Kiki."

Soupspoon sat on a long sheet of paper that the doctor had laid on the examining bed. All he wore was a pair of unbuttoned pants. Dr. MacDuff was seated on a chair that made her lower than him. Her long black hair hung down to her waist and her upturned eyes were almost black.

"I've recommended radiation treatment for you, Mr. Wise. It's at the Cooney Institute uptown in Washington Heights. It's expensive but I believe that it's the best for you."

"Yeah, but you know I ain't got two nickels an' Kiki don't make that much neither."

"The insurance will cover it."

"I don't see why you even wanna bother. Ain't nuthin' they could do about cancer."

The young woman stood up and threw her hair back. She took a seat next to Soupspoon on the waxy paper and opened a dark folder that had ghostly X-ray photographs of his bones. Soupspoon had seen these pictures before but only when Dr. MacDuff was showing them to the technicians or some other doctor on her floor.

"You see, the pain in your hip is coming from here." She pointed to a dark area above what he figured was his leg bone. "It's a tumor growing in the bone. Have the painkillers been working?"

"Well, least I can sleep through the night and walk some."

"This other scan is your lung. There's just the smallest little tumor there. We're not worried about that yet because it's so small and you aren't showing any symptoms there."

Soupspoon was looking at her elbow, which rested on his arm as she pointed.

A woman doctor. A white woman doctor treating him with her arm touching his.

"The radiation treatment has a high success factor. Seventy percent in cases like this one. I'm optimistic about it," she said. "But you're going to have to be careful. I'm giving you a prescription, because you have high blood pressure already and some of these procedures might make that a little worse."

"What's blood pressure got ta do with it?"

"Lots of things. It could bring about heart attacks, stroke."

"Nuthin' wrong wit' my heart." Soupspoon thumped his chest

like a one-handed Tarzan. "You gotta have a good heart to be where I been."

Kiki filled out the forms and took the train with him to the clinic for the first five days. She watched as they tattooed the little black points where the radiation was to be aimed. She waited on the other side of a lead shield as he lay flat on a table in the big green room while a giant robot arm shot atomic beams into his fragile bones.

They sat together with Dr. Fey, who had a large bandito mustache and shy brown eyes. He was cheerful and asked all kinds of useless questions about what baseball teams did Soupspoon like and how long had the couple been married.

Dr. Fey was suspicious when he heard that Soupspoon and Tanya were married. But when he saw the devotion the young woman gave her man he was reassured. The couple wore matching wedding rings that Kiki bought in the street and then got sized by a student in jewelry at the Fashion Institute of Technology.

On those five mornings Kiki had told Sheldon that she was going through physical therapy for the cuts in her side. She *did* go to the hospital twice. They had to check the stitches and examine the fluids she was leaking.

"They cut up the muscles down there and I gotta get my legs fit or else I'll be a cripple when I get old." She could have told him anything. Sheldon just nodded and said okay. He was better than a lover; he was afraid of her.

The pills Soupspoon took—Percocet, three at a time, six times a day; three times the dosage the pharmacist said to take—made him tired and listless. He'd sleep the day through, after going for his "zapping," and then wake up at night thinking, half dreaming, about the lost days of his life.

After the first week he took the long train ride to the clinic by himself. The women there were all nice to him. Only women worked for Dr. Fey.

Soupspoon brought them sweet rolls and hot coffee with skim milk and Sweet 'n Low just the way they liked it. Then he'd sit in the maze of cushioned chairs and bask in the slatted sunlight that came through the blinds. He'd doze in the chair thinking about the lazy rock lizards down along Water Moccasin Pond. They'd crawl up on the slate shore in the noonday sun. He'd imagine himself a lazy sunning lizard who didn't have the time or the mind to worry about cancer or the rent. All he had to do was to eat flies, and there were enough flies to last a thousand years.

A distant chime sounded whenever the pale violet door to the waiting room opened. Skeletal old men and balding children would come through. They all had the same look; as if they were concentrating on a question in their heads. Some deep religious problem or maybe long division. Old women came in wearing out-of-style clothes. Some of them wore pastel trousers and T-shirts with no jewelry. Many who still had some hair had given up their combs completely. They sat and stared out ahead trying to figure out that problem. They sat and waited for the nurses to call.

There were three nurses. Yvonne, a big brown girl from Tennessee originally, who had nine children and a husband who was no good but pretty. Wendy, who was blond and full of smiles even though she wore braces and had bad skin. And Bristol, a straight-backed English woman who made everything happen and managed to be nice even when she was pushing some poor old frightened dying woman in or out of the door.

Soupspoon liked Bristol. He was idly considering her big breasts and the little jade earrings that dangled beside her square jaw when the chimes sounded.

Two young men entered. They were as different as day and night. One brunet and the other blond. They were both tall, but Harry was sober and serious where Bob had a grin on him just like he must have had when he was three. Harry didn't like to talk. If you said hello to Harry he'd nod and look down at your hands. But Bob laughed as if you were some long-lost cousin and asked you how your life had been.

Bob was six foot one and weighed just over 120 pounds. His blond hair was in wisps now, and there were open sores on his face that oozed pus and blood. Bob couldn't walk without Harry holding his arm. They usually got in late.

After Soup met Bob, he'd save him a seat next to the nurses' station if he could.

Soupspoon felt sorry for everybody who had cancer and had to be shot through with atomic radiation. But he liked Bob, because he was one of the only patients who still had some humor.

"How you doin', Bob?" Soupspoon always asked.

Bob would look back as if he were thinking hard and then he'd smile and say, "If it was any worse I'd be better off than I am now," or some such blues humor.

While they waited, Bob and Soupspoon talked about things. They gauged each other's pains and treatments. Bob talked about his soap operas and events in the news. Harry kept out of the way and left the two to their gabbing. Every now and then he'd ask if Bob was comfortable or if he needed some water.

"You got a girlfriend, Bob?" Soupspoon asked on the day after they met. He thought that maybe he had one but she left when he got cancer and now he had to rely on his friend.

"Harry's my wife," Bob answered in a sly tone. He was looking Soupspoon in the eye when he said it, a smile tucked under the three or four hairs of a mustache that he had left.

"Oh." Soupspoon nodded. "You a homo, huh?"

"We say 'gay' these days," Bob said.

"Yeah, I know. But you know, sometimes a word just sticks in your mind and nuthin' else seems right. To this very day when I talk about my own people I got a inclination t'say 'colored.' I know I'm s'posed t'say 'Negro' or 'black' or 'Afro-American,' but I say 'colored,' 'cause that's what we said when I was a boy and it fits in my mouth right."

Bob laughed in a mild hacking way that he had, and they became friends.

Soupspoon found out what AIDS meant. How so many people had it and didn't even know. He found out that Harry had been tested and that he had it.

"I'm sorry to hear that, man," Soupspoon said to Harry one day. The hale young man nodded and smiled. Then Soupspoon understood why he stayed so somber, because when he smiled he also cried.

"We all sure do got the blues, don't we, Bobby?"

"At least we can sing together," he said. "At least for a while."

By the third week Soupspoon's pain was almost gone. He only had to take two Percocets a day.

Bobby was dead.

Harry sent a long letter, which Kiki read to Soupspoon. It said that Soupspoon had helped Bobby laugh those last two weeks. ". . . the only things he looked forward to were seeing you in the morning and watching *As the World Turns* in the afternoon," the letter said. It also gave the time and address of the service. It was in the Village, not far from Kiki's.

Soupspoon stood at the back of the chapel. Over four hundred people had crowded in to pay their last respects. The family took up the front row. Mother and father, his sister and her kids. They were all broken up. They cried for Bobby Grand. But what got to Soupspoon was the men who had come to pay their respects—they cried too; cried with that deep sort of bereft sorrow that people have when a great leader passes. That ragged kind of sorrow you feel when your best friend dies. A brave kind of man who you, in your ignorance, never believed could die.

It made Soupspoon think of Jolly Horner.

Jolly had a big black face bulging with shiny cheeks. He had powerful smiling teeth that could bite through iron nails. His big hands and legs were so strong that he could lift a barrel full of water and carry it a quarter mile.

When Jolly Horner clapped those big hands behind Soupspoon's guitar it sounded like artillery; cannonfire and the blues.

I hear a train a-comin'
bang!

You know you hear it too
Bang!
It's got a seat for me, Mr. Charlie
Bang!
I be sittin' right next to you

The floor gave way right under Jolly's feet. Seth Wyles made a bet with his uncle that Jolly could carry a two-hundred-pound spotted pig up the ladder to the top of Seth's barn. Jolly could do it, there was no doubt about that, but he didn't want to. He didn't want to play the fool for white men. But Seth made him do it anyway. He told Jolly that if wanted to keep his job then he had better tote that pig.

It wasn't much of a challenge except that the pig was scared and the boards of the barn weren't strong enough. Jolly made it to the top, but then the floor gave way and he came down, pig and all. They fell through to the plow mare's stall. The mare reared back and crushed Jolly's big face.

It was a hard life back then.

People died all the time. Young people died from hard blows, disease, and from taking their own lives. If you cried for every one of them you would have died from grief. Let their mother cry, their children; everybody else just picked up and went on. There was no holiday that you got to mourn.

But there was a holiday the day after Jolly Horner died. No one went to the plantation fields on that day. No one went to the farms or into the rich white people's homes to work.

Jolly wasn't meant to die, and Negroes from all over the county came out to say it. The night before, men went to Wyles's barn. They slaughtered his spotted pig and crushed his mare's skull.

And nobody ever found those killers, because when the white men came down into darktown the next day they found a funeral vigil with over a thousand people lining the road.

Jolly had friends everywhere. People loved him because of his strength and his loud, big-toothed laugh. You could hear Jolly laugh day or night because he didn't get tired.

A thousand men and women came out to tell Jolly 'bye. But they also came out to tell God something, that's what Soupspoon thought. The black population of the whole county came out to say that they would bear witness to the innocent death of a good man. A right man.

Soupspoon found himself crying at the back of the church, but he wasn't sure who it was that he cried for.

He got home by three and put water on for tea. He took two extra pills, because his hip bothered him that day. There wasn't a thing he could do to help that poor dead boy but at least he could do something about the pain.

When Kiki got home Soupspoon was sprawled out on the bed snoring. His shoes were in the middle of the floor and the dry sharp smell of burnt tin was in the air.

"What in the hell is this!" she shouted, flinging the hot pan against the wall over his head. Soupspoon rose out of his drugged sleep and peered at the wild woman.

She snatched his shoes up from the floor.

"You think this is some kind of pigsty?" She stomped across the room and hurled the shoes right through the windowpane. "This ain't no goddamn cat box!"

"I'm sorry, honey," Soup said softly. He tapped his toe on the floor as if, in his music mind, he were trying to slow down the beat, to bring them into harmony.

"You're sorry?"

Kiki moved with fast clipping steps from the shattered window to the bed.

"You're fuckin' sorry all right!" she shouted. The next thing Kiki felt was a sharp pain that ran from her fist up her right arm. Soupspoon grunted and fell sideways from the impact of the blow.

"Sorry?" tore from Kiki's lips. She swung with her left fist, hooking Soupspoon in the eye.

"Shit!" he yelled, putting his hands up around his face.

"Goddamn, goddamn . . ." Kiki kept hollering. With each syllable she punched or slapped until there was no more breath for either and she fell down on top of Soupspoon, putting her arms around him in a tight embrace.

Later Kiki went out to buy ground sirloin, canned collard greens, and lemon pie. She made ice packs for Soupspoon's swollen eye and asked every few minutes, "You all right, Atwater? You okay, honey?"

He met those questions with shrugs and grunts until she'd been brought to tears five times. Finally he said, "Don't worry 'bout it, honey. You a good girl. You done good by me. It's just all'a this havin' somebody stay wit' you in such a small place is too much. I'ma get myself together after this last few days'a treatment and move on."

"You don't have to go, Soup."

"Me stayin' here an' livin' off you ain't right, Kiki. An' I need my own place."

"But how can you pay for it? You don't have money."

"I can work. I might be past sixty-five, but somebody needs a sweeper or counterman. 'Cause if you can't work then you dead already."

"You can stay with me as long as you want," Kiki said.

E I G H T

They sat next to each other on the couch for over an hour without talking. Soupspoon took an old address book out of his guitar case and flipped through the pages, mumbling and musing over what he saw. Kiki slouched down next to him looking miserable.

"Why'ont you go over an' watch TV?" Soupspoon asked to show that he was over being mad.

"Don't wanna."

Soupspoon had put down the address book and was now rubbing his guitar with an oversized white handkerchief. He watched the young woman sulking and shook his head.

"Why'd you hit me, girl?"

"I don't know."

"You think it's right to hit somebody when you mad? You think that's gonna teach'em sumpin'?"

Kiki glowered and shifted her position—a petulant child.

"I didn't mean to hurt you," she said.

"But you did."

"No I didn't."

"You *did* hurt me an' you *did* mean it. An' you know I ain't done nuthin' to hurt you."

"You coulda burnt down the house!" she blurted out. "We coulda been killed!"

Soupspoon put his hand on her thigh and said softly, "But you saved us, honey. You saved everybody."

A free-roaming twitch moved around Kiki's body. First in her shoulder, from there to her foot. Her cheek jumped twice and then her stomach contracted, forcing her into a half-bow.

"I set my house on fire once," she said.

"You did?"

Kiki stared ahead, her assent more in her posture than in any gesture she made.

"Anybody die?"

Kiki seemed to enjoy the question. She smiled, then grinned. "No," she said. "Nobody died. They didn't even know that it happened. I lit a match in the basement and threw it in a trash can full of papers. Then I went back upstairs and waited for the house to burn down but I guess that it fizzled out."

"How old were you?"

"Eight."

All the anger and sadness was gone from her. She went back to her bed and turned on the Johnny Carson show.

Soupspoon took out his address book again and murmured over the scrawled names as if he were praying in a foreign language.

"Kiki?"

"Yeah, Soup?"

"You wanna lend me some money?"

"Sure. What for?"

"T'buy me a tape recorder."

It was late. Kiki was propped up at the head of her bed with a water glass and a bottle of Jack Daniel's at her side. The TV light played over her head, across the blank wall.

"What you need a tape recorder for?" Kiki asked out of a blue-gray haze of cigarette smoke.

"What that doctor say to you?"

"Which one?"

"Dr. MacDuff. What she say to you when you went down there?"

The television ran long flickering shadows across Kiki's face, but the sound was turned low. "She said that you were in remission—mostly. And that if you went in for checkups and stuff that you'd be okay."

"That all? That all she told you?"

"Well..." Weak laughter rose up from the TV and then a drumroll. "... You know doctors, they always got to say some things, but it's not because it's so."

"What things?"

Kiki's eyes, trying to be innocent, opened wide, making her, in that ghostly light, resemble the zombies that the old folks told about to scare children and keep them home at night.

Soupspoon had come to like this girl all over again. She had some kind of anger built up inside of her. That's why she hit him. But even those blows had come from her crazy kind of love. It was that same craziness that made her take him in.

Now she wanted to keep quiet so as not to scare him with what the doctor might have said.

"What things?" Soupspoon asked again.

"Well . . . they always say, even if it isn't true, that if you got even a little bit of cancer then you might only live for five years."

"Tops," Soupspoon added.

"It could be more." Just that quickly she was on the edge of tears.

"I once knowed a man name'a Bannon," Soupspoon said. "Ole roustabout down Mississippi."

"Was he your friend?" Kiki used the blanket to wipe her eyes and nose.

"In a way he was. I was a boy an' he was pushin' sixty. But back then, in the country way'a life, you could have friends all kindsa ages an' there wasn't nuthin' weird about it."

Soupspoon fingered a page in his address book as if he had found something that proved what he said.

"So what about your friend?" Kiki asked. Someone was shouting on the TV and then came applause.

"Bannon? Bannon was a thief by trade and a history teacher by nature." Soupspoon looked at the guitar on the couch beside him. "He played guitar too."

Carefully Soupspoon took up the guitar and put it back in its case.

"Bannon would take me out on walks an' tell me all about what he called *real history;* all the things he had learned from African students that he'd met in Washington D.C. when he was a janitor at Howard University."

"What did he steal?" Kiki asked.

"What?"

"You said he was a thief. What did he steal?"

"He only stole from white folks, but what Bannon loved was history; especially African history, which, he said, was hidden by white people who was jealous of all the things that the Africans had when people in Europe was still holed up in caves.

"He used to say that your African races was civilized six thousand years ago. Egypt and the Sudan, that's where it all started. Your first Jews and your first Christians was black folks. They made Babylon and the pyramids, they wrote the Bible and sailed the seas. Mosta your black people around today don't know all that. But I do. Mosta your white kids grow up thinkin' old is England, old is Rome. But they don't know shit. . . ." Soupspoon was the voice but they were Bannon's words. The dapper little man with fuzzy gray hair like a halo around the shiny black dome of his head.

Soupspoon laughed to himself.

"What's funny, Soup?"

"I met Bannon 'cause one day I was breaking inta his little old shack out past the Willis plantation. I just went in there t'take some apples but I didn't know that he was out back nappin'. He caught me by my ankle before I could get back out the windah."

"Did he beat you?" Kiki asked—she was wringing the blanket.

"Naw. He told me, 'If you do anything you gotta do it right.' I was sweatin' an' shakin' under the pecan tree that growed at the side'a his place. The grass was cold and them pecans was hard under my feet.

"Bannon was preachin' up to the branches of that tree, 'Here you got a black child comin' t'steal from a old black man—from his own people.' An' that's when the lectures started. All about how black people everywhere didn't know who they was an' didn't know how to be proud. 'Bout how writin' an' readin' an' arithmetic all started in Africa.

" 'All the white man ever made was weapons. But that's all they needed.' That's what he said.

"With those weapons they stole everything in the world. They piled their warehouses with every goddamned thing they could carry. An' when they couldn't carry any more they made slaves carry away their own things to put in the store. An' when the white men had so much that they couldn't use it all they made the slaves work and serve.

" 'White men the biggest thieves in history,' " Soupspoon said, making his voice deeper so that Kiki knew he was quoting from the long-gone Bannon. " 'And it's our job to steal it right back.'

"The old boy didn't believe in working, no sir! He say, 'Workin' for the white man is helpin' him to pick your own pocket. Work every day for your whole life and you might make ten thousand dollars. But it's in the white man's pocket and the white man's bank. An' here you livin' in the same goddamned shack from six to sixty-six an' you even payin' him rent. When you die the white undertaker pull the gold right from outta your teeth.'

"I was just a little boy really, 'bout ten I guess. My daddy an' my momma was already dead an' I didn't have nobody to talk to. I mean, I stayed with these two women that I called my a'ntees but I guess I needed a man to talk to. An' the way that Bannon talked was so great that I still remember all the stuff he told me. It was like I had been lied to all my life an' now somebody finally wanted t'tell me what's what.

"An' he needed t'talk too. Because Bannon knowed mo' than almost anybody I ever met, but he didn't know how to read. Everything he knew was in his head an' he had t'talk to keep it up—if you see what I mean."

Kiki took a deep breath and brought her hand to her throat. She looked as if she wanted to say something but the words didn't come.

"He say, 'So when you go crawlin' in a windah it should be a white man's windah. An' if you use a gun it should be against a enemy, not some lost African brother don't even know who he is.'

"You know I'idn't have no gun. Shit! I'idn't have a stick. But I knew that if I hadda had a stick I woulda swung it an' because I knew that I knew what he meant.

"I spent every day at Bannon's house, eatin' apples and pork rinds while that old man talked about the great black men of history. In the afternoon, when we'd take long walks, he'd tell me all about people like Marcus Garvey an' the return to Africa. We always found ourselves in the woods behind white people's houses. Bannon would not steal from a colored man, he said that stealin' from a colored man was wrong." Soupspoon cackled and sat back on the couch. "But if some white man so happened to be gone, and his door was locked, then Bannon didn't mind me goin' in through his windah an' openin' up. You see, he'd get mad when a white man had a lock on his do'. He figured that that white man had money he stoled from the coloreds in there. Yep."

"Did you ever get caught?"

"I didn't. I was s'posed to meet'im on a Tuesday mornin' and he was gonna start talkin' about Hannibal and the black armies that Rome drafted out of Africa. You see, I'idn't stay wit' him 'cause he thought that people might get suspicious and put two an' two together. So I still stayed wit' my a'ntees but I never told 'em what I was doin'."

The flutter in Soupspoon's heart had a small speck of pain inside it.

"By the time I got there the shack was burnt down an' Bannon was dead. They had took him an' piled stovewood on'im an' then set him afire. His arms was just black bones reachin' out away.

"I runned right back to Inez an' Ruby. And I prayed that the people killed Bannon never knew about me."

Kiki came over from the bed to hug him.

"So what does all that have to do with a tape recorder?" Kiki asked some time later. She turned out the lamp, leaving the room lit only by the blooming blue waves of television light.

"Only two men ever taught me anything," Soupspoon said. "Bannon Tripps and Robert Johnson. But they taught me a lot. You know I ain't never had no kids or no nieces or nephews even.

"But I once knew this man name of Early, William Early out in Chicago. He wanted to interview me twenty years ago for a book about the blues. He called it *Back Road to the Blues*. I didn't want to at the time. That was a bad time in my life an' I didn't wanna think about no blues."

"But now you do?"

"That's why I want a tape recorder. I wanna tell my story like Bannon told his. I know stuff now too. I got somethin' to say an' you done gimme a chance here to say it, Kiki."

"What?"

"I could die anytime now, girl. I need to say somethin' an' send it to Mr. Early before that happens."

"Why not just call him?"

"I don't wanna call'im, goddammit! I wanna tell it an' play it right here. I wanna tell it my own way wit'out all kindsa questions an' shit. I just wan' it, wan' it the way I wan' it."

"Okay, daddy," Kiki said. "I'll get it for you on payday. Next Friday, I swear."

N I N E

Soupspoon left the apartment at four the next day. He knew where he was going but was in no hurry to get there. His hip hardly hurt him and he hadn't had to take a pill all day.

"Good morning, Mr. Wise," Mrs. Manetti said. She was coming up the stairs as he was coming down.

"Ms. Manetti. How are you today?"

"Oh, all right I guess," she said, looking at his feet.

She was older than he; gray-haired with rounded blunt features and thick hands that had held many years of hard work. Arthritic legs forced her to put both feet on each stair before ascending to the next. She put down both of her plastic bags to greet Soupspoon and took in a deep breath.

"You need some help?"

"Maybe if you could take one bag." She smiled as if it hurt to ask for help. "It's all the way to the top."

Soupspoon carried both bags back up the way he had come. They went past the fourth floor where he stayed with Kiki, toward the sixth where the old lady had lived for thirty-nine years with Alessio Manetti—and another twenty-three years alone. It was Alessio's old wheelchair that Kiki had borrowed.

They took one stair at a time—in her fashion.

At the half flight to the fifth floor they stopped to rest.

"I'm sorry about what they did to you, Mr. Wise. I tried to talk to them, but you know these young people won't listen. All they care about is beer and baseball, and whistling at the girls in those little dresses they wear.

"I called Mr. Grumbacher and told him that it was wrong. Wrong to put out somebody when he's sick. God takes in the rent too, you know."

There was no answer to what she said, but the subject was too painful for Soupspoon to go on with small talk.

"How are you now?" she asked.

"Just fine. Kiki took me to these doctors she knowed. They did a damn good job on my bones."

Mrs. Manetti leaned forward peering through half-blind gray eyes that were a perfect match for her hair.

"You like her?"

"Kiki? Yeah. She took me in." Soupspoon could feel the swelling over his left eye but he believed what he was saying.

"I don't know. I guess," the stocky little woman said. "But, well, you know . . . she has a bad mouth half the time, and you should see the kindsa men she brings in with her. Mrs. Green lives right upstairs and she hears them. Loud and fighting. I just think that you should be careful, Mr. Wise. You know, she's all smiles when you see her, but not after a drink."

"I don't know. I guess." Soupspoon picked up the bags and took normal steps to keep ahead, to keep from saying anything bad about Kiki. He wanted to protect her from the old women's words. After all, what did those old ladies know about hard times, about drinking hard to forget? Of course Kiki got mad, but not for no reason. She had a good reason and a good heart. But Soupspoon didn't want to make excuses. He wanted to carry those bags like a gentleman is supposed to do and then go on about his business.

Up to the sixth floor Soupspoon kept a few steps ahead. He could hear Mrs. Manetti straining and puffing behind. He turned once and said, "Slow down. I just got to move quick, but you could wait."

She couldn't wait, though. The ancient widow worked her feet and tugged on the railing until she could almost keep up with him. Her breath sounded like a greedy little dog slobbering over a bone.

"Which one is it?" Soupspoon called down to her.

"Number sixty-three," she said, head down, pulling her way up the stairs.

She reached him at the door.

"She called me a witch. All I did was to ask if maybe Social Services could help more because that's their job. I didn't mean anything. I didn't say that there was anything wrong with what she did," Mrs. Manetti declared. "She doesn't have any respect. You can't trust a girl like that, Mr. Wise."

The whole time she talked, Mrs. Manetti was rummaging around in her purse. Finally she came out with a copper key that had a red plastic handle. She pinched the key between two fingers and waited.

"You want me to carry the bags in an' put 'em on a table or somethin'?" he asked.

"No, thank you. You did enough already. I can manage." She made no move to unlock the door.

Soupspoon watched her watching eyes.

After a moment she blinked.

"You know, Ms. Manetti, nobody could help it."

"What?"

"Kiki ain't a bad girl . . ."

"I didn't say . . ."

"Excuse me, ma'am, but just let me say these here few words. That's all I ask." Soupspoon put out his hands. She could have held them if she wanted to. "You see, Kiki kinda wild but that's just who she is. She drink an' she mean sometimes. But when she fount me downstairs she opened up her do' an' took me in. She couldn't help it. It's the way she learnt, just like manners. It's like when you know somebody for a long time an' you see'em ev'ry day you ask'em in for a cuppa coffee now and then, right?"

The gray-headed, gray-eyed old woman nodded, still pinching her copper key.

"We cain't help who we is, ma'am." Soupspoon looked at her a while longer—waiting.

Mrs. Manetti held up her key. "I have to be going now, Mr. Wise. I have to call my daughter in Miami."

Soupspoon didn't want coffee anyway. He wanted to be outside walking with no pain, and so he went. He walked down Avenue C to Pitt and then over, down toward Orchard. Before he got there he turned again, toward his destination.

He had music on his mind and on the streets around him. The blasting boom bass from the trunk speakers of a passing car. Phonographs out of apartment windows. The bouncing butt of a heavyset girl in short shorts listening to her earphones and licking a soft ice cream cone.

Music had been in his every day almost from the very beginning. He had pledged his life to music when he was still a boy in Mississippi.

"What you mean you gonna be a musician?" Cleophus Brown asked thirteen-year-old Atty Wise. "Have you lost your mind?"

"I'd'ruther to pick guitar strings than pick cotton, Cleo. Damn! I'd'ruther shov'lin' coals in hell."

For two years after his pneumonia, young Atty Wise had spent every music night right outside the Milky Way. He'd heard Jeff "Little Boy" Tynan, Willa Smith, and Job Landry with Rodeo Bob White. He never saw Cody again, but Elma and Theresa were there every night. He saw them dancing and drinking, flirting and fighting over men, for a year before either of them saw him again.

Nobody saw him because Atty would climb up the live oak out behind the Milky Way and peer in through a flap he tore in the tarpaper wall. He could sit out there all night and watch and listen without all that harsh talk and hard liquor, without the hot smells and hot tempers.

He'd seen two men killed in that first year. One was Shrimper Martins, a great big sharecropper who had left his girlfriend Maretha in Clarksville to go back home to his wife and seven kids in

Cougar Bluff. Shrimper, Atwater had learned in the days after his murder, was the kind of religious man who sinned on Saturday and begged the Lord's forgiveness on Sunday morning.

He was sitting at a card table with his friends making a big celebration out of his return. There was a lot of drinking and laughing. Atty didn't like it because they made so much noise that Oja called off the music for that night. It was all toasting and roasting and talking loud because Shrimper was a popular man at the Milky Way and they were happy for his return.

When Atwater realized that there wasn't going to be music he was ready to go. But he wanted to wait till it was dark enough that he wouldn't be seen. That's when he saw Maretha walk up to the moon-splattered door of the juke. He didn't know who she was at that time but he could tell that she was different. To begin with, she was dressed in good brown cotton, good enough for church. And she walked with steady one-after-the-other steps, not like the regular customers ambling to and fro, seeing and being seen.

Atwater saw her at the front door and then he saw her in the bar through his flap. Shrimper was sitting among his friends, smiling and lifting his tin cup. As he brought the cup to his lips, Maretha was bringing her pistol to his head. She said something that Atwater couldn't hear. Shrimper turned to look but the bullet caught him in the temple before he could face her. The floor around the man and his killer cleared of people. In between the screams and shouts five more shots sounded, each one like the hack of an ax into thick bark.

I told you you'd never leave. That's what Maretha had said. Atwater heard about it later when the law came to take Maretha to jail.

Six months after that, Atwater changed his name. It was just after "Big Mouth" Willa Smith spied him peeking through the hole in the wall. She stopped singing and went right outside.

"Boy!" she shouted. "What you doin' up there?"

"Listenin', ma'am."

"Come on down here."

She took Atty inside and pulled him up to where she played guitar and bellowed.

"Atty!" Elma shouted. Theresa was grinning right behind her. Elma reached for him but Willa slapped her hand down.

"Hussy!" Willa hissed. "Git yo' hand away. This here boy ain't none'a your'n. He a music lover. He 'preciate the art."

The Milky Way wasn't so frightening when he was with Willa. She wasn't tall but she had big hands and the big mouth that she was named for. She was drunk most of the time and well armed with a .45-caliber repeater.

Willa loved it that little Atwater had been watching her through that hole and she was determined to make him into a musician.

He'd never played anything, so she gave him four big pewter spoons and showed him how to hold them between his fingers; how to hit them on his chest, stomach, and legs.

"Play somewhere between the way my head moves and my foot stomp. Play it like you love me," she said. And he did.

He loved her and rattled his spoons behind the brick wall of her voice.

Ruby and Inez had given up trying to keep him at home.

"He's a man now," Inez told Ruby, disgusted. "A fool."

Willa paid Atty ten cents for every dollar she made, and so he was rich. He spent every extra moment he had trying to learn the guitar, because Willa had once told him that "a woman's heart strings is di-rectly tied to the strings on a guitar."

He was still playing spoons, though, on the night of the second killing. Willa was singing, making up a song, really, that might have been called "Ain't Gonna Be No Cotton When I Die." She was strumming on her big-bellied seven-string guitar and Soupspoon (that was his name by then) was clattering alongside. A commotion broke out in the bar. Soupspoon looked over and saw Vesey Turnot push Tree Frank. Tree fell backwards but helping hands kept him from falling and pushed him back into the fray. Vesey hit Tree's jaw so hard that it sounded like a convict's hammer on a ripe stone ready to crack. Soupspoon knew that that blow would lay Tree down.

But it didn't.

Tree waded in swinging. Vesey did too. They looked less like men and more like little boys settling a dispute before running home for supper.

But these were men. Vesey was fast and accurate with his fists. He hit Tree where he wanted, and he hit him a lot. Tree was slow and lumbersome. For all the times he swung he hardly hit Vesey at all. But every time he connected, that part of Vesey's body stopped working.

First Tree put a dent in Vesey's side. Then he made the left arm fall down. When Tree finally laid his fist against Vesey's head it looked to Soupspoon like a watermelon had been cracked open.

The blood came from Vesey's face like a red snake jumping from a stone. The proud boxer put up his right hand to catch the blood and then he shouted, "Oh no! No!"

He grabbed for Tree's right arm so that he wouldn't get hit again.

Tree swung his arm around, tossing Vesey this way and that, but the bleeding boxer hung on.

"Please don't kill me!" Vesey yelled. "Please! Please!"

Finally Tree threw Vesey to the floor. Tree would have left him there but poor Vesey had been demented by the sight of his own blood. He grabbed Tree around the legs, bleeding on his ankles and begging, "I'm sorry! Please don't hit me again!"

Vesey showed more strength on his knees than he did with his fists. Tree couldn't push him away no matter how hard he tried. He had Vesey's blood all over his clothes and hands.

"Let me go, fool!" Tree shouted.

Willa had stopped singing.

"Pull that man offa there!" she shouted.

Tree backed up against the bar. He reached behind and grabbed a crock that was filled with pickled pigs' feet. Tree hurled that thick crock down with all his strength, hitting Vesey on the top of his head.

The clay didn't give.

Vesey stopped struggling and yelling. The whole jar of pig gelatin spilled down over his head. He slumped back against the bar and everybody else in the room went still.

Ulla Backley finally checked Vesey's breathing and his heart. "He's dead."

They laid Vesey out on the longest table at the Milky Way. He was flat on his back, no longer afraid, with blood and pork gelatin clotted across his handsome brown face.

Many people left the bar when they heard that Vesey was dead. Those that were left were the jury for Tree.

No one called the law like they had with Maretha. Maretha had murdered a man. Tree had just hit somebody who then wound up dead.

"Vesey started it," Elma said. "He called Tree funny-lookin' an' said how his momma was probably a dog."

"Yeah," some slim sharecropper agreed. "An' when Tree said to stop, Vesey picked a fight."

Tree had his head in his hands. He never thought that he would kill a man and was brokenhearted at what might happen to his soul. That's when Soupspoon decided to become a professional musician.

"When I heard that they was fightin' 'cause'a name-callin' I knew that I had to do it," he told Cleophus the very next afternoon. "I knew my life weren't worf a damn. Might as well do sumpin' I want 'fore they get me."

"Are you a fool, boy?" Cleophus asked. He had a great thatch of wild hair and wore plaid overalls. People treated him like he was a clown but Soupspoon knew that Cleophus was the smartest man in Cougar Bluff—after Bannon died.

"Yessir I am," Soupspoon said. "An' the on'y thing make me different is that I know it too. If I was out there pullin' cotton you know I'd be every night at the Milky Way, all drunk an' surly. An' if I get drunk enough I'm liable as not to fight. An' if I fight you know thatta be the end'a me."

Cleophus scratched under his burly beard and considered the boy's words.

What did he say? Soupspoon couldn't remember. It had been too many years. Too many war stories and bad movies, and bottles of beer. Too many girlfriends who he lied to and who, in turn, lied to him.

Soupspoon was coming down the street. In front of him was a big vacant lot, with a few men lingering toward the back end. On the other side of the lot was a short, dead-end alley.

"Hey, mistah. Mistah." It was an old man wearing a spotty green T-shirt under a black-and-white checkered jacket. His pants were tan and he had on a Mets sun visor cap. White stubble sprouted along his black jawline.

"Yeah?"

"You got a quarter?"

"Hell," Soupspoon said. "I got fi'ty cent."

The Mets fan staggered forward, raised his head, smiled.

"Guy name Rudy got a club back here somewheres?" Soupspoon asked.

"They ain't gone let you in," the man said. "They ain't gone let you in. Might as well put yo' money wit' mines an' we get us some Colt 45."

Soupspoon took two quarters from his pocket. "Where Rudy's?" he asked.

"Ovah yonder." The drunk pointed with the hand that held his money. The coins fell but Soupspoon wasn't distracted. It was a black door—the kind of door superstitious people used to ward off curses—down the dead-end street.

Inside the dark hot room smelt strongly of beer. There was a long black bar across the back and a few tables to one side. The room was populated by half a dozen black men who smoked, drank, and were talking serious in low tones. Everybody looked up to see Soupspoon as he walked up to the bar.

"I'd like a beer," he told the barmaid.

"This a private club, mistah," she answered.

"Rudy Peckell the owner?"

"I *said* that this was private," she answered. "That means that I don't tell you nuthin' and you walk back out the way you came in."

"Because," Soupspoon said as if the woman hadn't said a word, "Rudy's a friend'a mines. Coupla years ago I run inta him an' he told me I should come on by if I ever get the chance."

The woman looked Soupspoon over. Her face was ready to be mad but he thought she looked sweet in spite of her disposition. She didn't know whether to believe that he knew Rudy, but, he could see, she really didn't care either.

She took a glass from under the bar and worked the spigot on it. "Thatta be one seventy-five," she said after serving him.

"What's your name?"

"Sono." The short woman took the two dollars from him and put them in her apron pocket. She made no move to give him any change.

Sono was short and well-proportioned. Her lips were pursed in a perpetual, if sour, kiss. Her skin was high yellow and there was a deep brown mole riding on the words in her throat. A big fly buzzed lazily above her head. Soupspoon couldn't hear its drone above the hum of the refrigerator behind the bar.

Soupspoon thought he knew this woman. Not that he ever met her but that he'd known many a woman like her. A sweet girl who loved her daddy and her kids. A girl who never understood why people treated her the way they did. And even though she'd had it hard she was still looking; looking for that one man. A pretty black man who could talk her out of her clothes; who could work hard all day and playboy at night. A man who could bear up under the hot and heavy love that she'd been holding inside her chest since she was a baby—maybe since before she was born. A man who could learn that that love she had was all he would ever need in this life. A hard man who she could crack open like a sweet pecan. A man who could give up his sweetness to her.

"Rudy here yet?" Soupspoon asked.

"Do you see him?"

"He here yet?"

"Uh-uh, no. Rudy don't never come in till later."

"Well, when he get in tell'im I need t'talk. You got sandwiches here?"

"Naw. All we got is some potato chips an' pretzels."

"How much?"

"Pretzels free if you drinkin'."

"Then gimme some'a them, 'cause I'ma be waitin' right ovah at that table till Rudy gets here."

Sono filled a round plastic bowl with thin pretzels and handed them to Soupspoon.

He was happy to be eating and drinking, seeing colors and breathing the rancid air.

The bar filled up as the evening came on. All kinds of black men came in. Some came in work clothes, overalls and boots. A few dressed in synthetic pastel-colored suits with big-brimmed hats and almost fluorescent shoes. There were old men with sad yellow eyes and threadbare trousers. One big guy, who Sono called Bongo, made his eyes big and told jokes full of curse words. Soupspoon would catch snatches of his foul humor, like ". . . ugly, *ugly* mothah-fuckah had a tongue so big that could French-kiss 'er an' be lickin' her pussy at the same time . . ."—lots of laughing—". . . you know ain't no black woman gonna give up somethin' like that!" Every-body broke up at that. Sono laughed so hard that she went down on both knees for a second there.

Rudy walked in at just about seven-thirty wearing a midnight-blue silk suit and a yellow shirt. His loose tie was the color of blood. He was followed by a large Hawaiian man. Soupspoon decided the man was Hawaiian because he wore a brightly colored shirt and even though he was fairly brown-skinned he had big eyes for an Asian and black hair that came straight down to his shoulder.

"Take the door, Cholo." Rudy grinned, showing pure white teeth against mahogany skin. "Who gots the bones?"

"Right here, Rudy," a man all in pink said. "I been keepin' 'em next t'my nuts so they know who's boss down there on the flo'."

Cholo took his place at the door. Some of the men followed Rudy to the back of the bar. They all crouched down around him.

He put his hand deep into his pocket and came out with a wad of money so thick that it would have made Soupspoon sweat if he were a younger man still dazzled by the luster of cash. Rudolph threw down a bill and said, "One hundred dollars! One hundred dollars on my first throw." Then he threw the dice so hard that they sounded like the report of a .22.

"Five! That's a lucky number for me. My little girl is five. I was five with my first woman. I got five thousand dollars in my pocket. Now lemme see some'a all you boys's green."

Rudolph looked up at Soupspoon then, and smiled. He showed his teeth and nodded, but he quickly looked back at the gamblers that surrounded him. Soupspoon knew that he'd have to wait. Rudy was the man now while Soupspoon was shrinking back to the size of a boy.

The men started shouting and throwing down bets.

Soupspoon sipped his beer and watched them from his table. It seemed like Rudolph was winning, but he couldn't tell. He'd never been a gambler, never cared about taking chances like that.

"What you thinkin' 'bout?" Sono was putting a fresh glass of beer on the table.

"Wonderin' how could you stand it."

"Stand what?"

"Bein' cooped up in this smelly old room with all these here yappin' hyena men."

"Boxcars!" a tiny workman cried. "Damn!"

Somebody cackled. Money passed from hand to hand.

"I told Rudy 'bout you," Sono said.

"What he say?"

"That if you still here when he get through that maybe you could talk."

"I'll be here."

Sono walked away from him slowly. She got about half the way to the bar, then she stopped and came back. She put her platter down and stood very close to the bluesman.

"Men are fools," she said in a low voice. "They hide it pretty good, though, so mosta your women be even worse than fools 'cause they believe in them.

"But I don't never trust a man," Sono went on. " 'Cause I come in an' see'em here, where they don't do no pretendin'. They might as well all line up an' lay they ducks down on the table. That's all they care about—who got the biggest dick an' who get the most pussy. After four nights'a bein' in this hellhole I got enough of men t'last me a year."

"Is that all men?"

Sono sneered at Soupspoon. She wasn't going to let him think that he was special.

"Yeah," she said. "All y'all."

"How 'bout yo' man Rudolph?"

"That's different."

"Different how?"

"Rudolph is a businessman. Ev'rything he do is business. All that big talk is t'get them men drinkin' an' th'owin' they money away. He always the house in a crap game. He always makin' money."

"So at least Rudolph ain't no fool, huh?"

"That don't mean he ain't gonna make a fool outta me, or some other poor girl."

"Sono!" one of the gamblers shouted.

She took her platter and went back to work.

Now and then during the night a knock might come, and Cholo would look through the peephole and then open up. Mostly gamblers came to Rudy's; he was the Atlantic City of the Lower East Side.

At about two, Soupspoon was ready to go. He was wondering about a last glass of beer when a knock came on the door. Cholo peeped and then whistled so loud that it hurt.

The dice stopped rolling and all of the men were up on their feet strolling aimlessly away from the game.

Cholo pulled open the door and a white man in a wrinkled tan suit came in. As he walked in the door he pushed Cholo aside.

"How you doin', man?" someone said at Soupspoon's side.

It was the man dressed in pink. He had a dark, scarred-up face and was chewing on a wooden match. He extended a hand to shake.

"Name's Billy Slick." His breath was sour.

"Soupspoon's what they call me."

"Hello, Officer Todd," Rudolph was saying. He had his arms extended like a halfhearted Christ and a smile plastered across his face.

" 'Gainst the law t'lock the doors if you're open for business," said the jowly-faced cop.

"A man just left here ten minutes ago an' said he was comin' back to settle a debt with Cholo there. We locked the door to keep trouble away."

"You should have called the police if you were threatened," the cop said.

"Don't look at'em," Billy told Soupspoon. "Pretend you talkin' t'me an' let Rudy do his thing."

Rudy was talking. "I didn't want to cause the man no problem. He coulda just been talkin' outta his head."

"What was this man's name?" The policeman took a note pad from his pocket.

"Why don't we go back to my office an' talk in private, officer." Rudolph gestured the way and the two went through a door behind the bar.

"Time for the greasin'," Billy Slick said.

"Yeah, I guess so."

"Have I seen you here before, man?"

"Naw. But I know Rudy. Ain't seen'im in a while, though."

"Where you been?"

"Sick. Sick and tired."

"That's too bad," Billy Slick said, not caring a damn. "But you better now, right?"

"When Rudy close?"

"That depends." The big man's eyes lit up when Rudy's name was mentioned. "If he got a woman waitin' he break about two,

two-thirty—a woman waitin' or a bad streak."

Soupspoon nodded and looked Billy up and down. He was maybe forty with big muscles under those pink clothes.

"What you want wit' Rudy?" Billy asked.

The older bluesman felt the smile come to his face. He heard the men laughing and shuffling and even that lazy fly buzzing around, looking for the barmaid's scent.

"You hear it?" Soupspoon asked at last.

"Hear what? I don't hear nuthin'."

"That's what I wanna talk to Rudy about."

"You crazy?" Billy asked.

"Uh-huh. I'm a musician, least I used to be. Maybe I could be again."

"You wanna play here?" When he smiled, Billy showed two missing teeth and a broken one. It reminded Soupspoon of someone but he couldn't quite remember who.

The air around them was sour from Billy's breath, but Soupspoon didn't mind. He liked the atmosphere.

"You come on back whenever you want, hear?" Rudolph was saying to Officer Todd. Todd was gruff and moved quickly toward the door. He made eye contact with any man who would look at him—but most men were looking down.

On his way out the door Todd said to Cholo, "Keep this door open from now on."

The Hawaiian grunted and nodded but when Todd walked out he slammed the door shut and threw the bolt home.

Billy Slick was on his feet the moment the door was closed.

"I'm lookin' fo' seven!" he shouted. "I'm on a mission for home!"

By three the game was over. The only people left in the club were Rudy's employees. Rudolph spent a few minutes talking to Billy Slick and Sono at the bar, then he strolled over to Soupspoon's table.

"Soup," Rudy said.

Soupspoon held out his hand but he didn't stand. "Rudy."

"What can I do for you?"

"It's a nice place you got here," Soupspoon answered. "Why'ont you sit down an' drink wit' me?"

"I got places t'be." Rudy pointed at his heavy gold wristwatch—it read three-fifteen.

"You ain't got five minutes t'drink wit' a old friend?"

The gambler looked uncomfortable for a moment. Soupspoon addressed himself to the boy he had known, not the man standing in front of him.

"Sono!" Rudy called.

"Yeah?"

"Bring ovah some Wild Turkey and a coupla glasses."

Rudy sat with a hand on each knee.

Sono rushed over with the liquor. She poured each squat tumbler one quarter full.

"I need a job, Rudy," Soupspoon said.

"A job?"

Soupspoon nodded and touched the rim of his glass.

"Hey, I'm sorry, man, but I don't have nuthin' for ya here. It's just me an' Cholo an' Sono here. Sometimes Billy do a odd job, but you too old for anything he do."

"I could play the blues."

"This ain't no music club. You know that, Soup. Shit, I'ont even have a jukebox."

Rudy was big and hale now that he was a man. He was sure of himself and people respected him. But Soupspoon remembered the skinny little boy in cutoffs and no shirt. He and his wife, Mavis, used to pick Rudy up at his mother's house and take him home for fried chicken dinner. They played tic-tac-toe and dominoes with him in the front room.

The first time he ever saw Rudy he was no more than six. Soupspoon and Mavis were out walking when they saw this little boy, all snot-nosed and ragged, breaking bottles in the street.

Mavis went right up to him and jerked him by his arm.

"Pick up that damn glass, boy! You think people want holes in they tires just 'cause you bored?"

From the look on his face, Soupspoon figured that that was the first time anybody had ever tried to make Rudy do right.

It probably was. His mother wasn't much use. She had seven kids—and a boyfriend for each one. When Mavis made Rudy take her to his sixth-floor apartment, up in Harlem, they found two babies eating peanut butter out of a jar on the floor while Mrs. Peckell was with one of her men in the back room.

"Maybe we better leave, Mavy," Soupspoon had suggested. He didn't want to come to blows with some man that he didn't even know.

"You could leave if you want to, Soupspoon Wise," Mavis had said. "But I will not sit by and leave these children to live like this."

"Oh yeah! Yeah, baby!" Mrs. Peckell yelled from behind the closed door.

Rudy stuck his finger in his ear, embarrassed by the lack of manners his mother displayed.

Mavis let Rudy take his little brothers out in the hall. Then she banged on the closed door.

The yelling stopped and Soupspoon could make out the sounds of clothes rustling, springs singing, and shoes sliding on the floor.

"What?" a woman's voice called out.

"Come on out here!" Mavis commanded. It was the first time Soupspoon heard her voice like that. It was the first notion he had that they wouldn't be together forever.

The woman who came out was a mess. Her Cleopatra wig was crooked on her head, her eyes were two colors, and the sheet wrapped around her big body was covered with stains—some of them still wet with bloody patches in them.

The man, who came out second, was small. He wore gray pants and a shirt with no sleeves.

"What?" the messy woman asked again.

"I come about your kids." Mavis was no taller than Mrs. Peckell but she managed to look down on her just the same.

"What about my kids?" Mrs. Peckell glanced at the floor where the two infant boys had been eating.

"I better be goin', Jessie," her little boyfriend said.

"Richard, sit'own!"

He almost did it. Even though he was nowhere near a chair he let his butt slump back as if he meant to fall down on the floor and await her next command. But instead of falling down he took a long step forward like a Russian Cossack dancer—then he took another.

"Richard!"

But he was gone out of the door. He took Mrs. Peckell's brass along with him. All of a sudden she seemed slack and flabby—aware of how messy she and her house were.

"What about my kids?" she asked Mavis again.

"I fount Rudy in the street breakin' glass."

"Is he hurt?" Jessie Peckell asked.

"He's fine. But now I come up here an' find yo' other babies eatin' wit' they hands on the flo' while you layin' up wit' that sorry li'l coward . . ."

"That's Juanita's fault," the sad mother said. "I told her to feed them an' take 'em to the park. I'ma beat Juanita's ass when she come home."

"Are they your kids?" Mavis's voice shook.

Jessie shook too, like a kid herself, caught smoking behind the house.

"Are they?" Mavis lifted her fist, causing Jessie to flinch.

"Are they?" Mavis asked again. "Are they yours? Because if they your babies—an' you don't watch'em ev'ry minute—then they gonna be dead an' not nuthin' you say to nobody else gonna bring 'em back. When you look at his chair an' ain't nobody there, ain't no flowers gonna, ain't no sea breeze gonna help . . ."

Mavis walked right up to Rudy's mother with her fist still raised. Jessie fell backwards, not because she was afraid, Soupspoon thought, but because of the hurt that Mavis showed her.

"I'm dyin', Rudy," Soupspoon said. "Got cancer in my bones an' I'm almost homeless. I did some radiation an' now I'm gettin' ready t'go on keemo. An' all I want is to play the blues."

"A'ntee know that?" Rudy called Mavis his a'ntee.

"Mavis in New York?"

"Uh-huh," the boy inside the man answered.

"Well, I ain't talked to Mavis in years. An' I don't want you t'tell'er nuthin' neither. All I want from you is yea or nay."

"I don't even know what you want."

"I wanna play music. I wanna play it here. All I need is a chair."

Rudy twisted his face like a little boy again. Soupspoon remembered the first time that Mavis took him home: his face was all twisted then too. He didn't want to stay for the night away from home. He didn't want to until he tasted the roast pork and potatoes with gravy; he didn't want to until he had buckwheat pancakes and bacon for breakfast and then a pony ride in Central Park.

"People don't come in here to hear music, Soup. They come here to gamble; gamble an' drink."

"I'ont care what they want. They gonna get me," Soupspoon said. "You know you owe me, Rudy. You owe me sumpin'."

"I cain't pay ya."

"That's okay. I take donations."

Rudy downed his scotch. He sat back in his chair and then he sat forward, bringing his elbows to his knees. Then he sat up again and covered his lips with his hand.

Soupspoon smiled to see the fidgety boy grown into a man.

"Keemo be over in three weeks. If that don't kill me I might got six months, maybe more. I figger I be strong enough t'come in in about a month or five weeks. We try it on, an' if it don't fit . . . well then, I'll leave."

Billy Slick and Sono were listening to the conversation from the bar behind Rudy.

"Do it, Rudy," Sono said.

"Yeah," chimed in Billy Slick. "Do it."

"You gonna take responsibility for it, Billy?" Rudy asked in a threatening tone.

"Sure I will. I'll set'im up an' break'im down too. Shit! I used to do that at the Palladium till they fired my ass."

Rudy nodded. Sono grinned at her new friend.

"Okay," Rudy said. "Listen, I tell you what, you call me when you ready in four or five weeks an' we see. All right?"

She slapped him hard across the face as he was tiptoeing in.

"Where the hell have you been?" Kiki stood only half a foot from Soupspoon—her breath was ninety proof. She cocked her fist and reared back. Soupspoon knew that if she hit him again he'd be on the floor, so he pushed out with both hands as hard as he could against her chest. He swung out to slap her but only clipped the top of her head as she was already falling.

When she hit the floor, Soupspoon took a step backward intending to get outside, but he bumped into the door and it swung shut. He couldn't open it because he didn't dare to turn his back on Kiki when she was wild.

But he didn't have to worry. Kiki rolled herself up into a ball and sobbed.

"Don't touch me!" she shrieked when he crouched down beside her. His hip throbbed along with his left cheek but the real pain was a hollow aching that came from the very center of his heart.

"I ain't gonna touch ya. I'm just gonna sit here next to ya. That's all. I ain't goin' nowhere."

While Kiki cried, Soupspoon pressed his fingers against the left side of his chest. The pain was like a hard pea lodged in his clenching heart. It was the memory of love and the onset of death all at once. It set off a wild glee in him.

"You didn't have to hurt me," Kiki said, her face still buried between her knees.

"I was just scared, honey. I'as afraid that you might start hittin' me an' then not be able t'stop."

"I didn't mean it," she said and then gulped. "I was just worried because it was so late and you didn't call or leave a note or anything. You were just gone and I was scared that you wouldn't ever come back."

Soupspoon put his hand on her heaving side. She brought her arm down and clamped the hand to her.

"Where'm I gonna go, baby? I'as just tryin' t'get ready for what I'ma do after this keemo shit."

"What do you mean?" Kiki asked as she sat up. She wiped the tears from her eyes and brushed back her hair in the same motion.

"Doctor says I'll be real sick for a while. She says that keemo is poison for the cancer. But I figure that if they got me takin' poison then I gots to be real sick already. Sick almost to dyin'—an' maybe even dyin'."

"Don't say that, daddy . . ."

"Don't cut me off now, girl. You know since you brought me up here I been thinkin'—I started playin' the blues 'cause I had a feelin' that I would die young an' all I wanted before that happened was to play. An' now that I'm dyin' for real I wanna do it again. I wanna make sumpin' an' leave sumpin' behind."

"I'm sorry," Kiki said.

"Yeah, baby. Me too."

"I didn't mean to hurt you," she said.

"I know you didn't, baby. I know it."

T E N

For the next three weeks Dr. Fey and his assistants administered Soupspoon's "keemo." The poisons made his ears ring day and night, took his appetite, and made the little hair he had left fall out.

He lost twelve pounds.

The first few days he staggered around the apartment—vomiting and shivering. He couldn't get warm no matter how much he wore. Even in front of the stove he felt the chill of death. His blood went bad and the doctor gave him transfusions one after the other. Soupspoon had to lie on a hard table six hours at a time with the blood leaking into his vein.

After a week they decided to keep him in the hospital because the doctor was afraid that the trip back and forth would kill him.

The head nurse had asked Kiki to stay away after the third day. She argued with the nurses and set up a racket whenever Soupspoon was the slightest bit uncomfortable—and he was under the pain of death most of the time. Kiki yelled and commanded and tried to stop them when she thought they might hurt him needlessly.

But it was when she knocked down the tray of syringes in a rage that Nurse Jones asked her to leave.

"You're not helping Atwater, Tanya," she said as kindly as she could.

After that Kiki had asked Randy to see after Soupspoon—but not as a request. The only way Randy could have any of her attention was to share it with Soupspoon in the cancer ward.

Randy had seen the way she pulled the blankets over Soupspoon while he slept. She'd refuse even to whisper if he was napping.

So when Kiki asked Randy to take some time to go into hospital, he did it. He knew that her temper would have ended their friendship if he had refused.

He was only twenty-five, younger than Kiki by over ten years. But in spite of their difference in age he was crazy about her. He loved her red hair and her pale sinewy arms. The slight southern twang in her voice always made him smile. He liked the way she couldn't be pushed around and how she was never shy about saying what she thought. If somebody did something that she didn't like, she told them—no matter who it was. It didn't matter if they were white or black. Kiki spoke her mind.

It was true that she used bad language and derogatory names, especially when she was under the influence of alcohol or marijuana. Randy didn't condone the use of artificial stimulants or bad language. His mother had brought him up to be a proper gentleman in Flushing, Queens.

Randy only had a mother. His father hadn't even been there to see Randy's birth. For a long time Randy believed that his father had died. That was the story his mother had told him. But when he was fourteen he found a stack of letters from J. Chesterton addressed to his mother.

There was no reason to believe that his mother had lied. It could have been some other J. Chesterton. Maybe a cousin. It couldn't have been old letters from his father; he knew that because the postmark was only six years old—way after his death.

Randy's father died, the story went, moving a shipload of Frigidaires from Bethesda, Maryland, to Morocco. Jamal, his father, was a blue-eyed Arabian of ancient stock; a rare Caucasian Arab who had merchant blood running in his veins. Esther, Randy's mother, was from South American lineage—descended from the conquistadors. Her blood, she said, was ninety-nine percent Spanish, because the upper classes didn't mix much with the natives. "Most of your mixing," she told the boy, "was done among Indians and common soldiers." When Randy asked her why her skin was so tanned all the time she said that as far as she knew the only documented case of *mixing* in her family tree was with a Mayan princess over three centuries earlier.

"But you know that royal blood is powerful," she told the impressionable boy. "It shines through the centuries."

But one day a Negro couple with two small children came to the front door claiming to be cousins of Jamal Chesterton, whose father was an English explorer. Mrs. Chesterton told them, with great patience and reserve, that their cousin and her husband must have had the same name but were in reality two different people.

"But we saw Jamal just last week," the big brown woman said. "He gave us this address. He wanted to know how his son was doing."

"That proves it," Mrs. Chesterton said. "My husband died fourteen years ago and never knew that he had a son. He died in a shipwreck off the coast of Africa."

"Jamal's not dead," the dapper little man in a doe-gray suit said. "He's in Atlanta."

Atlanta was the city in the postmark on the letters that Randy had found.

"I don't know what to tell you," Mrs. Chesterton said. She held the door wide open as if to prove that there was no secret in her house. "This cousin of yours has made some kind of mistake. Tell him that I hope he finds his wife and son, though."

Mrs. Chesterton gave the couple a big smile and waited for them to leave. Randy could see that they wanted to say more, but instead they gathered their small children, a boy and a girl, and left.

After they were gone, Randy's mother sat down at the kitchen table in a foul mood. She refused to answer any questions about the couple that had come or make guesses as to how they made the mistake.

The next day Randy looked for the letters but they were gone from the desk.

Three weeks later a moving van came and took them to a new address in Long Island City.

Randy knew that the move had something to do with those letters and the visit from the Negro couple. His mother had always discouraged his relationships with Negro children in school and would get coldly angry when anyone mistook him for anything other than what he was—an exotic Caucasian.

Randy never disliked coloreds when he was a child. He liked it that his hair was so curly, and as soon as he was old enough to defy Esther, he grew dreadlocks. He didn't mind black people. He had a lot of black friends. He got along so well with black people that many people often mistook him, probably because of his hair and royal Mayan blood, for a Negro himself.

But that's where Randy drew the line.

You had to be true to your race.

He was an exotic; a white man without clear European lineage. But white still and all. Black people, he felt, could never truly understand his world. Because of slavery and racism the world of blacks could never encompass the path that he intended to travel.

Upon graduation from Pace, Randy would enter an Ivy League law school. From law school he would go to Wall Street, using the connections he'd made. Randy knew that from a position of power he'd still have gentle feelings for the deserving oppressed.

He saw these feelings reflected in the way Kiki saw the world. He imagined them not only married but as a kind of a team. Two conservative white people who made the black people they assisted toe the line in order to receive help from the various charities they would endow. Of course, he'd have to get Kiki to stop using the word "nigger." But he overlooked those flaws for the present because he loved her. He wanted her to be his wife. And if she clung to her resolve never to bear children, they would adopt; maybe even some African child—that would prove that their hearts were in the right place.

But before any of that could happen he had to take care of Soupspoon. He had to because Kiki had such a sensitive heart that their love might not survive his refusal.

At first he didn't care about Soupspoon. He was just an old man who smelled like rotted corncobs. Somehow he'd figured out how to take advantage of Kiki's generosity—that's what Randy thought.

But even though he didn't care about being there, Randy saw how terrible the treatments were. Soupspoon suffered nausea and great pain without a complaint. Sometimes when the nurse would just lightly touch Soupspoon's arm Randy could see a shiver run through the length of his body.

"Oh, no!" Soupspoon's lips mouthed the words, but he never made a sound. He let the poisons into his body but his eyes seemed to be stronger than the pain.

On his third visit Randy noticed a change in his feelings toward Kiki's friend. He'd brought a book to read but it lay unopened while he gazed into Soupspoon's sightless eyes. He felt like looking away but couldn't; he felt like going down to the rest room but he didn't have to go. When he finally went outside the room a nurse smiled at him and he turned away quickly so that she couldn't see him cry. It was then that he knew the feeling that had come over him—it was shame. He was ashamed of how naked the pain was.

"Yo' daddy's dead?" Soupspoon asked during his ninth six-hour transfusion.

"Yes, sir. Died when I was two—shipwrecked."

"I'm sorry to hear that."

"It was a long time ago. I guess I'm used to it by now."

Soupspoon took pleasure in watching the young man.

Randy brought textbooks to read when Soupspoon was dozing. Books like *In the Street* and *Investment Strategies for the Eighties*. He also brought the *Wall Street Journal*. He'd read the national and international news items from page one to Soupspoon when the sound didn't jangle the sick man's nerves.

Sometimes the needles and poisons and fluorescent lights got to be too much for Soupspoon. He'd start shaking from weakness and the nearness of death. Randy would put down his book and hold the dry old hands in an attempt to stop the tremors. Once Soupspoon shook so terribly that Randy got scared and so upset that he actually kissed the older man's forehead.

A kiss.

Soupspoon looked up into the worried face of the youngster, still feeling where the lips had touched him. He tried to remember the last time someone had loved him so much that they wanted to kiss him. Not some love partner, not sex, but when was the last time someone saw his pain and wanted to kiss it away? Maybe Ruby and Inez did it, he didn't remember. He'd been kissed before. Kissed and licked and sucked dry. Kicked and shoved too. He'd been in love with Mavis and other women. But none of them had ever tried to kiss his pain. He'd been in love with the whole world, everything, when the music was right. But Randy's kiss was something special. Something he'd missed.

That day Soupspoon got his sickest. A fever took him over and he fell into nightmare. Sometimes he was having chills on the transfusion table and other times he was in a plantation barn, surrounded by corpses that had known his name.

"Where's your family from?" Soupspoon asked. He and Randy were at Kiki's apartment the day after they'd sent him home. It was two weeks after his final "keemo" injection so his ears were only buzzing slightly.

"North Africa—that is, Morocco—and Brazil." He looked away as he spoke.

"I guess we everywhere, huh?"

"I don't know what you mean."

"Colored people, Negroes, niggahs. We everywhere."

"Oh, I see," Randy said, looking down at his own brown hand. "No sir, you're wrong about me. I'm not a Negro. My father was pure Arab and my mother was from Brazil. A lot of people think I'm black but I'm not. Not at all."

Soupspoon just stared, dumbfounded by Randy's claim.

"That's why I have such light eyes," Randy went on.

"That's from the Arab or the South American?"

"Some Arabs have blue eyes, it's considered a blessing to have them. There was a whole blue-eyed Semitic tribe in the eleventh century. They were great warriors and scientists."

"Yo' momma come down from them?"

"My father. He was a tradesman."

Soupspoon had known many Negroes who'd *passed* for being white. Some would just get dressed up and go out to white restaurants and white churches for a hoot. Some, who couldn't bear being what they were, moved into white neighborhoods and lived like they really were white. They'd marry, raise children and explain their curly hair as coming down from Greece or Ireland or some other exotic Caucasian land. They belonged to the Junior League and the Ku Klux Klan, voted for conservatives, some even ran for office. They spoke the white man's language better than he did, because nobody knows white people better than blacks. A black man knows the white man inside out. And why not? They took old clothes, old cars, old books, and old food from white people. They lived in a world where they had to be better than white. White men never had to worry about how they talked or walked or laughed. They took being white for granted. Anything a white man did was okay because it was a white man doing it. But a black man was different. No matter how hard he studied or how righteous he was, a black man still had the mark of Cain on him. All you had to do was look.

But if your skin was light and your hair was *good* then you were treated better. Whites liked light-skinned Negroes more, and a light-skinned lover was the dream of many a dark heart. Light-skinned Negroes had better jobs. The lighter the better. And if you were light enough you might even slip through a crack and make it into heaven.

Soupspoon knew them. Sometimes he'd catch one sitting down in a hotel lobby. By his profile or the way he folded his hands Soupspoon suspected their common roots. He'd be certain when the man would catch his glance and look quickly away. That man would have bad dreams for a month over that look. But he didn't need to worry, because Soupspoon wasn't going to tell. Nobody had to tell him why colored brothers and sisters passed. There wasn't a thing of value to being black in America back then. You didn't have a damn thing and anything you might get could be taken away. Maybe white people had it hard too, but you couldn't convince a black man of that. His porridge was so hard he'd put rocks in it to help him chew.

It was a hard life that made people want to pass, but, Soupspoon thought, Randy had it harder than anybody.

At least the people Soupspoon had known knew where they came from. They were passing—making it in the white man's world the way all colored people do: looking the man in the face and lying about what you feel and what you know—what you were inside. Everybody did that. Lying to the white man was both sport and survival.

The people Soupspoon had known lied to the white man, but Randy lied to himself. Look at him and you saw what he was—a gray-eyed Negro. But when he looked in the mirror he saw a white man. He imagined himself in the white man's history books and as the star of TV shows. Maybe he loved opera.

Soupspoon used to laugh about people like Randy, made up funny songs about them. But not anymore.

"Well," the old man said, "I guess we all just folks makin' it any way we can."

As Soupspoon's strength returned he felt the tide of cancer receding. And in forgiving Randy he felt cured of the disease that made black men want to be white. All of his dreams and memories about the Delta and the pathways of the blues became sharper in his mind.

The memory of Robert Johnson was so strong in him that he sometimes felt that he could actually talk to the guitar man. He'd walk around Kiki's studio apartment, while she was at work, imagining RL was at his side talking about women he'd known and how many records he could play from memory.

It all came in one big rush; too much for him to make sense of. He tried to write it down but the words were flat and toneless. He turned on the cassette recorder that Kiki brought home from Radio Shack and tried to talk out his stories. But when he played the tape back he was reminded of a hapless baby-sitter trying to tell a fairy tale that he couldn't remember.

Finally he asked Kiki to help.

"Just listen to me," he said. "I'm a storyteller. Storyteller need somebody wanna hear what he got to tell."

ELEVEN

"I run into RL at harvest time in Arcola, Mississippi. He told me t'come on later and join'im, but by the time I got there he was already at work, playin' his guitar. He was playin' a new song like I never heard the blues played before. It was his own words and they was somethin', but I didn't care 'bout the words at first. I was moved by his wild voice and the way he th'owed his head back like somethin' in'im might break if he didn't holler it off with a song. He was like some righteous Baptist minister rapt in prayer. Not that religious folk would ever claim ole RL an' his devil music." Soupspoon turned to Kiki and winked. She'd come home with a bucket of fried chicken, a six-pack, and a quart of Jack Daniel's. She laid out the feast on the dining table and sat down, all attention.

"He was a skinny boy," Soupspoon continued, "with one good eye and one dead one that floated in its socket. With that dead eye they said he could see past all what we see, into hell—where everyone knows the blues come from anyways.

"His hands was like angry spiders up and down them guitar strings. No two men could play what RL, Bob LeRoy, Robert Johnson could play. He was a field nigger too lazy to pull cotton. He was scarred and scared and smallish. He loved his momma an' almost ev'ry other woman he ever met.

"But like I was sayin', it was late in the day an' there wasn't too many people out 'cause it was cotton-choppin' time in Mississippi an' all the colored folks was workin' except for me an' RL an' maybe five or seven lazy souls like us.

"I remember four nappy-headed boys and a old man called Crawdaddy an' two young girls. The girls was Linda Powell and Booby Redman. The boys was all stampin' they feet an' noddin' they agreement with what RL sang. An' old Crawdaddy shook his shoulders like he was a young man again, ready to get out on the dance floor or pull down his terrible Texas jackknife.

"It was like hurricane weather that day, both warmish and cool, with a wind comin' up from the Gulf and mockingbirds wheelin' across the sky at every note.

"At first he played 'Love in Vain' but it was when RL sung 'Me and the Devil' that Booby's jaw dropped down. She had on a plain cotton dress with a bright red rag across her head. She was a healthy girl with upstandin' bosom and sturdy legs, but when she heard RL her jaw hung open and her hands dangled down at her side. By the time RL told us that his evil soul would catch the Greyhound I thought that Booby might just fall down and cry.

"That boy could play the clothes right off a woman's back."

"By the Rolling Stones?" Kiki asked.

"What?"

" 'Love in Vain,' isn't that the same song that the Rolling Stones did?" Kiki was all excitement and grins.

"Girl, do you wanna let me tell this here story or do you wanna ask all kindsa stupid questions?"

Kiki took a wing from the bucket of fried chicken and puckered her lips into an air-blown kiss for her friend.

"Now, where was I?" Soupspoon asked. "Oh yeah, we was out on the street. RL stamped his hard soles and sung new blues. I mean he was playin' music that nobody ever heard before, he was makin' history right there in front'a our eyes. The people come, more and more, and the nickels fall into his old bean can. When there was enough of a crowd I went across the street and took out my own guitar. I was just sixteen but you know I could play.

"Bluesmen in the Delta liked to play both sides of the street. It made us kind of a spectacle that the country Negroes wanted to see. And it didn't hurt too much if you was on the road an' you had somebody willin' t'jump in if some field hand got mad at the way you made his girl laugh.

"I guess RL's music was too much for Booby, because she come across the street, really it was just a graded dirt road, to hear my soft sweet blues. Satan wasn't after me. That's why I'm still here in the flesh.

"That was a day to remember. It was the end of a hard day in the fields. People was so tired that they fingers dragged in the dust, but they still come to see what everybody else was doin'. Even the sky was curious. Big ole fat clouds rushed over and then passed for a glimmer of sunshine that would blind for a minute. People was yellin', 'Play it!' an' 'All right!' Some of the girls was movin' they feet and the boys was soon to dance with'em because back then when a woman got the urge to dance she was serious. If her boyfriend didn't wanna dance she'd take her another man by the hand. That's just the way it was.

"We played and played. The nickels fell like hail. Everybody was movin' to RL's evil moods. And when they got tired they'd come over to me an' I'd sooth'em with songs like 'Got Me a Country Girl' or 'Blind Catfish Blues.'

"There must'a been forty people listenin' an' dancin' to me and Bob. Forty poor-as-the-day-they-was-born colored souls. We was higher than a holy roller's shout when the county sheriff come up.

"Heck Wrightson was a white man big as two men and meaner than a hungry rat down yo' pants. He threw his billy stick on the wood sidewalk so that it rolled and clattered on the slats. He called out, 'Everybody better hit the ground by the time that stick stop rollin' 'cause I'm shootin' waist-high.'

"Booby was the first one to scream. Then black folk started runnin' with they heads down and they hands up. Colored souls piled one on the other, and Heck was true to his word. He held a forty-one-caliber pistol at his beltline and squeezed off shots at a leisurely pace.

"POW! Bang! Heck was smilin'. Linda Powell hit the ground with this loud *humph!* I seen'er boyfriend, Lyle Cross, run away from her an' go 'round the general store.

"I was in a awful state 'cause of my guitar, which I had received from my Uncle Fitzhew and which I named Bannon after my murdered friend. I couldn't just th'ow it down or run wild with it. So I tried to lower myself down off the side of the wood walkway. People was still yellin' an' runnin' an' I was leanin' over the side, prayin' t'God that I'd save my life along with my guitar.

"Then there was this hard boot next to my head.

" 'Git up from there, nigger,' the boot said. An' I knew right then that Heck Wrightson had got me.

"I look up an' seen Heck towerin'. That ugly gun muzzle looked back down at me. With his other hand Heck had RL by the scruff of his shirt.

"The look on Bob's face spoke the whole history of Mississippi colored life. RL was a brash young man and he was conceited and wild. But when that lawman grabbed him he just slumped down and took it. His good eye was starin' out beyond the dirt road and his bad one searched a thousand miles further on. Even his lips sagged. Because when a white man, especially a lawman, grabbed a nigger, that was all she wrote. If you gave him any trouble or any mouth, or if you stood up straight and looked him in the eye—if you did any'a them things there, death waitin', death just as quick as my momma's biscuits.

"Heck dragged us down to the white barbershop where his uncle extracted teeth and cut hair. They kept a cell in the back. It was just a closet with a cast-iron doorframe that sported five metal bars. But it wasn't much of a jail. They didn't even have bars on the li'l window but we had enough sense not to try an' get away.

"Bob sat himself down in the corner like he had been punished at school. He sat on the floor, because there wasn't no furniture or even a stool in the room. The only thing there was was a tin pail that smelt powerfully of sour vomit and shit.

" 'Hey, Bob,' I whispered when Heck went out to talk to his uncle.

"RL shook his head so hard that his cheeks made a flappin' noise, but he didn't say a word.

"I turnt away from him to the cell door an' looked out into the barber's room. Heck had put our guitars in the corner, underneath where the customers hung their bags and coats. I wanted to yell out for that white man to put our guitars somewhere safe, but then I worried that if I said somethin' he mighta popped a string or worse just for spite.

"That's when Bob started in. 'Ohhh, momma yeah. Yeah, yeaaaaahhhh,' he sang out.

" 'Ohhh, momma, I,' he cried. Then he th'ew his head back and crooned a long high note.

" 'What's that?' I heard Heck say. I could see the barber, a red-headed man, look up from the head bowed down in front of him. I grabbed RL and shushed, 'Quiet, Bob. Sheriff don't like no noise.' But by then Heck was at the cell door. He had on Levi jeans and a snap-down-the-front cowboy shirt. There was a awful green patch of skin across his left cheek. He was chewin' on a nail as most men might chew on a toothpick. He says, 'What's goin' on in here?'

"I said, 'Ain't nuthin'.' But just then RL go, 'Ohhh. Oh.'

" 'What's wrong with him?' Heck had his fist around one of the bars. I was afraid that he'd yank that pole right out the door and beat us both to death.

" 'RL got spells,' I told him. I figured it was true.

"He go, 'You tryin' t'mess wit' me, boy?'

"An' I says, 'Nawsir, nawsir I ain't.' I fell right into the planta-tion nigger's stoop. I mean, I was sittin' on the floor but I stooped just the same. I let my head hang down and my lips hang loose when I talked. I know you don't wanna hear 'bout how somebody might act like a nigger when the white man crack his whips. But you never lived through the early south like I did. You ain't never been on the floor with a man like a bear lookin' down on yo' weak flesh."

Soupspoon had begun to breathe hard at this point in his story. He reached over and picked up a glass of whiskey that Kiki had poured. He finished it before he started speaking again.

"Heck swung the jail door open and went right over to RL. 'Stop that growlin', boy!'

"And RL says, 'Ohhh, momma!' an' he sway from side to side. Heck hit Bob so hard that the poor boy rolled across what little floor they was. But he jumped right up into a crouch and scrabbled back to his corner and started singin' again. And Heck hit him again. But this time RL had his behind anchored. You could see how hard the slap was but RL just shuddered, shuddered and moaned.

"The sheriff was a little worried when he seen that his slaps didn't bother RL. So he turned to me and said, 'What's wrong with him?'

" 'Spells,' I said. I hunched my shoulders up to my ears. 'Had'em since he was a babe,' I lied.

"That time Heck used his fist on RL. That boy's head rolled back and so did his eyes. He slid down on his side but he was still singin', 'Ohhhh, momma yeah. Yeah.' And a sweet smile crossed his beat-up face.

"Heck backed on away from him then. He looked down on that po' bluesmaster with a kind of awe.

"He whispered, 'Spells.'

" 'Bad ones,' I tells him.

"Then he says, 'Get this nigger up an' get outta here!' He banged out of the door and walked out to the barbershop.

"I helped RL up an' half drug him through the shop. An' all the time he was moanin' and rollin' his eyes. I pulled him outside and propped him up against a wall. Then I went back in for our guitars.

"I got them both and slung'em around my neck. Then I stood there, lookin' at the floor. An' any brave soul who mighta thought I was a coward to bow my head in that cell might wonder at me bowin' now with courage. Because I was standin' my ground with Mr. Wrightson right then.

" 'Sumpin' wrong, boy?' he asted me when it come clear I weren't goin' nowhere.

" 'Our money, suh,' I said.

"An' he sneer and he say, 'What money?'

" 'That tin can RL had,' I told'im. 'I had one too but he had a bigger crowd.'

" 'What you sayin', nigger?' Heck said, and you know it was a sore on my mind to hear him talk like that.

"But I answered in a civil tongue, 'I just want the can, suh. That's all. Can is our'n. We the ones played for it.'

"When Heck grinned I seen that his teeth was green too. He say, 'You broke the law playin' 'fore sunset, son.'

But I told him, 'Nawsuh. Nawsuh, the law just say that you cain't play on Sunday in Washington County. You cain't play day or night on Sunday.' And he knew that it was true.

"To this day I remember that one lonely drop'a sweat that trickled down my spine. In them tiny little seconds between my last protest and Heck's reply I saw a mouse come out of a crack in the corner of the wall. That li'l thing looked at us and got so scared that he th'ew hisself against the wall three times before he could make it back into his hole.

"Heck stroll over to his coat and pull RL's can from out of his pocket. He held the can up to his ear an' shook it. Then this bitter stain cross his face, what some folks might call a smile.

"The can hit me in the shoulder before I seen him th'ow it. Silver clattered all over the floor. I was down on my knees pickin' up whatever I could while them white men laughed and stamped around my fingers.

"After I got almost half'a what fell I jumped up and run outta there. They stamped their feet like they was comin' after me, but the door slammed on behind. The guitars banged together and cried. The white men was laughin' in the barbershop but the street was quiet.

"Robert Johnson was gone.

"I went down Germaine but I didn't see him. I cut down there to Winslow and into the colored part of town. You could always tell the colored neighborhood because the flower gardens got scarce and the shotgun houses ran in rows.

"I saw RL goin' down toward Carver's Road, which led out to the farms and plantations.

"I shouted, 'You, Bob!'

"He started to run.

" 'Bob!' I goes after him.

"RL was runnin' like I used to in my dreams. A giant be comin' after me an' I'd be huffin' but my feet hardly made no progress. RL was runnin' like that, movin' his legs from side to side. When I caught up to him he fell to his knees.

" 'Bob!' I says. 'Bob, it's me, Soup, Soupy!'

"RL huddle down in the yellah dirt and sobbed. I helped him up and got'im t'walk wit' me. I told'im that we could get some whiskey if we went back to Mary's general store. Back then the general store was also a juke joint, what they call a nightclub nowadays.

"RL says, 'Why you got my guitar, man?'

" 'Just carryin' it till you want it back, RL. Ole Heck almost busted it.' RL looked at me so wary I didn't think he knew who I was.

" 'Where my money?'

" 'Right here in my pocket, Bob.'

"He stopped walking and I dug out his change. I kept a few coins in my pocket though, I figured I earned that.

" 'This all they is?' he asted me. And I told him that Heck Wrightson took all the rest and th'owed it on the jailhouse floor.

"RL took his guitar and we headed for Mary's. He didn't even say nuthin' 'bout bein' in jail. I don't even think it was real fo'him. It was more like we had passed through a dream and now we was back to where we was.

"Mary's store was a big square room with a counter running across the back wall and shelves full of canned and boxed goods behind that. In the middle of the floor she had a pool table that had been shipped all the way from Ohio.

"There were tables and chairs around the room for nighttime when people came out to drink.

"Mary, who was a big woman, sat next to her cashbox behind the counter. She eyed every soul who came through the door. So when me and RL come in lookin' like yesterday's po'k chops she say, 'What's wrong wit' you an' yo' friend, Soupspoon Wise?'

"I told her that Heck Wrightson had us in jail but she says, 'I know that. What I mean is why do yo' friend look so beat-up?'

"RL was lookin' 'round the room like a man comin' awake after a long afternoon nap. 'You got music tonight, Mary Wade?' he asked her. She said no. It was a weeknight and the juke joint wasn't gonna have enough customers to pay musicians to play.

"But RL says that we'd play for a bottle'a whiskey and a hat on the table. 'Yeah, momma,' he said to Mary. 'We play the house down for a quart bottle and a hat for some tips.' And RL cracked a smile that woulda made a sweet girl's photograph cry.

"He said, 'You know we bluesmen, Mary Wade. Bluesmen born to trouble in a land Christendom never seed.'

"Mary was no saint. She loved the blues and the men and women who played it. She got all coy and toothy and said, 'You and Soupspoon can play okay. I give ya a pint right now an' if we get some people in here like you had outside then I'll pass you over another pint.'

"We took our bottle and sat at a table in the corner. I told RL that I couldn't play too well because of my shoulder. It was stiff from where Heck hit me. RL rubbed his swole chin an' said, 'You just strum on behind me, Soup. You just follow me an' I show you how t'get there.'

"Booby and Linda got the word 'bout us an' come by t'help us drink our liquor."

"Hmmph," Kiki said. She got up from the table and walked, unevenly, over to the bed. The small tape recorder caught the sagging springs of her sitting down and the loud scratch of the match she used to light her cigarette.

"... When we finished our pint, RL came up with two bits for another one and then I scraped together my change for a third.

"Booby sat down next to me but her eyes were fixed on RL's baby face. Linda was laughin' an' grabbin' onto RL's shoulder whenever anybody said the least funny thing.

"Lyle Cross come in and sits down on t'other side'a Linda, but she acts like he ain't even there. You see, she was mad at him fo'runnin' off when Heck was shootin'. For all I could tell, RL didn't even know that Lyle was there. RL'd put his arm over Linda's shoulders an' laugh and make friendly just like they was onna date. I thought he shoulda showed a little more sense because, like I said, RL was a small man—and Lyle Cross was as big as a sharecropper comes.

"But nothin' happened because Lyle was ashamed of the way he acted and because we were the musicians. Mary's was gettin' full about then and the people wanted to be entertained; they didn't want no mess wit' they music.

"We started playin' Robert Johnson's blues, naturally. I don't remember him or me sayin', 'Let's play,' all it was we had our guitars in our hands and the music started.

"RL played music that told you how it was. He'd sing like a miserable hound yowling after a bitch in heat and here he cain't get through the fence.

"Booby Redman and Linda was right near us. Linda'd give Bob a kiss now and then. Lyle moved back toward the door to show he didn't care. And sixty or more other people danced and nodded, put their hands together and drank whiskey.

"You don't understand how it was for us back then. You think all that drinkin' and consortin' an' playin' wit' danger was too much an' why didn't we do sumpin' else? But you don't know our place back then. We was the bottom of the barrel. We were the lowest kinda godless riffraff. Migrants and roustabouts, we was bad from the day we was born. Blues is the devil's music an' we his chirren. RL was Satan's favorite son. He made us all abandoned, and you know that was the only way we could bear the weight of those days.

"We played until early mornin'. Our hat had more than five dollars in it and we put a deep hole in Mary's whiskey supply. Lyle shamed hisself by cryin' over Linda and left Mary's store.

"Later on, outside, RL told me that Linda took care'a her bed-ridden grandmother in a big house just outta town. This grand-mother stayed upstairs and we could go on downstairs with the girls if we wanted. RL made it clear that was what he was gonna do.

" 'Ain't she gonna hear us down there?' I ast'im.

"He says, 'Naw. She deaf 'less you shout in her ear. An' she all alone out there 'cause they keep this wolf-dog called Lupe. Man be a fool to go in there wit'out Linda 'cause he'd have to shoot that wild dog an' they ain't nuthin' in that ole house worth the bullet.'

"Booby an' Linda come up then an' ast if we was ready. They walked us out the main street into the Mississippi moonlight. The dark clay road was hard as cobblestones under my shoes and the Delta spread out into the hot, heavy Mississippi night.

"For all that it was barren, the Delta was a beautiful land too. It was a hard land but true. It had the whippoorwill and the hoot owl and crickets for music. It had pale dead trees that stood out in the moonlight like the hands of dead men reaching out of the ground. And the Delta smelled of sweet earth and jasmine and magnolia.

"I remember our feet trudgin' and the sound of nickels and those lovely girls laughin' at nuthin' at all.

"When we came to the house the wolf-dog slavered and snapped but Linda took him and locked him in a room offa the porch. She lit a single kerosene lantern and Bob turned it down low. I had a quart of shine from Mary's, so we drank for a while at first.

"Linda sits on RL's lap feedin'im whiskey, laughin' an' stickin' her tongue down his throat. Booby would watch them kiss for a while and then she'd kiss me. Once RL ran his long finger down Linda's blouse an' Booby shivered in my arms.

"Between hugs I just had to ask, 'Where you learn t'play blues like you do?' We was all settled on a big bed. The girls was draped on us an' our hands was all in their clothes.

" 'Made a trade fo'it, Soup.' That's what he said! Give up his right eye to the blues. Made a blood sacrifice with a witch woman down Clarksdale. Soiled his hands in the blood of a animal, then goes out to the crossroads. He said that and then he jammed his hand under Linda's skirt. Booby saw that and stuck her hand into *my* pocket. You know you add that to whiskey and the room will start to spin.

"But then all of a sudden somebody yells, 'I kill ya!' The lamp was turnt over. RL shouts out, 'Hey!' but then his voice is cut short like somebody grabbed his windpipe. I jump over to his side'a the bed an' wraps my arms around a body I swear was carved from stone.

" 'Lemme go!' the statue yell. And then there's this flasha light from the lantern gettin' set straight. I was huggin' on Lyle Cross an' he was killin' RL. Lyle takes one hand from RL's throat so he can th'ow me 'cross the room. Booby was on the floor yellin' at Lyle. Linda was nowhere to be seen.

"And then it was like everything in my life just stopped. I was on the floor next to my uncle's guitar. RL was dyin' on the other side of the room. And what I thought of was the music RL had played that day. Music I never even dreamed of until I heard it. But once I heard it, it seemed like I had always known it. Like Bob had found the truth somewhere and give it to me for a lark.

"And then I was moving again. I slammed the side of that dear instrument into Lyle's flat nose. I hit him so hard that the strings snapped back at me. Blood was spoutin' from the sharecropper's face. Bannon turned to splinters in my hand.

"I heard Linda say, 'Get'im,' and the dog that was half wolf was on Lyle and Lyle was screamin' and runnin' from the house."

Soupspoon sat back a minute. Kiki took that moment to take the cassette out and flip it over to get whatever else there was for him to say. Soupspoon looked over at Kiki. She looked him in the eye in a way she never had before.

"Is that all, Mr. Wise?" she asked after finishing with the recorder. Soupspoon looked at her a long moment before saying more.

"RL an' me lit out that night. We hitched a ride on a hay truck that went all the way to Leland. RL wanted to stay with Linda but we finally got him to go. He swore that he'd get back to her one day.

"Years later I heard that Lyle had lost a hand to Lupe, which ruined him for sharecroppin'. He went down to New Orleans to live with his a'ntee. But he was broken after that tragedy and took to drinkin'. Two years later they brought him home to be buried.

"I traveled with RL for a while after that, but one night, just outside'a Panther Burn, there was this fire. Me an' Bob was playin' hard an' things got so wild that the juke joint caught on fire. The whole place burnt to the ground. I ate too much smoke and had to rest for a while. I guess I coulda caught up to RL later but I just couldn't.

"I didn't hear 'bout him again until I hear one of his songs on a phonograph record that a rich colored undertaker had in Florence, Alabama.

"A few weeks after that I heard that Robert Johnson was dead.

"They said Satan come got him in a little place outside Greenwood, Mississippi. Satan or a jealous man."

Soupspoon sighed and left three blank minutes on the tape. When he finally spoke again his voice was deeper and hoarse like a man who had just recently awakened from a full night's sleep.

"You know I played a whole lotta music in these fifty years since he died. I made a lotta people happy and a lotta people dance. I could play anything on my guitar. Sometimes I'd look out in the crowd an' see women with tears in their eyes. But the music they was hearin' was just a weak shadow, just like some echo of somethin' that happened a long time ago. They was feelin' somethin', but not what Robert Johnson made us feel in Arcola. They cain't get that naked. And they wouldn't want to even if they could, 'cause you know Robert Johnson's blues would rip the skin right off yo' back. Robert Johnson's blues get down to a nerve most people don't even have no more.

"I never played the blues, not really. I run after it all these years. I scratched at its coattails and copied some notes. But the real blues is covered by mud and blood in the Mississippi Delta. The real blues is down that terrible passway where RL traveled, sufferin' an' singin' till he was dead. I followed him up to the gateway, but Satan scared me silly and left me back to cry."

TWELVE

Neither one of them spoke for a while after he finished his story. Kiki sat back holding a cigarette, just letting it burn. Soupspoon leaned forward on his elbows. He looked like a man does after completing a long and difficult job.

"They ain't nuthin' Robert Johnson did worth rememberin' except the way he played guitar and how he made livin' just that much more easy t'bear. You got botha them things now, here today. They got his records t'listen to an' me t'bear witness." Soupspoon slapped the table and showed his teeth.

"I gotta get to work early, Soup," Kiki said from her bed. She had a glass of whiskey in one hand and a burnt-out butt in the other. Soupspoon saw by the way her head lolled to one side that Kiki was drunk again.

She winked at him.

Kiki put the cigarette in her whiskey hand and got to her feet with some effort. She grabbed onto the head post of the bed to keep upright. Then she spilled the whole glass of whiskey out on the bed. It looked like she did it on purpose but Soupspoon knew that she was just drunk. He jumped up and grabbed a towel from the sink. While he toweled the liquor from the bed he said, "If I had ever done that my a'ntees woulda hung me up by my ears . . . my wife woulda kilt me."

"What wife?"

Kiki wore a light green dress with clusters of tiny red apples printed all over. She went up close behind Soupspoon and leaned against him. It was a drunk woman's weight he felt against his back.

"What wife, Soup?"

He could feel the hot breath, smell its liquor.

"You better get to bed if you wanna make work tomorrow, Kiki."

"Come to bed with me, daddy." Pale arms snaked around his chest. Kiki's fingers pressed at his breastbone.

"How's your hip?" she asked.

"It hurts some."

Kiki put her mouth to his ear and breathed for a while before saying, "I could ride you so good you wouldn't even feel it, baby."

Soupspoon went still like the levee lizards of his dreams. He let his hands hang down and whispered, "You got to get to bed, honey."

"Come with me." Her arms tightened. With controlled strength she began to pull him toward the bed. She kissed his ear and said, "I liked your story."

"You did, huh?"

Soupspoon stumbled and they were at the foot of the big bed. It loomed out in front of him and the weight of his savior began to bear him down.

"I never knew all that stuff about you, honey."

As they lowered to the bed, Kiki's thigh rose over his leg. He remembered a feeling almost lost in the pain of cancer.

"I could play you a song," he said as the slippery tongue tickled the hairs in his ear.

"You could?" Her hand ran the distance between his knee and his navel.

Soupspoon almost forgot what he'd been saying.

"Yeah, uh-huh."

"What kinda song?"

"A love song. A song I heard when I'as just a boy down in Cougar Bluff, Mississippi."

Soupspoon sat up and looked down on Kiki. She was a plain

woman but her red hair was beautiful. She hiked her dress up to her crotch and looked deep into his eyes. He felt his heart skip once and made it to his feet before she could reach out for him. He went behind the couch and brought out his red guitar.

"I want you to fuck me," Kiki said so loud that Soupspoon was sure that Mrs. Green upstairs could hear.

He sat on the bed next to Kiki and started tuning his guitar. His fingers felt stiff and clumsy but the sound was still in his mind. The strings whined a little from long years without play but they came half the way back to life for him. Kiki became silent while Soupspoon cocked his ear to make sure that his chords were just right.

He picked the words, note by note, as he sang, hearing an old man in his voice—a man he'd never heard sing the blues before.

> *I got a half-blind woman*
> *her eye's out for me.*
> *Got a half-blind woman*
> *her eye is out for me.*
>
> *I cain't do nuthin'*
> *but Ann-Marie don't see.*

Inez insisted on painting the porch pink. Sweet peas she had planted crawled up string, half the way to the roof. He remembered the little rays of sun making hotspots on his arms and Fitzhew singing "The Half-Blind Woman Blues" while Inez and Ruby leaned next to each other behind the slanted screen of sweet pea blossoms.

> *I got a peg-legged momma*
> *run all 'round the town.*
> *I got a peg-legged momma*
> *run all through the town.*
>
> *Outstep the freight train*
> *run her daddy to ground.*

He remembered his ex-wife, Mavis Spivey, and how she was miserable and drunk when they met in a Texas juke. He married her and loved her. He still missed her after thirty-two years and two months.

On the day they were married, Mavis made pig tails and black-eyed peas. All the blues men and women from miles around came to Reverend Crow's backyard and played music until late in the night. After the wedding Mavis came to bed crying. He begged her to tell him what was wrong until the sun was bright through the lace curtains her cousin had given them. He finally got so frustrated that he left and went down to a friend's house for two days. When he came back, Mavis had stopped crying. She was sitting at the kitchen table, her suitcase packed and her traveling clothes on.

"Where you goin', Mavis?" Soupspoon asked.

"I don't know. Somewhere where I can start up new."

"Can I come?"

When he asked that question she started crying again. She fell to the floor and moaned. She was saying something but Atwater had to get down on his knees to hear her weak words.

"I cain't give you no chirren, daddy," she sobbed. "I had bleedin' after Cort and the doctor cut me up on the inside. He cut me an' now I cain't have no more kids."

Soupspoon said that he didn't need any kids as long as she could stay with him.

"I wouldn't want no kids that wasn't ours, Mavy," he whispered to her. "So I guess I got to take you like you is."

> You know my baby died
> Lord I wailed and moaned.
> You know she up and died
> pneumonia come to her home.
>
> She still come to me at night
> never leaves me alone.

Kiki was sound asleep. Soupspoon moved her hand away from her crotch and pulled her dress down.

He looked at that pale face, pondering a life filled with hard-pressed women and shadowy, disappearing men. Ruby and Inez, who had little love or respect for most men but who loved him just the same. Mavis Spivey, barren and childless since her one baby son, Cort, died in a flash flood. Mavis, who married him without joy or dreams. And then this redheaded white girl, drunk and jagged, who thought slaps were kisses and whiskey was milk.

Bannon, RL, Fitzhew, and a thousand other blues boys crushed down into the mud without making a sound. Dead, buried, and forgotten all on the same day. Trampling each other like a stampeding crowd making for the door. Men who sought out love in women's tears.

He sat on the bed next to Kiki and touched her cheek. She smiled in her sleep. Soupspoon knew that it was a pleasure she'd never remember. The small touch of love and the smile to go with it that she couldn't know when she was awake.

He thought again about Mavis. How her face hardened year after year. The love of life drained right out of her; her smile went with it. He wondered, looking at Kiki's ignorant bliss, if Mavis even smiled in her sleep.

THIRTEEN

From her window she could look down on the Lower East Side of Manhattan. Glancing over the clusters of electric light, she was appalled again by the large areas of darkness. Evil-looking patches where people were being slaughtered and raped—right out there, in the world outside her eighth-floor room. She concentrated on the headlights and taillights moving slowly up and down the avenues. The stoplights switched colors at a steady beat, the faint sounds of engines and horns broke through the window now and then. A scratchy seventy-eight on the turntable played early Jelly Roll Morton, more static than sound to hear, but more music for her than all the junk they played on the radio twenty-four hours a day.

All the lights in the one-room apartment were on; were always on. In the closet next to the front door, Mavis Spivey kept a large carton of one hundred 100-watt bulbs. Sometimes in the middle of the night she'd feel a dimming on her eyelids and get right up to change the dead bulb, in one of two dozen porcelain lamps she kept burning. The walls of the living room had been painted antique white; the sofa and love seat were upholstered in almost exactly the same hue. The curtains were pale lace, as was the tablecloth over the round blond table in the dining nook. The kitchen, separated from the rest of the room by a waist-high counter, was a brighter white. All along the wall white-enameled pots and pans hung from white plastic hooks. Above the pots dozens of red roses hung upside down by wire from the ceiling. Fifteen bunches of twelve roses each hung over the sink and drainboard; some still soft and deep red while others had already dried to a spiky, rich black. Nowhere in the room were these flowers on display. Mavis bought the bouquets when they were old and wilted from a fruit stand on Eighteenth Street for a quarter each. Then she "cured" them as she called it and arranged them in lovely bouquets for Angela's Curios on Madison Avenue near Sixty-eighth Street. Her small earnings along with Social Security paid the rent and electric bill. She didn't need to eat much. Mavis hadn't had much of an appetite since Cort had died.

She wore a pear-green housecoat with golden swans embroidered on it and tan house shoes that burst open at the tips, exposing her blunt and ashen black toes. She was darker in old age than she had been as a girl. Her cheekbones were still high and her eyes still shone brightly, even though part of her had been sad since the day of the flash flood in southern Texas.

Raising the window, she first felt the arthritis in her fingers, then the cold air falling from the sill to her exposed toes. Somewhere a woman was yelling in anger; a radio played loud music with shouts and electric drumbeats; a siren got louder from the distance, horn honking every now and then, at the intersections, probably. All of these sounds carried on a river of traffic, along with Jelly Roll playing through the static that slowly, year after year, drowned out the light-skinned pianist.

Just when the cold began to hurt her feet a sound, like a cicada chirping, exploded in the house. Mavis looked at the console next to the door. She looked at it for half a minute and the buzzer blasted again.

"Hello?" she said while holding down the talk button on the brass console that she'd painted white last Christmas. "Hello?"

The sound of shuffling feet and a cough were the only answers; then a door opened and closed.

"Prob'ly lookin' for somebody else," Mavis said after a while. It was cold in the apartment. She went to shut the window.

Five minutes later the loud chirping came again. Mavis didn't even look up from her chair. The bell sounded three more times before she returned to the console.

"Who's down there?" she commanded.

"Rudolph Peckell, A'ntee Mavy."

"Rudy? What you want? I ain't got the time for you now. I'm up here wit' my flowers."

"Did you get my checks, ma'am?"

"Yeah. Now I told you not t'come by wit'out callin' first." Mavis lifted her finger from the *listen* button but then she put it back.

"But you never answer the phone and I got somethin' t'tell you—somethin' important."

"What?" Mavis shouted at the speaker.

"I got to come up."

"I cain't talk to ya now, Rudy. I got things to do, I tell ya."

"Uncle Atwater's dyin', A'nt Mavy," Rudy said in a man's voice. "He's got cancer."

A grin and then a frown flitted across Mavis's face in fast succession. "Oh no," she whispered. She brought the flats of her fists to her mouth and raised her left thigh to ease the tightening in her stomach.

Jelly Roll Morton hissed out a quick melody from the record player. In the bright whiteness of the wall Mavis caught the flash of Soupspoon's smile as he looked up sideways from his guitar onstage. When he was playing was the only time that he was ever happy. And she was only happy in the presence of memories and bright white light.

The intercom cried again.

"I heard ya, Rudy! Go on home now! Call me tomorrah, in the daytime. I'll put in the phone at three."

Mavis took her finger from the intercom and went back to the sofa. She wrapped herself in a thin white sheet and reclined, thinking about Egyptian queens laying up in their coffins, wrapped in fine white silks—their hands over their breasts.

She didn't think about Soupspoon; about him dying out there in all that smelly darkness. But he *was* out there. She thought about orange peel, about squeezing the skin of the fruit close to her nose, about the bitter sting. She thought about the crisp odor of new leather shoes and, with that, the stale grainy smell of her first lover's penis.

She thought about flowers.

Mavis folded her feet up under her body and covered her head with the sheet. She closed her eyes and imagined the whiteness of the room. The last Jelly Roll record fell from the stalk-stack. Before the song was over Mavis was far away watching a boychild play with his new spinning top. He wanted to know how flies landed upside down. When she reached out to stroke his head he looked at her with big vacant eyes. The boy was her young son but he was more than that. He was every little boy who had to grow into rough, and finally broken, men. He was happy because he was ignorant.

She started to say something but the boy laughed and ran away.

"Catch me," he cried.

He ran, impossibly fast, across a field of wildflowers. The sun began to fade. And when he was out of sight, night descended and Mavis was asleep.

FOURTEEN

Mavis had been Soupspoon's last chance at any kind of normal life. He didn't mind that they couldn't have children. He didn't care that she cried, sometimes for days. He was happy to get away from the heartache and despair of the deep south. Up north he played in nightclubs and at barbecues. The upper states were loaded with Negroes who wanted a taste of down home—and he was better with his guitar every night.

There was some time away from home, there had to be. By bus usually, but also by train and even a car now and then. Never in his whole life had Soupspoon been airborne. There were times that he was away from home for two months and more. But he was always glad to come back to Mavis. She always had something good on the stove in their uptown cold-water New York flat. Pig tails and black-eyed peas was a favorite; collard greens and cornbread on a plate of their own on the side.

Mavis loved her daddy's foreskin. "Come on to bed, baby," she'd say in the early days when the sadness only came now and then. "Let's go shuck that corn."

He saved up his money and all his love on the road. Didn't play with the B-girls, didn't play with himself either. He held Mavis in his arms until it was quiet, even in Harlem. When he was through his mind was as dark as the night sky and that was all right with him.

But then a chill came into his mind one night and Soupspoon woke up to an empty bed.

Mavis was in the kitchen. All the lights were on and she was smoking Pall Malls and drinking beer. Her elbows were up against her side and her legs were tight together. She was perfectly still but tears ran freely from her eyes.

"Woman was the saddest thing I ever seed," he once said. "She didn't even get no release from cryin'."

One time he came home from the road and there wasn't anything cooking on the stove. Everything in the house had been painted white. The walls, the floor, the wood chairs, and even the little dolls Mavis had saved from when she was a child. There wasn't a bottle of liquor left in the cabinet.

"It's just a style," she said. "Ain't nuthin' wrong with it."

She couldn't go to bed without a light on, couldn't even take a nap in the dark.

He wanted to say something but the light made him quiet.

Mavis would throw a fit if he dirtied something or left a stain. She put everything of his into a closet to keep the house clean—even sealed the sofa and stuffed chair with plastic because he might sit on them.

He knew he should have said something. But even when she shamed him—by saying that the only reason he even wanted her was to put his thing down where RL's thing had been—he didn't fight. That night he tried to sleep on the couch but it was too sweaty so he curled up in a sheet on the floor. They never slept together again, and finally he moved out. He'd heard a year later that she'd gone back down to Texas to keep Cort's grave covered with fresh flowers.

He couldn't even hold on to his woman. He never missed her after all the crazy things she did and all the terrible things she said—he was lonely and didn't want a friend.

His music was empty too. Just an old bastard style. Singing the same words every night to people who didn't care, who didn't even know what it meant to dust your broom. He felt like an old dog that rolls in a carcass out in the woods. Maybe a long time ago his ancestors did that to throw prey off the scent, but now he'd just come home and smell up the house.

He put his guitar down and became the day janitor at the Calumet Building. At night he'd roll out a sleeping bag so he could call the cops if anybody tried to break in. They let him go after thirty years. He didn't even have Social Security.

Kiki's drunken snore filled the room.

"I'm gonna lay me down in a bed fulla blues," he sang softly to himself.

"No, daddy," Kiki answered from her sleep.

Soupspoon laid down on the couch and fell right into a dream about the Delta.

After the fire at Terry's juke joint young Soupspoon went to heal at Darnell Calter's house, which was on an unnamed tributary of the Potato River. Rich white people had fancy homes along the Potato at that time.

In the dream Soupspoon had gotten better and was with Darnell under the deck of Judge Whitestone's cabin. Darnell used to like to go there because it was cool under the shade and you could let a line down in the water and no one would know. Mrs. Whitestone had passion fruit vines growing down the side of the house, so the underpart wasn't even visible from the rare passing boat. Darnell and Soupspoon had crawled down to the water's edge under the house and had their poles stuck in the mud so they could see if a catfish or carp was pulling on the line.

"You a fool to follah RL, Atwater," Darnell said. "He ain't no good. An' he got the kinda bad luck fall on people 'round him."

"Uh-uh," Soupspoon replied. He was laying on his back letting the dappled light through the vines fall on his face. "That man play some music I got to know."

"You almost got kilt already, boy. What got to happen t'wake you up?"

There was the lazy swish of an alligator diving in the river and the flitting of hummingbird wings and cicadas crying. Soupspoon knew he was dreaming. He kept his eyes closed like a guitar man who's hit a good note and just wants to feel it in the dark.

"Man gotta settle down, Atwater," Darnell continued. "All RL want is that pussy and that whiskey."

"That's all you want, Darnell." Soupspoon sat up to look at his friend. "Only you too scared to go out there an' get it. You hate it, down snatchin' cotton and haulin' it. You hate how hard it is but you ain't got nuthin' else to do. I'm tired'a every day just doin' my business an' fallin' into my bed. I could just as well be you an' it wouldn't make no difference at all."

"But you follah RL an' you be dead in a year. Somebody shoot you or stick you with a pick."

"We all gonna die," Soupspoon said.

And the images of a lifetime flashed into his mind. Kirkem Bowers pushed to the ground by stupid Willy T. and stabbed until his head nearly came off. Mother Babbet thrown from the window by JoJo, her boyfriend at the time. Her neck was broken and a scream frozen on her face; it looked like she was holding her head back in a laugh that needed more room than a live person had. After the flood of '26 they gathered the bodies and stacked them in the Curry plantation barn. White on one side and colored on the other; forty-seven dead souls stretched out and piled high. Soupspoon thought that that barn was more God's house than any church. He imagined again in his dream barefoot God walking among the dead and judging their sins.

Lisa Harding poisoned by her own sister over a man who wouldn't marry either one. Sly Fox Nathan Mull shot in the head for cheating at cards. He ran six blocks to Ruby and Inez's house. They laid him out on the porch and sat with him as he had one hand on his hard cock and the other over his heart. "Boy!" he shouted at Soupspoon more than once. "Never gamble with a nigger. Nigger can't take the joke."

As a boy Soupspoon had followed the men; Rayford Benoit, Toy Bennet, and Alfred Fixx. It was after a gang of white men had robbed and murdered JT Ott. Rayford heard from his mother that June Bell had seen Grig Plothdell coming from where they found JT. The men drank at Soupspoon's house until they were drunk and then they went out past the old bridge near Grig's farm. They waited and Soupspoon waited behind them. Old man Grig never came, but Justin did. Justin was Grig's nephew, a pale boy who had a girl somewhere nearby. When he got to the bridge the men surrounded him. He cried out loud but was slapped down by Toy's cudgel. The men kept around Justin and every time he tried to run out of the circle one or the other would hit him with a stick. Poor Justin begged to be free and then he'd make a break and get struck back to the center. The men never said a word. Justin went down on his knee and there came a flash of silver. Soupspoon heard a scream that ended in a gurgle, then something like a spray. When he opened his eyes again Justin was just a lonesome heap on the rill's edge. He was just a pile of bones.

Then he heard a knocking. He imagined the sound of a hammer banging on a slender pine coffin, then he saw that Darnell had taken out his pipe and was knocking out the ashes by banging it against the timbers that held up Judge Whitestone's porch.

Soupspoon was suddenly afraid that the judge would hear, that he'd come running down underneath his house and arrest them. He wanted to tell Darnell to stop but he couldn't catch his breath to say it. Darnell just kept on banging. It was loud enough to wake the dead.

While Soupspoon was counting dead bodies in his sleep, Kiki called out, "No, daddy."

Her dream was southern too.

She went down in the basement with her father, Keith, to his new photo lab. He'd started a photo development darkroom in the old house and did people's photographs right in town instead of them having to send off and wait weeks for their pictures. When that went well he went into other little towns around Mississippi and Arkansas. He liked to go into a town where there was already a developer and put him out of business. That way he knew that he already had people who needed the service and he could lord it over anyone else who tried to stand up to him.

He was a smallish man with blue-black hair, not a trace of gray, and small hands. He was clean-shaven and his round face looked like it was waxed. He never washed much and he sweated a lot, so any room he was in reeked of him.

Down in the basement Keith Waters separated and saved the silver from the film developing process and made it into one-ounce coins that were imprinted with the rough-rendered profile of his tight face. Every once in a while he'd tell Kiki to come on downstairs and look at his treasure.

If she said no he'd slap her and then ask her again—sweet as corn syrup.

When she got there he'd ask her to get something from the high shelf. She'd get up the ladder and he'd come to steady her, talking about his silver and the men he'd destroyed for her future. First he'd put his hand on her behind and then he'd slip his hard little fingers between her thighs. She couldn't fight him off because he'd get mean. All she could do was stay still and bring him what he needed as fast as she could. Sometimes her just being scared was good enough for him.

But not then, not in that dream.

"Daddy, stop it."

"What's that you said?"

"I said stop it. You got your wife right upstairs."

He was even stronger in the dream. He held her over his head and threw her down on the chemical table, breaking glass and throwing everything everywhere. When she looked up he was taking off his belt. She turned to run but only managed to fall off the table. She fell on her knee. It hurt but the pain was nothing.

"Come here, Kiki Waters."

"No, daddy. Let me be."

"Come here, girl. You cain't talk to me like that and not get it."

"Daddy, no!" she yelled. Somebody somewhere had to hear that.

Keith sat down on his old wooden chair. Kiki remembered that chair from when she was a little girl. She hated that chair. It had always been there, it had even followed them to the new big house.

"Please, daddy."

He didn't say anything else, just waited there with the strap in his hand. Kiki had to go lie across his lap and pull up her dress. She knew not to pull down the panties, that was for him to do.

The strap lashed against her backside twelve times. She screamed and he smelled stronger with each blow. The pain was real in Kiki's dreams.

She felt his fingers and hand. He was hoarse from heavy breathing and made her say everything he wanted to hear. If he rasped, "Does it hurt?" she had to answer, "Yes, daddy," making sure to hold back any tears or rage.

When it was over she went up the basement stairs while he washed off his hand in the sink. Her mother stood at the door holding a tight ball of handkerchief. Kiki tried to let her skirts hang down to cover the red welts on her legs. She could hear her father's heavy footfalls across the cellar floor.

Kiki couldn't hold in the shout. "YOU WHORE!!!" So loud that her mother was buffeted backwards against the plasterboard.

"YOU GODDAMNED, GODDAMNED WHORE!!!" Kiki ran her hand up the crack of her ass and came out with fingers covered in blood and shit.

Then there was the sound of her father's feet coming from somewhere. She knew the feet were headed for the gun case. She wanted to get there first but she'd forgotten where it was. The steps moved faster and louder. Kiki was afraid. She wanted to wash her hands. Her father's footfalls sounded like gunshots.

FIFTEEN

omebody was hammering down below. Kiki jumped out of bed and Soupspoon lurched up from his couch. Kiki was breathing hard. Soupspoon had lost his breath. They stared at each other with no words on their lips or in their heads. After a while, quaking in her bed, Kiki got up and came over to her friend. She put her arms around him and buried her face in the crook of his neck.

Her tears felt thick on his skin, oily. He looked at his skinny arms wrapped over hers. Then they both shivered like cold dogs huddling up to get warm.

"No," Kiki whispered.

Soupspoon didn't answer, he just held on tighter and closed his eyes. His slow breath coming only once for three of her gasps.

The hammering continued.

It wasn't a carpenter driving nails but some kind of vicious pounding that was designed to tear down and rend. It was a wall, Soupspoon thought, that wasn't ready to come down yet.

Kiki dragged herself to the table, where there was a half-drunk cup of day-old coffee. She downed the dregs and grimaced.

Soupspoon watched the sunlight from the window climb up on the pale skin of her thigh. She didn't look sexy—except where the sun struck her leg.

That same sun shone under Judge Whitestone's house.

Kiki took a dirty juice glass out of the sink and filled it with beer from the Frigidaire. She drank it down and poured another. Then she came back to the couch and the same sexless embrace.

The hammering got louder.

Kiki held on to Soupspoon, but his hands were laid down on either side of her. He tapped his fingers in an off-beat; played against the ripping hammer.

"Somebody should complain," Kiki said. Maybe it was half an hour later. The beer had gone flat from the heat of her hand. "Let's take a walk, daddy."

"Walk where?"

"I don't know. Around."

"Why you always goin' down around Chrystie Street, girl? What's down there for you?"

Kiki pulled away from him while trying to stand at the same time. Instead she fell off the couch.

"Then I'll go my own damn self!" she yelled from Soupspoon's feet.

"Noooo, no. I'll go wichya." He pushed himself up from the couch. "Just lemme get my pants on."

"You don't have to come. I can go myself."

Now the sun was on her knee.

"You don't have to be mad at me, girl. I said I'd walk wichya. I will."

Kiki's nostrils flared and her breath came hard. Soupspoon was wondering if she was going to try and hit him again, but then the hammering stopped.

"Okay," she said, suddenly quiet herself. "Okay. Let's get ready to go then."

They went down through Little Italy on Baxter to Canal. The whole time Kiki was looking, especially when she saw little boys wandering or playing. Little black boys running ragged; no different, really, Soupspoon thought, from him when he was down on the work farms and plantations of the Delta.

They went up and down Mott and Mulberry, Bowery and Elizabeth. There wasn't much traffic, because it was early in the morning and Sunday. Only a few pedestrians were out.

Kiki stopped at Hester and Chrystie and peered at the sidewalk as if it held some kind of secret.

"This is where they did it," she said.

"Where they stabbed you?"

"Right here."

Soupspoon looked down the bare streets. It was safe now but he knew how an empty, nowhere place could become an awful mean place.

Anywhere a man can walk, the blues is on his tail.

"Mr. Wise?" It was a man's voice.

A gray man was standing there before them. Not old and not young. His shirt had a hint of green from when it was new and his pants were once blue. Both had aged, under the sun and in the rain, from many months of hard living. His hair, blond at birth, had whitened too from the elements and neglect. His skin was almost colorless but dark from bright sun and processed red wine. White men would have a hard time claiming this man.

"Who're you?" Kiki asked. As she spoke she stepped between the stranger and her friend.

"Hare?" Soupspoon said. "Hare, is that you?"

The big man grinned.

He had been in the shelter when Soupspoon got there. He was stupid but nice. Whenever Soupspoon couldn't get out of bed, Hare was there to help him. It was Hare who helped him down to the exit when he ran from the shelter.

The director had come to examine Soupspoon when he told them that he could barely get out of bed. They said that they'd have to take him to some hospital. Soupspoon knew what that meant— they'd take him into some ward of dying men and leave him to die all alone, not even a friend like Hare to smile and say good morning. He knew that if they piled him into that ambulance he'd be a dead man.

While they went to the director's office to discuss how to move him, Soupspoon asked Hare to help him escape.

The big gray man had said, "Sure. Let's go."

"You hear about Norman Braddock?" Hare asked. It was as if he had run into a neighbor from down the hall and had stopped for a chat. "You know—Brandy?"

Soupspoon didn't want to remember. He didn't want even to think about the shelter.

But he couldn't help himself.

"Brandy?" Soupspoon had tried to put everything about the shelter out of his mind. About how they locked them in at night; how they told them when to get up and when the lights went out. One man, a big toothy warden of a social worker, even told him that the pain in his leg wasn't so bad. "I got a toothache," he said. "But you don't see me complaining."

If you had a nickel it was gone. If you had to crap you needed permission first and had to have someone, probably a woman, go unlock the toilet for you. Cancer grew like milkweed in the men's shelter and Soupspoon didn't want any of it.

But Brandy was different. Big-eyed, Buddha-looking, sienna-colored Brandy. Big old stomach he grew so he could rest his hands there. Brandy sat at the end of his cot most of the time. Every morning he took the disposable razor, the tiny bar of hotel soap, and the toothbrush wrapped in plastic paper to do his toilet down at the sink. Then, when he was all clean, he'd put on his glasses and sit at the end of his bed reading scraps of newspapers he took from the trash. He didn't bother anybody. Nobody stole anything from Brandy, because he didn't have anything to steal. His broken-down brogans were too big for anybody else. He did his laundry naked in the basement twice a week.

Soupspoon never talked to the Brandy-man. But he respected him. Brandy was a clean man, happy reading and comfortable in his fate. He'd given up everything but being a man.

"How'd he die?" Soupspoon asked. "He wasn't sick. He wasn't even that old."

"Stabbed."

"Stabbed? Stabbed for what?"

"His glasses," Hare said simply, accepting the fact as reason in itself. "Somebody tried to steal his glasses."

"Steal the fillin's right outta your mouth in the mortuary when you dead," Soupspoon said, remembering Bannon and his hatred. He had the taste of mealy apples on his tongue.

"Um, hey, Mr. Wise?" Hare shuffled from side to side in a show of humility. "You got a coupla bucks? I could sure use two dollars. It's for food." He added this last for Kiki, who had been looking away most of the time, but who turned to look at him when he asked for the handout.

Soupspoon touched his pocket. Kiki had given him a little cash to carry around. He hated to take from a woman, but he couldn't help it. He wanted to give to this big dumb white man because he had helped when nobody else seemed to care. But he didn't want Kiki to get mad either. He didn't want her to go off because he was giving her money away to some bum in the street.

But before he could speak, Kiki asked the gray man, "You hungry?"

"Yes, ma'am!"

"We could get some food at Bernie's Delicatessen and sit in the park across the street."

They walked back up to the East Village, stopping at Randall's one-room apartment on Avenue C. Kiki went in and came out with the gangly boy to meet Soupspoon and Hare.

"I thought you be out on St. Mark's on a nice day like this, Randy," Soupspoon said.

"I try and do my math work on Sundays, Mr. Wise. It's quiet almost all morning on Sundays and I can really get into the work."

"What school?" Hare asked. He tried to stand up straight and look Randy in the eye but he kept squinting, nodding, and looking down.

"Pace," Randy answered, then he looked his question at Kiki.

"Hare's a friend'a Soup's, Randy. We're gonna go get somethin' and sit in the park."

They went to Bernie's, which sat opposite Tompkins Square Park. She got cupcakes and a bulbous can of Japanese beer. Soupspoon and Hare split a pressed turkey sandwich and they each had coffee with lots of sugar poured in.

Soupspoon didn't eat his sandwich half—he was still thinking about home.

The sun was strong and there was no shade on their bench. All around them were the people of the park. Young white men and women in tennis shoes that matched their exercise suits and shabby folks like Hare. There was a game of basketball going on between middle-aged men, some of them balding, who sported headbands and fading tattoos. The Sunday paper was everywhere being read. Children played on skateboards and with balls. Kiki drank her beer and studied the boy children. Randy and Hare were silent.

Soupspoon watched the sparrows and starlings at first, then the flies darting from place to place. From a tree nearby he spied tiny albino worms descending on invisible webs. On the ground ants made their ways haltingly, stopping now and then to rub antennae and move on.

"Everybody's doin' their business. The world don't stop for you or nobody else," Soupspoon said at last as he watched two hard-eyed starlings chase a sparrow away from a crumb.

"What's that, Mr. Wise?" Randy asked.

"Spider hatches spinnin' her web. That's what she do. Ain't no stoppin' her, 'cept if you gonna kill her, stomp out her life and wipe away all the beauty she was and don't leave a thing."

Soupspoon was remembering the broken men and women of his dreams; the cowering of everyday life like a spider crouching when she senses a shadow. The shadows came every day in the Delta. So many shadows where it hardly seemed that a colored man ever got the chance to stand upright. Men and women wore shadows like cloaks and shawls; like the hundred-pound sacks of cotton they carried on their backs. Sacks bigger than they were. Like God's big white toe about to crush out what little misery they had to let them know that they were alive.

The only time they got a chance to stand tall was when the shadows turned into night. And even then they didn't stand—they jumped. Jumped and twirled to the music. The weight of a normal man under cover of darkness—darkness where no shadows could find you—was freedom for them. And freedom had a name. It was called the blues.

Hello blues, hello Satan.

Robert Johnson evoked the devil with a clear call. You might have been scared that morning—scared that your woman was gone; scared that your baby was dead; scared that the bottle was empty or that poison was scattered on your floor. But when RL tuned up you weren't scared anymore, because that man told you, "Yes, it's all true, so you better lap up the gravy while you can still lick."

Soupspoon sat up straighter with these thoughts. He found himself looking across the park—straight into the eyes of Robert Johnson.

He was sitting at a small round table leaning over to kiss a pretty brown girl. She let him kiss her on the side of her big red lips, pouting almost angrily. Somebody who didn't know black women might have thought that she resented the kiss but Soupspoon could see her pleasure.

The young man sat back (but how could he be so young?) and took a drink from his brown bag. He looked right into Soupspoon's eye.

It was him. He cracked an evil smile, the smile that broke all the girls' hearts, and raised his bag. His girlfriend looked over jealously. She didn't even see Soupspoon. She was looking for some other girl. When she didn't see the one RL was flirting with she gave him a full kiss on the mouth to mark her territory.

"You want a job, Mr. Wise?" Randy's voice was severe and thoughtful.

"Yeah. Yeah, I sure do."

"What could he do?" Kiki asked.

"Can you still play your guitar?"

"Yeah. I mean, not like I used to. Not like at the Savoy or Billy's Room. But I can do a blues chord. Better'n these rock'n roll boys can do."

"You see, I'm gonna do this T-shirt sale on Carmine Street at a street fair two weeks from Saturday. They do it every spring."

"What's that?"

"It's a like bazaar. You rent booths outside and if it doesn't rain then a lotta people come and buy what's bein' sold. They got food and jewelry and clothes."

"Yeah yeah, I got ya. I seen that happenin'. But you know, I never really went inside'a one. Too much of a crowd."

"You'd be right inside the T-shirt booth with me. And you could just play. I bet lotsa people would come over and then if I had the right shirts I'd make some money. What do you think?"

"I don't know . . ."

"Come on," Kiki said. She even smiled. "Let's do it. It'd be fun."

"I don't know, Kiki. But maybe. Maybe we could."

Kiki smiled again. This time at Randy. She reached out and took his hand.

Soupspoon glanced over toward RL. He was gone. An empty park bench was all he saw.

"What's wrong, Soup?" Kiki asked.

"You seen that man over there?"

"What man?"

But Kiki wasn't looking at the bench. She was looking at Randy, rubbing his hand.

Soupspoon and Hare walked back toward the Beldin Arms without her and Randy. On the way they picked up a jug of red wine.

"You cain't sleep here, Hare," Soupspoon told his friend. They were nearing the bottom of the bottle. Hare had drunk most of it but Soupspoon had had enough that his fingers tingled and music played over and over through his mind.

"That's okay, Soup," Hare said. "I got me a girlfriend."

"Shit!"

Hare couldn't repress his grin. "Sure do. SallySue. Live right down under this side'a the Williamsburg Bridge. They got a li'l trestle house down under there from a long time ago. Sally took it."

"She got free house under the bridge? Shoot. Boy, you better put down that bottle, you know the wine done got to your head."

"No lie, man," Hare said, sounding almost like a black man talking. "She's big an' she got a twenty-two pistol—nobody mess with her. Nobody."

"And she's your girl? Big old smelly boy like you?"

All Hare did was to shake his head and grin.

Soupspoon felt an urge deep down somewhere. He wanted a big woman with a trestle house under the Williamsburg Bridge; carrying a sleek pistol and calling him home.

Hare got up and waved. "See ya on Carmine."

"Huh?"

"When you do that street fair. I'll be there with SallySue." Hare went to the door. He waved again and then went out.

"SallySue," Soupspoon intoned. He got that feeling again and felt relieved that Kiki probably wouldn't be coming home that night.

SIXTEEN

The next day Soupspoon dialed a number from his address book, but it had been disconnected. Then he called information. His old friend Popeye Peter Laneau, who played mouth harp and who was Leadbelly's uptown barber, was unlisted. His cousin Mattine was in the book but she was stone deaf. Mattine's grandniece told Soupspoon that Mattine hadn't heard from Uncle Popeye in twenty-four years.

He found a listing for Alfred Metsgar, a bass player who backed up Howlin' Wolf and Quickdraw Marrs in Chicago. Alfred lived on 147th Street off Broadway. Soupspoon decided to go straight to there. Even if Metsgar was deaf he might be able to talk.

He packed his tape recorder and two bananas in an old tan briefcase that he'd found under Kiki's couch. It would be the only testament of Quickdraw Marrs's demise in the Black Sparrow Bar in East St. Louis forty-six years before.

The door to apartment 3L was slender, it reminded Soupspoon of a coffin's lid. There was a straw mat on the floor that read GOD'S WELCOME. No fanfare for the musician, just a plain pine door stained maple and sealed. There were two deep dents in the door made by something hard and jagged and a large green smudge almost dead center. Graffiti, Soupspoon thought, that somebody tried to wipe out.

Before he'd gotten up the courage to knock he was startled by the door coming open. An ancient woman, small as a girl, stood there leaning on a new aluminum walker. She wore black slacks, a puffy white sweater embroidered with beaded white flowers, and a lopsided gray wig. She had on black-lensed sunglasses with white frames in the shape of swans whose wings arched out beyond the width of her small head.

"You the ice man?" she asked clearly. Her lips were beautiful. Full and large. They wrapped around the words as if she were eating an overripe pear.

"No, ma'am, my name is . . ."

"You got a cigar, mister?" she asked. " 'Cause I hurt my hip and I sure could use some release."

"No, ma'am."

"Ain't you Bobby?" The old woman had begun to struggle with her walker. She reminded Soupspoon of somebody who couldn't do one more push-up. Her head sagged down between her shoulders and tremors went through her arms. But that didn't stop her. She cocked her head sideways and looked up.

He caught the dry, slightly sweet scent of old age. He was looking at the cockeyed face with the beautiful lips, ready to say no again, when a deep voice boomed out, "What you doin' here, man?"

Behind the little woman was a long dark hallway. From the gloom a large man appeared. Three hundred pounds of hard fat in short-sleeved orange overalls. His face was brown like a tree trunk with a wiry mustache that ran down his chin and throat disappearing into the collar of his T-shirt.

"Come on, Miss Winder. You shouldn't be out at this door."

As soon as she heard the big man's voice the woman started making her way back into the house. Soupspoon saw the rhythm of it. She waited for the big man to be watching a basketball game or maybe to get on the phone, and then she'd sneak out to the door looking for ice cubes, cigars, and a man named Bobby.

"What you want?" The big man held the door ready to slam it shut.

"Alfred Metsgar."

"What you want him for?" His neck was as wide as his head. The mustache ran down the lines of a normal-sized neck. It was an optical illusion to make him seem normal.

"We used to be friends, I mean . . . we was musicians together a long time ago. I just thought I'd come on by an' shout at'im."

The name MIKE was stitched over the man's left breast. Mike was breathing hard—as if maybe he was getting ready to fight.

"Is Alfred here?"

Mike's eyes were dark and unhealthy. His scowl was mean and Soupspoon was sure that he was going to be sent away.

Mike surprised him when he said, "It's the door down on your right," and backed away allowing Soupspoon to enter. After Soupspoon had gone halfway down the hall, Mike yelled out, "Mozelle!" A door came open and a woman stuck her head out. She was tall and skinny, somewhere in her late forties with a salt-and-pepper Bride of Frankenstein hairdo.

She didn't say much. "Down yonder," to say that Alfred was just down the hall. "Naw," when asked if she was his daughter. When Soupspoon asked if he could talk to the old man she said, "If you wan'."

Alfred Metsgar's room was no more than a cell. It even had bars on the unshaded window. This window looked into another room where, in a single bed, Soupspoon could see the back of somebody's head that poked out from under a mound of covers.

Alfred was too busy looking into that bedroom to notice his old friend. The shrunken old man was sitting in a wooden chair, hemmed in by squared armrests. He was leaning forward and peering toward the bars. The bed beyond him was neatly made. A bright-orange-and-yellow quilt covered the lower half.

Alfred wore a threadbare T-shirt and had an army blanket over his legs. The pitted wood floor was swept and there was no dust on the short two-drawered dresser that stood beside the window.

"Sh!" Metsgar said, even though Soupspoon hadn't uttered a word. "She still sleep."

Soupspoon looked over at the head and then back to Alfred.

"She like to sleep late, late." He kept his voice low—a proud parent letting a spoiled child get her rest.

"Alfred?" Soupspoon said, partly to get the old bass player to recognize him and partly because he wondered if this actually was his old friend.

His skin seemed to have become liquid. It had seeped slowly downward until it molded almost perfectly over the bones of his face; the effect was to make him look like a brown skull. Below the eyes the flesh had bunched into downward-rolling waves. The deep ocher skin at the top of his head was so thin it seemed that a hard breath would separate skin from bone.

"Yeah?" Alfred jawed.

"The musician, right?"

He turned away and whispered, "She still sleep."

The room stank of urine, like the men's shelter had. Because of the smell, Soupspoon didn't want to sit on the bed. But there was no place else to sit. His leg was hurting him some—from the long walk, he told himself—but he decided to stay on his feet for a while more.

Soupspoon was about to ask his question when Alfred put his hand out and pointed Soupspoon to come somewhere, or to go.

"Over there! Over there! Right chere!" Metsgar waved his hand around meaninglessly. Soupspoon wanted to obey his urgent commands but he didn't know what to do.

"Go ovah an' sit on the dresser. Then you could peek around the side."

Soupspoon sat on the short stack of drawers and opened Kiki's briefcase across his lap. He took the cassette player and pressed the record and play buttons.

"Alfred?" he whispered.

"Shhhhh! Look!"

Soupspoon followed the the direction of the lizard-skin finger pointing over the sill and into the room across the way. There again he saw the head lying in repose. He saw now that it was a woman's head.

Soupspoon felt like a child again waiting by the side of his mother's bed—waiting for her to rise.

He'd wake up with the sun through homemade cardboard shades. Then he'd be roused by the racket of his father's ax chopping wood for the stove. In the season when his father had plantation work, Soupspoon would wait in the bed with his big brother Holden until he heard heavy bootsteps marching away from the house. He'd take his blocks down from the loft and go up next to his mother's bed and play very quietly, watching her round brown face.

That was greatest feeling of love in Soupspoon's whole life: guarding over his mother while morning birds played and his brother snored up in the loft. His stomach gurgled but he loved to see his mother sleep and would wait all day rather than see her get up and go off to the cotton mills.

When she finally opened her eyes she would smile so nice and say, "Mornin', baby. You et?" He'd shake his head and then she'd kiss him for being so good and letting her sleep. More than sixty years later Soupspoon still felt a pang against his heart when he thought of her rising up from the straw-filled bed.

"See? Look," Alfred Metsgar said.

The woman in the bed had turned over and was now sitting up. She was naked as far as she could be seen. Plump and the color of a dusky orange, she was young. Soupspoon moved closer to the wall so as not to be seen looking. But he soon realized that he had no reason to hide. The young woman never once looked into Alfred's room. She got up from the bed with her naked back to the window and pulled on a loose pair of underpants. Alfred leered as she walked from one corner of the room to the other—picking things up and putting them down again.

The show went on for two or three minutes. She finally went right up to the window and stood on her tiptoes to reach the shade. It took her a few moments to grab the string and pull it down. When Soupspoon saw her face she was smiling, and then she was gone.

"That stuff sure is sweet," Alfred Metsgar said. "I'd die wit'out my dancin' girl. I'd die."

Soupspoon got it on the tape recorder.

"You remember me, Alfred?"

The old man was still looking at the shade. He turned toward Soupspoon and squinted. After a long time he shook his head, no.

"Atwater Wise. They used to call me Soupspoon. I played twelve-string with Hollis McGee and Triphammer Jones."

Alfred smiled and nodded but his eyes didn't know Soupspoon.

"You remember, Alfred. We did a whole circuit around California in '57. You know."

Alfred looked back toward the window but the show was over.

"Don't you remember, man? You the one told me about Quickdraw Marrs. You know—how he got killed at the Black Sparrow in East St. Louis?"

Alfred turned toward Soupspoon. "Who told you 'bout that? Who told you?"

"You did, Alfred."

"Who you said you was again?"

"Soupspoon. Soupspoon Wise. Guitar player. We played at the Sour Bowl in Pasadena—with Holly Gomez."

"Holly," Alfred said with a smile. "Cook some damn good red beans and rice."

"Yeah, yeah," Soupspoon said hopefully. "You remember Holly?"

"That gal could cook."

"An' you remember Quickdraw Marrs?"

"Who you said?" The curtain came down over Alfred's eyes again.

"Quickdraw Marrs. You told me back in '57, '58, that you was playin' with Quickdraw when he died back in East St. Louis, back in '36."

"Drummer boy?"

"Guitar," Soupspoon said.

"Uh. Um. Oh yeah. Yeah. That was somebody else." Alfred held up his hands and smiled. Then he looked out of the window again. "Shade's down," he whispered.

"Don't you remember?" Soupspoon asked.

Alfred shifted in his chair and a wave of urine odor rose in the room.

"No sir," Alfred said. "You want some coffee, mister? You could make that lazy girl go'n get us some coffee."

"You told me at the Sour Bowl that you saw the man shot Quickdraw. You told me that you knew who did it. You told me that you was there."

"Maybe I was," Alfred said clearly. "I coulda been. But you know I ain't never killed nobody. An' if I don't get me some coffee in the day then I gets headaches. But that girl won't let me have it. She say that it ain't good for me, but that's some shit. I'm the one say what's good for me an' what ain't. Thas only right, ain't it, mistah?"

"You don't remember anything, Alfred? Nuthin' but Holly?"

"Will you talk to her for me?"

"Talk to who?"

"Mozelle. She wanna take all'a my money. She plottin' 'gainst me wit' Mike." Alfred nodded his head to back up his claim.

"She all right, Alfred," Soupspoon said. "She sure enough keep this room clean."

"She wanna p'ison me."

"No."

"But that's okay." Metsgar bounced in his hard chair. "I gots her number. I ain't dead yet."

"How did Quickdraw die?"

"Who are you, man?" Alfred asked, angry. "What you be comin' in here for—messin' wit' me?"

"I'm yo' old friend, Alfie. Soupspoon. We used t'play together. I wanted t'tell the story about that night if I could get you to remember. I wanted t'tell some stories 'bout the blues 'fore they all gone. You. Me . . ."

"You could read?" Alfred asked.

" 'Li'l bit."

"I wanted t'go to school. But a black man couldn't be nuthin' where I come up. All you could do was to clean up after the white man, an' you know you had better brang your own broom.

"They didn't have nuthin' for ya. So . . . if somebody did some-thin', an' maybe it wasn't right, what could you expect? We ain't had nuthin'. An' if somebody wound up dead it wasn't nuthin' lost. He knowed that he had it comin' an' he were grateful not to be bur-dened with the when an' wherefore."

Alfred Metsgar sat back in his chair exhausted by all those words. Every breath stopped at the end of the exhale that might have been his last.

Soupspoon was tired too.

"So you don't remember nuthin'. Right, Alfie?" Soupspoon asked.

"I played the music but I didn't kill nobody. You cain't pin that one on me."

"I'm not sayin' that *you* did it, Alfred."

"People die all the time, man. All the time. You cain't s'pect me t'keep up wit' all'a that."

"Alfie, I know you didn't do it. All I wanna know is the name'a the man that did. I want to say about us and what we did. I don't want them to forget. But I ain't blamin' you."

"But I did do it," Alfred said.

"What?"

"It was me—my fault."

"You shot Quickdraw Marrs?"

"I played the music."

"But did you shoot'im?"

Alfred Metsgar raised his yellow and brown and green skull face to regard his younger friend. "What difference it make if it were me or that other man pult the trigger? What difference if Quickdraw turned the bullet on his own heart?"

Soupspoon turned off his tape recorder and locked it away. When he stood, Alfred looked up at him with fear or maybe awe that people could still stand on their own.

Soupspoon held out a hand which Alfred took into both of his. Alfred was grinning. He didn't shake so much as he felt the hand, moving it back and forth.

That embrace lasted for three minutes.

In the hall Mozelle stopped Soupspoon.

"What he say about me?"

"He said that you wanted his money."

"That old fool don't have no money. All he get is a check from the Social Security. We spend that on keepin' him alive. You from them?"

"Who?"

"Social Security."

"No. I'm just a old friend. I wanted to talk about the old days."

"Alfred don't remember nuthin'. He just sit in there. He wouldn't even go to the bathroom without me helpin' him."

"Yeah, uh-huh." Soupspoon wanted to get out from there. The whole apartment smelled of urine.

"Do me a favor, will ya?" he asked Mozelle.

"What's that?"

"Touch him ev'ry once in a while."

"Say what?"

"Put your hand on his forehead like you feelin' for fever. Then tell'im that he's cool as a cucumber. That's all he need now. Believe me, I know."

Pig Ears Mackie, Big Time Joe Harker, Blues Belle, Nessie Montgomery. They were all dead or disappeared. Soupspoon went through his address book and all of his memories. Few were to be found. Of those few, none had anything to say worth turning on his recorder for.

SEVENTEEN

"Kiki, could you come into the office a moment?" Sheldon Meyers asked.

She could have said, "Later, Sheldon, I got to get the change list down to production or they won't make the run tonight," just to make him wait. But she didn't because there was sweat on his upper lip. Sheldon's lips only perspired when there was something seriously wrong.

"Have you ever seen this?" he asked, handing her a blue policy folder.

She wished that she was sitting down when she saw the names Atwater and Tanya Wise next to INSURED. There was all the information she'd keyed in two months before. And under that was a list of payments made for radiation treatments, doctor's visits, and medicine. The total was $186,042.28.

The speed of light, Kiki thought. The moon entered her mind; the cold moon and the darkness that surrounded it.

"No," she said with a dry throat. "Never, ahem, never."

Kiki handed the folder back to Sheldon and sat down, trying to look natural. She crossed her legs and sat back.

"It came through my office," Sheldon said. "You know I sign a lot of these things, but when the money's this high I usually check it.

I usually send it down to the adjusters. I mean, I don't just sign everything that comes across my desk."

Kiki felt the dull thud of a hammer against the inside of her chest. An urge came over her to run, run right out of there. She could go back down south. Down to Arkansas. Nobody could find her in the small towns. She could work anywhere, live in the woods. Her father would never have to know she was there. She could never let him know where she was. For years after she'd run from home she worried that he would find her. He used to whisper in her ear, while he had his whole fist up in her rectum, that she could never get away; that he knew people all over the country and if she ran he'd send her picture to everyone he knew and they'd be looking for her and the police would bring her back home. He could find her anywhere and pull her right off the street, no one would even try to stop him. He'd whisper all that while opening his hand inside her. She'd gasp, helpless as he gripped her on the inside, and she believed him—every word.

"They've been investigating it for two weeks," Sheldon said. "They didn't even tell me about it until this morning."

"Why not? Do they think you did something?"

"No," he said reassuringly. "Not at all. They think that it was somebody in computer operations working with this couple." Sheldon turned the folder and pointed at the names. "They routed the papers and checks to an interoffice box and then forged the name with a stamp from the VP's office."

"How'd they get that?" Kiki asked, trying to act like she didn't have the guile to figure it out.

"There's at least half a dozen of them floating around operations. And there's one in the locked box at the end of the hall. It's locked but almost everybody has the combination.

"It doesn't matter, though. Now that we know, we'll be able to trace it down."

"How long will that take?"

Sheldon hunched his small shoulders.

Hot needles poked from behind Kiki's eyes. She couldn't get a full breath. Sheldon was talking again but she didn't, she couldn't make out what he was saying. Her intestines started rumbling and she was on the verge of throwing up. The stitches in her side, almost healed now, began pinching.

Then came the sound.

At first it was a distant booming, like someone playing a kettle-drum down in the basement with all the doors closed. But as it got louder it became harder and less resonant. And then, for one moment, Kiki was back in the dream. Her father's hard soles banging around in the basement and then loud knocking . . .

A jolt went through her body. Suddenly everything was all right, everything was calm. The cool of a fever breaking passed over her forehead and down the back of her neck.

"Whatever it is that's wrong," she said, "it beats gettin' fist-fucked up the ass."

Sheldon's mouth dropped open.

Kiki reached across the desk and picked up the folder.

"I'll see if I have anything about this in the files, Sheldon." She went out to her desk and put the folder in its alphabetical place in the file cabinet. That was at ten-thirty in the morning.

Kiki came home early that day with an armful of groceries. She had hamburger and sweet peas and French bread. She brought home lemon and apple pies with vanilla ice cream and two six-packs of Old New York beer. In a separate bag she had her every-other-day bottle of sour-mash whiskey.

Soupspoon and Randy were at the table, talking blues. Soup-spoon had his wedding suit on and his guitar out. His tape recorder was plugged into the wall and running.

"Hi guys," she said with a big smile.

"Hi." Randy waved.

Soupspoon looked up and scowled. He'd never seen her home from work early. He was half worried that Kiki would be mad to find somebody else in the house. But she didn't seem to mind. Soupspoon was relieved, because just that morning, when he'd been tuning his guitar, he felt a twinge in his chest and a sharp jolt down his leg.

"That's what music's all about, Randy," Soupspoon had been saying before Kiki came in. "It's all about gettin' so close to pain that it's like a friend, like somebody you love."

"Why don't you stay for dinner, Randy?" Kiki offered.

Randy had brought with him sample T-shirts, mainly buxom women in impossibly small bikinis and hard-muscled superheros all pumped up and in a rage.

"People buy this shit?" Soupspoon asked. "I wouldn't wear sumpin' like that in the street. Damn! Anybody could see I don't look like that. I ain't got no girlfriend look like that neither."

"Kids buy'em up for the superheros and pinups. I almost always sell fifty shirts, but with you, Soup, I bet I sell all hundred and twenty-five."

"Hamburgers and sour mash." Soupspoon lifted his glass in a toast. Kiki's eyes sparkled.

Soupspoon gave Randy a tin spoon and a mayonnaise jar. He showed the boy how to follow a beat. Then he started playing his guitar. He strummed and sang,

I got the travelin' blues, momma
Kansas Special on my mind.
Three locked doors in front'a me
and all I got is time.

Kiki showed that she had a rough, sexy voice by the second chorus. She cried and sang and laughed with the men.

Soupspoon realized somewhere near midnight that they were playing music. These children weren't even born when he came around but they were playing his music. They were living it too.

He felt the arthritis in his fingers as they traveled up and down the strings. His hip and leg ached dully under him.

Kiki started to dance and Randy rocked with her. They didn't know a thing about dancing. But you didn't need to know anything to dance to those tunes.

After a while Randy left Kiki to dance by herself while he

slapped the table, almost in time with Soupspoon's song. It was like back in the days when Negroes broke stones and one man was their voice. Every line ended with a grunt and the impact of the sixteen-pound hammer.

They played music until the liquor was gone. Then Randy kissed Kiki on both sides of her face and shook the bluesmaster's hands.

"I'll pick you up at seven on Saturday, Mr. Wise," Randy said. He looked at Kiki hopefully, but when she didn't take his hands he knew that he was going home alone.

The phone rang at three-thirty in the morning.

"Hello?" Kiki said in a drugged voice. She could see Soupspoon still seated at the kitchen table. He was asleep on his folded arms, next to the lacquer-red guitar.

"I know what you did, you cunt."

"Fez?"

"If you don't tell them what you did I'm gonna come over there and slip my knife up your goddamned pussy. You understand me?"

Kiki hung up.

She got up and went over to the old man. When she touched his shoulder he turned up his face and cried, "What?" in a small-boy voice. Then he wrapped his arms around Kiki and shuddered.

She took his clothes off without him really waking up and helped him into the bed, pulling the covers snug under his chin.

On the top shelf of the closet, under a stack of three straw hats, was the box Hattie had given Kiki after she came running out to Hattie's house, crying and bleeding from her ass. A tall thin man as black and shiny as tar was sitting in the front room of her two-room shack. He came into the bedroom after a little while and said, "You cain't leave that chile here."

"What I'm s'posed to do, Hector? You want me t'put her out there in the dirt? You more worried about some goddamn white man than you scared'a God?"

"God knows the trouble I got. He ain't gonna blame me for this here."

"If you scared then go on," Hattie said. "An' git yo' butt outta here anyway. This girl don't need to be 'round no men."

Hector went out but Kiki could hear him from time to time in the other room. She had a fever again like when she had flu. She could always come to Hattie. Hattie listened to every word she ever said.

"Tell me a story," Kiki begged.

"Shut up, child."

But Kiki remembered that all she had to do was keep on asking and finally the story would come.

Once there came a loud knock on the door. Hector came in, picked Kiki up from the bed, and took her out of the window and into the woods. He held her rough and tight the way her father did when he wanted to do it. When she tried to scream he held her mouth. She fought against him but he was too strong.

Her nose was stuffy from crying and the skinny man's hand was clamped tight over her mouth. Kiki went silent as she concentrated on sucking in the slender stream of air through her almost fully clogged nostril.

She got fuzzy-headed.

The light from Hattie's house looked to her like big colored snowflakes and the loud voice of her father was just a jumble of mad words. "Mr. Waters! Mr. Waters!" was all she could make out from what Hattie said.

When the shouting came out back, Hector pulled further off into the wood. He whispered in her ear, "Sh!" Then he released his hold on her mouth.

She had never, before or since, tasted anything so rich and pure as the air in that deadly wood. Her lungs tingled with the beginnings of pneumonia as her father blundered around lost, unable to find her.

"Kiki! Kiki, you come on out here!" he shouted. "You cain't run from me, girl! Come out here!"

She was only fourteen but she understood that he had come

alone. Alone because he was ashamed and didn't want his friends to see the blood at the back of her skirt.

But tomorrow, she knew, he'd have his white friends come down. She didn't care much about that, though. Not while she was sitting on Hector like some old comfortable chair; hard but made to hold her.

She passed out and didn't come to again until she was in a hunter's cabin with Hector, deep in the Arkansas woods. The dark man sat next to her cot. The sun shone through a paneless window illuminating the old newsprint used to paper the walls. Hector was washing her bare legs with alcohol, using an old rag and a battered tin pan. He slathered the rag up over her belly and chest. When he let the liquid run cold over her throat she wanted to touch him, to let him know how good it felt, but she was still too weak.

He turned her over and went from between her toes and the soles of her feet all the way up to the nape of her neck. The alcohol burned where it seeped to her rectum but by then she knew that Hector didn't mean to hurt her. He was trying to save her life.

Hector bathed Kiki at least six times that first day, and he not saying a word. He fed her soup and water, and watched her sleep. He was always touching her, feeling for fever, and whenever he found heat he bathed her in cold.

Kiki suspected that Hector had never been so intimate with a white girl and that he probably enjoyed rubbing her all over. But she didn't mind his eyes and hands. She didn't mind him being there when she roused. He could do anything he wanted, because he was Hattie's friend and his hands were cold and he smelled like the deep Arkansas wood.

The next day Hattie came and clucked and watched over her. Hattie made Kiki drink much more soup than Hector had. She took her outside to pee. She told the half-asleep girl that her father was looking for her and that Hattie had to be careful. She'd only come out twice a week.

Kiki didn't care, though. She liked being alone with silent Hector.

After three weeks Kiki was strong enough to eat bread. The

fever had broken and the pneumonia was almost clear. Hattie had a hundred dollars put away and offered it to take Kiki on a bus to California where her cousin would take her in. Hattie also gave Kiki Hector's pistol. It was a .32-caliber six-shooter that Hector's old boss had given to him after a good year.

Hattie taught Kiki how to oil her gun and how to keep it clean. She told her to buy bullets every three years. Kiki went to target practice on her own. She wasn't a dead shot but she wasn't afraid to shoot either. She could hit a man at ten paces, that's all she'd ever need.

On the day she was to leave, Kiki went outside Hector's shack while Hattie was still packing her bags. Hector was seeing to the litter he'd made to drag the bags down to the road where the Greyhound passed.

Kiki stared at Hector but he kept working as if she wasn't there.

Finally she asked him, "Would you come with me, Hector?" She hadn't planned to say it, didn't even know what she meant. "I mean, come with me to California."

"What?" That got his attention.

"We could sleep in a big brass bed and eat oranges and work for the movies. You could be a gardener and I'd do makeup work for the stars." She was surprised at herself—that she had it all worked out.

Hector moved to turn away, but Kiki grabbed him and dug her fingernails into his forearm. Blood came from the deep scratches.

He looked at her again and shuddered. She knew, or thought she knew, at that moment he was almost ready to go. But he was too strong. He pulled her hands away and was lost to her. And that loss was the worst thing, up until this night in New York, that she ever experienced.

Kiki took the gun out and cleaned it sitting next to Soupspoon's guitar. Then she went back into the closet and found a shoulder purse that she'd be able to carry with her around work.

She brought the purse with her to bed and slept better than she had since she was just a child, sleeping in a big black woman's arms.

E I G H T E E N

The day after Kiki came home early, Soupspoon called Rudy.

"I'ma play at a street fair on Saturday, Rudy. Down on Carmine Street just offa Bleecker. You could come on down an' hear me t'see what you might get."

"Okay, Uncle Atwater. How you feelin'?"

"Like I was dead an' then I died again."

Rudy laughed at Soupspoon's blues. "I told A'ntee Mavy 'bout what's goin' on wit' you. She said she'd like to talk if you wanted."

He found himself pressing her buzzer at about noon. She didn't live far from the Beldin Arms. Fourteenth Street and Avenue A.

All those years and we was just walking distance, Soupspoon thought. *Might as well been a million miles.*

"Who is it?"

"Me, Mavy. Atwater."

There followed a long silence. In a corner of the vestibule a water beetle was dying on his back, waving his hairy brown legs at the light. Soupspoon raised his foot but then put it back down.

Who knows what he thinkin'.

"Rudy said that you got cancer," Mavis said at last.

"That's what the doctors say, babe. That's what they say."

"Elevator's straight back when you walk in. Eight G," the talk box barked. Then there was a loud buzzing and Soupspoon pushed his way in.

She was old and skinnier, dressed all in white. Her skirt and her shirt and shoes, even the shawl over her head, which she clutched with both hands at the chin, was white.

He couldn't kiss her standing like that; couldn't even shake her hand. So he stood there, briefcase hanging from his fist.

"What's that?" she asked.

"Tape recorder an' my lunch."

"Tape recorder for what? A Walkman?"

"Naw."

"What is it then?"

"Can I come in your house, Mavis?"

The question caught her up short. Maybe she thought that they could stand at the door and say what they had to say. After that he could go home to die and she could fade back into white.

There was music coming from an old phonograph behind her.

"That the same old Victrola, Mavy?"

"Yeah, sure is."

"Where you find a stylus fo' it nowadays?"

"I got six dozen of'em at a flea market down North Carolina 'bout fifteen years ago." She frowned, angry that he got her talking. "You could come in for a little while, Atwater, but I got work to do."

He perched on the edge of her antique white sofa while she sat up straight in a blond chair. As the minutes went by she got younger-looking. Her face, at first hard, was now regal. He caught a whiff of perfume, Forest Rose. She was wearing that scent when they met over forty-five years before.

He told her about the cancer treatments, but not too much. He told her about his whole life since they'd parted—it didn't take long.

"One day been just like t'other these last twenty years. Sometimes I even forget what year it is," he said.

If anything Mavis's life was even simpler. She'd left Texas after only a few months because being next to where her son had died was too painful to bear.

"I got a driver named George pick me up every Tuesday at eleven-fifteen. He take me up to Angela's Curios and I let off all my flower arrangements and she pay me. She got seven shops here and on Long Island an' dried roses always sells good. Then George take me up t'get my groceries an' I pay'im fifteen dollars cash."

"Where you get your flowers from?"

"Korean place. Usually their little boy, Kwan, bring 'em up. I give'im fi'ty cents for that."

And that was it. Neither one had done a thing special in years. Except now Soupspoon was dying. Now he missed things that he had never even noticed before. But he didn't talk about those things to Mavis—he didn't have the heart.

Instead he said, "You know now I'm sick I figger I better do all the things I left till later."

Mavis took a long white cigarette from a porcelain cigarette case on her glass table.

"An' one'a them things," Soupspoon went on, "is to put down what I remember about the blues."

"Like a histr'y book?"

He nodded. "Only I put it down on tape. Stories and songs too. When I'm through I'ma send it to Mr. Early. You remember him?"

"Him! Mo' shit about Robert Johnson's all it is."

"Him too. He was part of it. Why not him?"

"Cain't you even die by yo'self, Atwater?" she asked. Then she brought the back of her hand to her mouth. "I'm sorry, honey. I shouldn'ta said that. That was wrong."

"You never really told me everything about that one time you met'im." It was all Soupspoon wanted.

"You ain't s'posed t'talk to yo' huzbun 'bout some ole boy-friend you had. That's wrong too."

"But I ain't yo' husband no more, Mavis. We ain't even friends. This is all I got left, baby." He pointed at his briefcase. "I ain't never made no records. I ain't got no heir."

"Well? What you want from me?" Mavis's voice was both small and angry. "What can I do about that now?"

Soupspoon opened his briefcase and took out the recorder. He pressed two buttons and smiled.

"Just tell me about it, Mavy. Just tell it like it was."

"You mean . . . just talk?"

"Uh-huh. That's all I do. Usually I start tellin' somebody like Kiki or Randy a story an' then I just forgets that they there."

Mavis didn't know who Kiki and Randy were, but she was afraid of the recorder box. She scowled at the thing and balled her fists so tight that her knuckles popped.

Soupspoon moved down to the end of the couch, nearer her chair.

"Tell me 'bout the night you met RL," he whispered and then he touched her thigh.

She jumped when he touched her, but she also looked away from the box.

"What you want me to say?"

"Just talk," he said, and he touched her leg again. "Start with Rafael. He was your boyfriend back then, right?"

"Yeah," she said. "Yeah, Rafael was my common-law huzbun."

"But you never really married him," Soupspoon primed her.

"Naw, uh-uh, Rafael wasn't no good, he was just all I had is all."

"He was a bad man?" Soupspoon asked.

"Naw. He wasn't bad, he just wasn't no good." She paused for a moment and shivered. "The only good thing ever come'a Rafael was my son Cortland—and he's dead all these years."

Through the window Soupspoon could see the dark and overcast New York afternoon. Inside there were at least two dozen bright lights blasting silently against white walls, white rugs, and white furniture. Mavis took out another long white cigarette and lit it. Her head was held back in elegant fashion, reflecting on many hard years. But the only indication of her age now was the two deep furrows in her cheeks and the wrinkles about her eyes. She opened those eyes dramatically and Soupspoon knew that he had her.

"Yes. Rafael was a wild man, but I wasn't too tame back then myself. I loved my baby somethin' terrible an' Rafe loved us—the way a hard-lovin', hard-drinkin' man loves. Sometimes he'd come in all mean and worked up. The way he'd talk was like a animal growlin'. Cort'd start whimperin' and I'd get up and tell Rafe to get-ass away from us until he was civil."

Mavis sat back and dragged deeply on the unfiltered Pall Mall. She exhaled the smoke into the air above Soupspoon's head.

"He wasn't afraid to hit me," she said. "An' he knew I wasn't afraid t'hit him back. You know my fists is big like a man's. . . ." Mavis balled her left hand to prove the point. "I had some power too. And if we'd fight an' get so worked up we had to make love, I'd tell'im that he had to carry me outside on the porch 'cause I didn't want Cort to see that. Rafe'd pick me up and he'd be shakin' he wanted it so bad.

"Rafe would love a woman hard. I could feel my back hittin' the flo', and later on I'd always be pullin' splinters outta my rear." Mavis exhaled and stubbed out the cigarette; she only smoked it halfway. "I used to think I liked a hard-lovin' man. Like when you see a stallion or a bull bitin' and fuckin' wit' that crazy look in they eyes."

Mavis gave Soupspoon a look that reminded him of the first night they met.

"What about Robert Johnson?" he asked. "Did he meet Rafael?"

"Hell no! Rafe woulda et that po' boy up. He was a big man an' mean when it come to what was his." Mavis lit up another cigarette. "When I met Bob, me and Rafe was livin' with Number Seven, Rafe's youngest brother, in a old ruined sawmill on the river. Number Seven and Rafe made moonshine up there and I picked flowers and did things for the white ladies in town. On weekend nights we'd get inta Number Seven's Terraplane an' drive down to town, that was Panther Burn. That is, we did used to go down there—until Terry's juke joint burnt down.

"We were down there on the night of the fire. A crowd was already gathered by the time we come and the music was goin' strong.

"Pete Hollis was there that night.

"Pete was a big ole boy like to dance wild. I mean, he'd get all the way down to the floor, if you see what I mean. *All the way down.* You know he grabbed me the minute I come in an' th'owed me around till all I could do was laugh an' laugh." Mavis was lost in the story now. Soupspoon could tell by the way she breathed. "An' when the song stopped and another one started, Rafe grabbed me an' spun me so hard that I couldn't even see straight. The musicians would hardly take a break between songs and so they got the crowd hotter an' hotter and I felt like the hottest momma there bein' th'owed from Rafe to Pete Hollis. The floor cleared out around us for every dance and them boys got wilder an' wilder tryin' to outdo the steps the last one done.

"One time Rafe th'ow me so hard that I falls down an' hurt my butt an' tear my dress. You know that shit made me mad." Mavis cut her eyes the way young women did in Soupspoon's day. "Girl like a li'l rough handlin' don't mean she wanna get th'owed to the floor. So I go over to Pete an' he smile all evil an' we start shakin' our shoulders an' holdin' hands. First he th'ow me down between his legs an' then he pull me up so I go flyin' an' twirlin' in the air. But he caught me. Ev'ry body was watchin' us an' cheerin' us. I was wearin' this big skirt that twirled open but I didn't have no underwears on.

"Number Seven come up right then an' grab Pete. Before I could say 'Hey!' Rafe had me dancin' again. But it really wasn't like dancin' at all. He had my wrist hard and was just th'owin' me out and back again like a sack'a beans. He tried to th'ow me down between his legs but I dug in my heels so he couldn't do it. Then he tried to twirl me in the air. I let my weight hang down, but Rafe was real strong, he got to hold'a me under the arms an' th'ows me so that I hit up against a kerosene lantern on the wall." Mavis opened her eyes in real fear. "Fire spread over the floor so quick that nobody could stop it in time. We was all runnin' for the door. My hem had caught fire an' I was runnin' an' yellin' till somebody caught my arm an' put me down in the mud to put out the flame."

There was a loud thought in Soupspoon's mind. He never knew that Mavis had met RL at Panther Burn; at the fire that marked the last time he was ever to see his friend. He felt a double loss. It seemed to him that RL had raised up out of his grave to steal his wife away. Mavis had never been his because she had never, even from the start, opened her whole heart to him.

The hard truth of his thoughts was reflected in Mavis's cold stare.

She lit up another cigarette and gazed out of the dark window. After a while she got up and pulled the curtains closed. This had the effect of making the room even brighter.

When she came back to her chair Soupspoon was very quiet—afraid that the spell would be broken and he'd miss the story he wanted so bad. But when he saw the sneer that Mavis gave him he knew that she wouldn't stop. He knew that she had to talk just as much as he needed to hear.

"The man who put out my dress," she said, "helped me up and walked me back down to the wreck. The whole place burnt down in ten minutes flat. Musta been a dozen people ate smoke so bad that they was stretched out. Four'a them died, but not for a coupla days. I looked for Rafe and Number Seven but they was gone—run off wit' Pete Hollis. The three'a them got scared an' run down to a place called Mud Town. It wasn't no real town then, just a place where colored people made their beds for a while.

"I was sick at how terrible it all was. My leg was hurtin' from where I hit the wall and I was caked wit' mud. But then the man who helped me touched my arm. He was a hush young man and I saw that he had a guitar. It was Bob Johnson. He took my arm and walked me away from the fire. Everybody was leavin' because nobody wanted to be there when the law came. I took Bob on a path that led up to the mill. We was alone and he was quiet, just holdin' my arm.

"It was too quiet for me, so I asked him, 'You the one playin' music tonight?'

" 'Yes, ma'am,' he says as respectful and sure as a deacon. And then he turn t'me an' says, 'Could I come home wit' you?' Just like that." Mavis was still amazed by the bluesman's audacity. "I didn't know him from Job but he askin' me t'share my bed. And here I am puttin' my filthy arm 'round his shoulders an' hopin' that Rafe wouldn't be back that night."

Mavis stubbed out her half cigarette, savoring the last drag. Soupspoon saw a small roach making its way along the base of the wall behind her. He tried not to stare at the insect for fear that Mavis would turn to see. Maybe she'd burn down this house if there was a bug in it.

"He made me to take off my dirty clothes out on the back porch. Then he filled up this bucket full'a cold water and soaked my dirty things in it while I washed the mud off. Then he find my room an' come out with the prettiest dress I got. There I am, naked to the world, an' here's this pretty man holdin' the dress up on my titties. I steps right into it an' he done up the buttons. You know I started to shake for that boy the same way Rafe'd shake for me.

"He was sweet in bed too. Real different from Rafe. You know a man like Rafe squeeze till you don't know where you stop and he start. But I knew where I was wit' RL. When I come he jump up t'look me right in the eye like he was scared'a what he called up. An' you know he had to be lookin' me in the eye like that all night, just about. Mmm." Mavis leaned her head back and brought the new cigarette down to her mouth with sensual pleasure. The smoke came out of her nose and drifted down her dark face in white rivulets.

"When I woke up it was still dark. I thought I mighta heard sumpin' and I worried that it was Rafe comin' in. So I jump outta bed and go out to the porch. We had mosquito netting out there and a couple's old chairs. The whole mill was up on stilts above the river. The moon was shinin' back there, half-faced and yellow. And the woods was a rough black color under it. Bob was naked an' sittin' on a empty five-gallon shine barrel. He was huggin' on his guitar like it was a woman or a child.

"I asked him what was wrong an' he says, 'Nuthin', momma,'

in this sweet li'l voice. He mighta been talkin' to his own momma as well as me. The tears was comin' down his face. He was so sad and beautiful out there naked to the moonlight. I was drawed to him. I took his guitar an' put it down real soft next to the banister and then I pulls him down to the floor with me. All there was was a burlap sack there for us to lie on, but we didn't mind. My chest was slick with his tears. And the bare breeze called up goose bumps.

"He told me all 'bout his girl down around Robinsonville. Just fifteen but she still died with their baby. He cried like chirren do, all lost and sad. I could see by the way he felt her death how he could play such strong music.

"He told me how everybody hated him. First his stepdaddy who beat him and then later all the folks who made fun'a him not workin' in the fields. Even the musicians didn't want him to play nuthin' but mouth harp. They bad-talked him until he trained hisself to play right. . . ."

"He tell you about how he sold his soul?" Soupspoon asked.

Mavis shook her head, still caught up in the memory. "He never said nuthin' 'bout that to me. All he could say was how he had been pushed around. Everybody was jealous of him. They stole his music and blamed him for all kindsa things. Maybe they blamed him for sellin' his soul.

"There I was layin' back naked with a man, legs open for him to do whatever he please, but there wasn't nuthin' like that. When he turns t'me an' ask, 'Could I stay here with you?' I almost told him yeah. I wanted to ask Rafe t'let me have that boy. I thought that if I took him in I could p'otect him."

Mavis laughed and shook her head at the white floor. "I know better now. Men like him ain't never had no chance at no normal life. If that child-wife'a his woulda lived it wouldn'ta mattered. If that baby had lived he woulda been left with some woman in some town suckin' on a wet rag an' cryin' fo' some daddy he never had."

Mavis smoked and stared directly into the lamp behind Soupspoon.

"Bob left in the mornin'. I kissed him goodbye. Then I got Cort from down at my cousin's where I left him t'go dancin'. I found out from her about where Rafe an' them had gone. After two days I heard that two men and one woman had already died from smoke. The county law was askin' questions about me, so I took up Cort an' run down to La Marque, Texas, where my older sister Martha lived. I did it 'cause Cort needed his momma an' I couldn't go to no jail. I mean, it wasn't my fault that them people died, but they woulda taken me down to the women's prison if they wanted. So I run. An' 'cause I did my baby is dead today."

Mavis lit the last cigarette and smoked it slowly while she stared off.

He remembered all the years that they had together. His broken leg, her first job with the church choir. They had come from the deepest, saddest south—not much better than slaves—and made it up into the twentieth century with automobiles, telephones, and indoor plumbing. He remembered everything but it all seemed like a play. He had said his lines and Mavis recited hers.

Not one moment of that life was like the two weeks after he met RL in Arcola. Those days went beyond everything. What they discovered was new and nobody could predict what would happen next. It was a hard song of disease and death. A wild dance and Soupspoon and Robert Johnson played the tune.

He remembered the fire. He was scared out of his mind. But somewhere he knew that this was the last great moment of his life.

Now he saw that the same was true for Mavis.

He had met her later, down in Texas. But that was after Cort had died. She was never wild again.

"Thank you, Mavy." Soupspoon reached down to touch her again but she stood up.

"You got what you wanted?" she asked him.

"I don't know. I thought that Rudy said you wanted t'see me."

Mavis took a half-smoked butt out of the ashtray and struck a match.

"I did," she said. "But you come on in here wit' yo' tape recorder an' yo' questions 'bout Robert Johnson. Well . . . I done answered yo' questions. Is there sumpin' else?"

"I don't know, Mavy. I just wanted to talk."

"Well, you done talked an' now it's time for me t'get back t'my flowers." She turned her face toward the door.

He watched her back, knowing that there was something he should say. He wanted it; she did too, he knew. But all he had left in him was the truth. A barren marriage behind a bare blues life. He never cared enough to find her again after they broke up. He didn't even know that she was back in New York until Rudy told him.

All he really wanted was on that tape recorder.

"I'm sorry, baby," he said.

NINETEEN

On Tuesday Kiki went to work, pistol stashed in her shoulder purse. Her friends didn't talk to her. Sheldon Myers said hardly a word. At noon, while she was outside eating a hot dog for lunch, she ran into Motie and Clive Tooms. They were smoking a joint near the statue across the street from the office building.

Motie told her that somebody had forged a million-dollar insurance policy. That building security had come to Fez's desk, thrown all of his stuff into a box, and escorted him from the building. He was fired but there might also be criminal charges. They stopped the numbers game and the bar.

"I hope they deep-fry the motherfucker," Motie said. Kiki didn't say anything. She could tell that Motie hadn't connected the files he routed for her with Fez's problems. She didn't even take a hit off the joint when Clive, a tall and redheaded black youth, offered.

"I gotta get back," she said.

That night she dreamed about the stone boy again. This time he caught her. He cut off her arm with his black blade.

On Wednesday Soupspoon borrowed fifteen dollars from Randy down at the "bookstore" on St. Mark's. He went to a music store on Forty-sixth Street and got strings for his guitar. The subway stairs were hard on his hip. He could feel the pain, but he had a trick that kept the feeling at bay. He "walked around" the pain. He took one step with his right leg, then he'd look quickly to the right, or left, and take a fast step with his painful side. That way the ache was contained, almost forgotten. Soupspoon made it a point to look at something special when he took his walk-around step; like a pretty girl or an interesting face. Often he watched babies at play or the domestic and wild animals of the city. Soupspoon loved the wildlife of the big city. Frisky dogs, hungry squirrels, and feral rats. Some of the bigger cockroaches reminded him of old men dressed in their stiff tuxedos. Sometimes he'd point his gaze up high, because in New York there was always something to see up on the sides of buildings and rooftops. There were gargoyles and statues, trees that sprouted right out of the concrete it seemed, brooding men and women looking back down at him.

That day he saw a hawk just as it swooped down from a ledge and snagged a pigeon by the throat. The hawk arched high with its prey, leaving a few tattered feathers to float down toward the street. Soupspoon turned to see if there was somebody else who saw that poor dove's angel of death—but he was alone.

Kiki was sitting at her desk on Thursday morning. She glanced down at her nails. They were ragged and rough. For a moment she thought of doing them but decided against it.

A small bald man in a light green suit was coming down the hall. He wore wire-rimmed glasses. Behind him were three large men in good dark suits. The men ran from slender to fat but they all looked powerful, as if their work was in a rock quarry instead of an office.

"Miss Waters?" the green-suited man asked when they got to her desk.

Kiki felt for her pistol in the bag at her side.

"Miss Waters?"

"What?"

"My name is Mr. Cause," he said.

Kiki found the name funny.

WALTER MOSLEY

"Do you know me?"

"I don't think I'd forget that name."

"I'm vice president in charge of personnel, Miss Waters. Your position here has been terminated."

"What?"

Out of the side of her eye she could see Sheldon peeking around his door.

"You will leave the building now, escorted by myself and these men . . ."

Kiki saw a red cloud around Mr. Cause. She felt her finger on the trigger inside the handbag. There was a loud bumblebee in place of the words the little man was saying. She felt an intense, definitely sexual pleasure down her body. A cool sweat went across her face— even into her mouth. When she smiled, Mr. Cause got a quizzical look on his face. One of the men, a dark-skinned white man, moved to help Kiki out of her seat.

"Thank you." She allowed the man to help her up by her gun arm. A potent attraction for this man went through her. His face was lean and his tapered ears were back against his head like a wary hound's ears. His eyes were truly black. He had no smell at all that Kiki could sense.

The little man was still talking. He said that she could only take her purse and her jacket. Everything else that was hers would be sent home. His high-pitched voice hurt her ears. She waved around the side of her head as if waving away the bees that hovered about the magnolia tree of her childhood.

She was wobbly on her feet toward the elevator doors. The olive-skinned man's long finger lit the button sensor. She leaned against his hard chest. "My things?"

"They'll send them." His voice was shallow. No resonance, no music. He was everything Kiki thought he was.

People shied away from the elevators when they saw what was going on. Kiki's friends didn't ask any questions. They stared from down the hall. But Kiki didn't care. She was thinking about the man who held her elbow. She thought how she could shoot him the way

Jack Ruby shot Lee Oswald in front of all those people. The dark man would hunch forward, his mouth forming a tight little O. He'd go down to the floor, the light fading into pain as he went. . . .

When they left Kiki in front of Number Two Broadway she was all right. She hadn't shot anybody. Nobody was dead.

Whenever she came running in to Hattie with all her problems the big black woman would always ask, "Anybody dead?" That question always knocked the tears right out of Kiki's eyes. She'd look up in wonder at the woman—who, to Kiki, was the perfect image of God—and shake her head, no.

"Well, if ain't nobody's dead we better get back to work."

"They what?" Soupspoon asked her that night.

"They came up to my desk and escorted me to the door. Wouldn't even let me get my stuff."

"Why they wanna do sumpin' like that?" Soupspoon was cleaning his guitar.

"They found out about the policy I faked for you."

"No."

"I don't think they could prove it, daddy. I never signed a thing. I used a stamp that they keep locked up on my floor, but they can't prove that I knew the combination. I didn't have the priority on the computer and nobody can prove that I did. They just fired me, that's all."

"But what if they come here?" Soupspoon felt a sharp jab that went from his chest all the way down into his legs.

"What's wrong?" Kiki got up and went to his side. She reached out and touched his head.

"Nuthin'. Nuthin' at all."

Days later, at Sono's apartment, Soupspoon would say into his Radio Shack tape recorder, ". . . that was the first time I ever figured it all out. There I was in shit up to my lip but they wasn't nuthin' I could do. That girl did everything she could t'help me. She saved my life. What could I say? I knew it was the cancer in my lung just like I knew it was the guitar on the table. Wasn't a damn thing I could do. I kissed that girl right on the lips an' told her that she was best thing happen t'me in years. . . ."

"Take a walk with me, daddy," Kiki said in a drunken little-girl voice. "Let's walk off this food."

"Kiki, girl, you not gonna find that boy. He scared away since he stuck you." Really it was the pain he'd been feeling in his leg and chest that made him want to stay home. It wasn't a bad pain. It was only late at night, when he was lying in bed, that it really bothered him. He told himself that it was just an old man's muscle, that if he rested it would go away, but he knew better.

"Just this one more time, daddy. After this, if your singin' don't do it, we'll have to move away anyway." Kiki had put away a cupful of whiskey already. There were tears in her eyes. "And this is the right time'a day, and it's Friday too. . . . Just one more time and I'll give it up."

When Soupspoon handed Kiki her small purse he felt the weight of it. But if there was a pistol in there he didn't want to know about it. It wasn't anything to worry about anyway. That boy was nowhere to be found. He was lost; that's why he was what he was—like Robert Johnson.

That's what he had told Randy on the tape recorder.

"All bluesmen are lost. Bluesmen. Black-and-blues, that's what they shoulda called it. Black men who only ever traveled at night, in the dark. Goin' nowhere and findin' hard fists and bone-breakin' rock in their path.

"You could yell out pain in the blues. You could kill that woman that played you wrong. You could shout, 'Oh no! Lawd!' And even the white boss would smile.

"You could show a mean bone or cry from down deep in your heart with the whole world as your witness.

"You could demand freedom in the blues. But it wasn't so much freedom a poor black man wanted but release. That's a slave's freedom; a sharecropper's freedom. Release from his bonds and his bondage. Release from hard hunger and even harder fear. Release from the pain of work so hard that you'd say it was impossible for a man to do all that. Work so hard that it hurts even to think about it.

"And when we asked for release we knew that it meant freedom—but it meant death too. We was bound for nowhere. Bound for a heavy iron ball on the chain gang or just at work on the plantation. Bound to die—that's what we was.

"Bound for freedom."

"Bob?" young Atwater had asked Mr. Robert Johnson. "How come you don't leave outta here an' go up north? We could go up there an' make a whole lotta money playin'. Real money. An' no green-toof sheriff gonna dare an' take it."

"I been up there," RL said. "I seen it—seen it all. Me an' this other blues boy go on up there. Chicago, New York. But you know it ain't real up north. Niggers don't even know they names up there, baby. Naw. They crazy."

"But we could make us a race record. Git that on the radio an' you gots all kindsa money."

Soupspoon remembered his friend's sad smile. "They ain't no gettin' away from yo' stank, Soup. Rabbit run, man, he run—maybe he even make it down into his hole. But you know that fox still out there grinnin' somewhere. He grinnin' right now."

Soupspoon still remembered, remembered each word that RL had said. He worried over the lines like someone might do over a song that moved them but, still, the words just didn't make sense.

"There he is," Kiki hissed.

She started walking at a slant across Chrystie. The gang of boys was just moving past where she'd come up on the sidewalk. Soupspoon followed her as she stalked the pack of children.

"It's the one in the black Spider-Man T-shirt," Kiki whispered when Soupspoon came up beside her. He didn't say anything. He just stayed beside her. This was a debt to her and he meant to pay it—a note come due.

There were about nine of them—little boys not one over ten. They were singing and laughing and trying to talk the talk of the street. Their hips and shoulders moved as they walked along because they couldn't keep all that energy in. They were happy and scared and wild, and, Soupspoon knew, they weren't thinking a thing about a crazy woman stalking them.

When they cut down a small alley, Kiki sped up to close the gap. She looked up over their heads and then back at Soupspoon. When she was satisfied that there was no one else around she took the pistol from her purse and ran right in the middle of the pack of boys.

"She got a gun!" a high voice screamed and boys were running everywhere. One of them fell but he never hit the ground because his arms and legs were moving so fast that he just touched the asphalt and somehow kept moving. Four of them sped past Soupspoon while the rest cleared out of the other end of the alley.

All of them got away except for the boy in the Spider-Man T-shirt. Kiki had him by the arm with her pistol jammed underneath his jaw.

They were both yelling but Soupspoon couldn't make out a word. Then Kiki dragged the boy behind a big green Dumpster and threw him on the ground. He was trapped in the corner, facing the trembling woman and her gun.

"You know me, nigger boy?" she yelled. Soupspoon came up behind her and stopped.

"Do you know me?" She had torn his shirt so that all he had left was a black collar around his throat. His face was strained and contorted, shot through with creases like the wrinkles of an old man. He was trying to say no, that he didn't know her, but there was no voice, just a high whine.

Kiki pushed him down on his back and stepped over him so that she had a foot on either side of his chest.

He was a brown boy but his sweaty skin glinted orange with blood from his hard-pounding heart.

Kiki grabbed him by his short dreadlocks and pulled his head up to meet her pistol again.

That's when he cried like a little boy, like what he was.

"Shut up!" Kiki screamed. "You don't remember putting that knife in me?"

The boy put up his hand to plead but Kiki slammed it down with the barrel of her gun.

Soupspoon saw a short piece of lumber lying nearby. He stooped to pick up the heavy stick.

"You don't remember?"

"I'm sorry. I'm sorry." The boy cradled the broken fingers. His breath sang from down below his throat.

Soupspoon came up close behind Kiki.

"I know you're sorry," she said. "And you gonna be even sorrier, 'cause I'm gonna shoot you. I'm gonna shoot you in your legs"—she touched his knee and he pulled back—"and then in your eyes."

The boy covered his face and sank even further into the ground.

"But first I'm gonna get you down where you got me." Kiki brought the muzzle down toward the boy's genitals. Soupspoon moved quickly then. He thrust the board between Kiki and the boy.

"Here! Beat'im wit' this," he said.

"What?" When Kiki looked up he could see the tears and the pain in her eyes.

"Beat'im wit' this here board. He don't deserve no shootin', Kiki. So gimme that gun an' beat'im for what he done."

Kiki didn't move at first. She licked her thin lips with a pale tongue. A quizzical look came over her face. Soupspoon still offered the thick board.

She let the pistol swing down to her side.

Immediately the boy was up and gone. He was running down the alley, holding his broken fingers and moving fast.

Kiki turned to watch him, and Soupspoon took the gun from her hand. He put on the safety and pocketed the piece.

Kiki fell to her knees and hugged him around the waist. Anyone looking from down the alley would have sworn that Kiki was performing some sexual act. But nobody looked. Kiki hugged Soupspoon and cried into his crotch. She cried for a long time and would have gone on but Soupspoon helped her to her feet. Then they walked home, arms wrapped around each other for support, Soupspoon holding on for his aching leg and Kiki staying near for love.

That night Kiki couldn't stop crying. She blubbered and snorted and drank a whole bottle of sour mash. She started talking and couldn't stop that either. At first she said terrible things about her mother and her mother's sister who had come to live with them when she was dying of cancer. She hated them. Hated the way they dressed and smelled. She hated how they went to the toilet and chewed their food. For over an hour she said things about them. Until finally Soupspoon asked her about her father, and if she liked him.

He was sorry about that question.

He didn't want to know all the things that went on in that childhood basement. The things that went on while one woman held her hands over her ears and the other one died.

Water hoses, hard fists, and the smell of sweat over cologne that still made her want to vomit—that's what Kiki remembered about her father.

Soupspoon held her, his mind devoid of anything—even music. He held her and hoped that the tears would wash away the filth caked in her mind.

But the more she cried the sadder she became. She cried and moaned and walked all around the room. Finally Soupspoon took her to bed. He had to lie with her because she couldn't lie down alone.

He remembered the smell of whiskey and sweat, and the touch of dry hot skin that was past passion.

> *He broke your heart li'l darlin'.*
> *Ain't no red in the rose no mo'.*
> *He tore that white dress, baby.*
> *Ain't no thread can sew it up.*
> *You know the beesting it feel like kisses*
> *Hershey's chocolate taste just like chalk.*

TWENTY

When Randy arrived the next morning he found Soupspoon dressed and ready to go. The old man had his guitar case, a harmonica fixed to wear around his neck, and a tambourine to tie around his leg.

Kiki was in the bathroom throwing up.

"You coming, Kiki?" Randy shouted through the door.

"Maybe later."

Randy's booth was in front of an Italian restaurant on the east side of Carmine. He had a long table that was just an unfinished door covered with piles of folded T-shirts. At the back of the booth T-shirts hung from wires that were suspended between two long poles anchored to cinder blocks on the street. The shirts were all sexy and macho in bright colors. Randy got them from Ralphie Dee, who worked for Wild Chests of Brooklyn. Ralphie loaded the shirts he'd taken over the months into his station wagon and left the keys for Randy.

To the left of Randy's booth two young men had a concession where they sold bootlegged audiocassettes that were counterfeited to look like the originals. To the right a group of potters sold wares from their studio; heavy cups and wobbling plates that old ladies swooned over before passing them by.

People sold toys, novelties, batteries, antiques, and clothes.

There were a lot of clothes. Designer overalls in psychedelic colors, natural wool sweaters from Chile, straw hats, old suits.

And then came jewelry. Earrings mainly, from gaudy cheap plastic to delicate handmade. Nose studs and nipple rings. Lots of silver, but no gold to speak of. Garnet rings and freshwater pearl necklaces, silver-plated bracelets and silver skulls for your fingers, toes, throat, and ears.

At the corner near Bleecker they had food. Italian sausages with peppers, fresh deep-fried doughnuts, flavored ice, fried rice, and hot dogs with pretzels and mustard.

"Hey, Claude," Randy called across the street to a man in a booth over which flew a banner that declared, TATTOOS. Behind the little black-haired man was a white screen covered with the decals he could give you to pretend for a day or two that you had the courage to be marked. He had skulls, butterflies, naked women, and MOM surrounded by a big red heart. He had an American flag but no swastikas, because Claude was a Frenchman and he hated the Nazis.

"Hey, Randy," he answered. "You got a lot today."

"Got entertainment."

"Wet T-shirt?" the little man asked, completely serious.

"No, uh-uh, we got a blues guitar man." Randy gestured toward Soupspoon, who was getting himself set up on his stool. He had on a three-button black dress jacket with slim dark slacks and black-and-white patent-leather shoes over red silk socks. He wore a red shirt with fake onyx buttons and a short-brimmed, olive-colored Stetson hat that sported a yellow feather held in place by a red-enameled hat pin.

Everybody who walked by noticed Soupspoon with his bright red guitar and his old-time fancy clothes. People were asking about T-shirts before they got their doughnuts. Mrs. Rich, the Carmine Street fair administrator, asked Randy about Soupspoon, but she wasn't mad. Music is a great thing for a street fair. It makes people just wandering through want to stop; and when they stop they're more likely to spend.

At first Soupspoon wanted to get to know his guitar again. He strummed a few chords and then, almost like that day in Arcola, he began to play. No singing at first, he just fingered out the words while strumming the chords on behind. "Placated Woman" was the first thing he played, then "The Sophisticated Blues," a song he learned up in Chicago when he and Mavis first left the south.

He played "Hangman's Blues" and "Momma's New Shoes." He played those songs without singing a word. It wasn't until the second song that he stomped his tambourine foot. It wasn't until the third one that he blew his harmonica.

People came around the booth nodding their heads and tapping their toes. The sun was beating down hard, but Randy put up a big yellow parasol that colored the air around Soupspoon's eyes.

Hare showed up. He wore the same weathered clothes, and he had an umbrella too. It was broken on one side but he held the good half over a large buxom woman who wore tight denim overalls. She had a good deal of facial hair and very little practice smiling as far as Soupspoon could see. He did see why no man could take away her trestle house. SallySue was the size of a football player. And it wasn't soft fat that she was made of either.

Hare had a brown paper bag in his hand that had molded itself into the shape of the bottle it carried. He offered the bottle to his date but she declined.

"Hey, Mr. Wise!" Hare shouted.

"Hey, Hare. How you doin'?"

"It's Saturday. I told you I was comin' t'see ya!"

"You sure did."

Soupspoon was a black visage against white T-shirts. A spectacle and a witness all in one. He saw the little children with their snow cones and their mothers in halter tops and shorts. He saw the swaggering men who found the rhythm of their bluster in his songs. He saw the way people walked with music in their step even when they didn't stop to listen, and he saw the clouds pass by, ignorant and grand. When the music got good, and he closed his eyes to feel it right, he saw the backside of his life—the people who he'd walked with and left behind.

The women who raised him because he just showed up one day

and asked if they knew his mother. They didn't, but they made him wash up and eat grits at their table. They bathed him and saved him and shared their love for eight years.

He went out on the road at fourteen and never looked back for them again.

There was JoDaddy Parker, who taught him to play guitar in the whorehouses where white men came to meet Negro women. He learned to live on tips from JoDaddy, who was gray-haired and wide-eyed from the time he was a boy.

He remembered grim-faced Bannon and the apples and the burglaries; the days and days of talk padded with history, hatred, and love.

He remembered meeting Mavis in Pariah, Texas. She was shattered and sad and on the way to drinking herself to death. She was distraught and lonely over a boy she lost in a flash flood. Soupspoon tried to comfort her, and then one day he found that she had spent a night with Robert Johnson. He made love to her that very night with a passion that surprised them both and then wanted to marry her, to save her. He tried.

Everything was already set. He remembered decades between notes. He had everything right there in his heart. Every time he stomped his belled foot, pain traveled up his leg. When the pain got bad he began to sing.

> She's a big-hearted woman
> Lord there's room enough for me.
> Got a big-chested momma, yeah
> washin' clothes so I could eat.
> I got the mountains for my bedroom
> backyard's the African Sea.

Randy sold fewer T-shirts than usual but he put out a Tupperware plastic bowl and people were putting down their money for Soupspoon's pain.

Thousands of people passed by, hundreds stopped to listen to the blues. Almost every black man and woman stopped and cocked their ears. They heard something in Soupspoon's notes. Something that some people call Africa. Soupspoon would have told them that he didn't know a thing about modern Africa except that "them po' people sure got a hold on some blues. From starvin' to slavery they sure done paid the tax."

Rudy came by in black jeans and a cream silk T-shirt. Sono was with him, followed by a small girl that she had by the hand and by a teenager who carried a baby in her arms. Cholo and Billy Slick came behind them. The men looked out of place in the daylight. They kept looking around from behind black-lensed sunglasses. They walked in a cloud of smoke that came from their own cigarettes and cigars.

But Sono took off her shades when she first heard Soupspoon play. The teenager didn't even have sunglasses. She leaned up on Randy's table like she wanted to rub her face in Soupspoon's music.

Harry came by. He had a new boyfriend, another young blond. They stood back and listened, holding hands and whispering back and forth. He said hello to Soupspoon with a nod and a smile.

Kiki came around noon, already drinking, already drunk.

Soupspoon's music was for everybody and everything. He saw the plastic bucket fill up with quarters and dollar bills. He felt the pain and saw it too. He played his guitar until he knew he'd have to stop, but he kept on for one more song, and another. Every now and then he'd wink at the young girl who came with Sono—the girl with the baby on her hip. He liked it when the baby and the young girl smiled.

> *She's a homely woman*
> *plain as brown paper wrap.*
> *Never see her on the dance floor.*
> *Sunday mornin' she way in back.*
> *But I see my baby Tuesdays*
> *when her husband's up to Hyde Park.*
> *She got me screamin' "Lord Jesus"*
> *brown legs wrapped round my heart.*

When Soupspoon finally broke down and took a rest the people put their hands together for him. Rudy came up after the music was over. But the young girl, with a baby girl in hand, walked up first.

"You from Arkansas, uncle?"

"Mississippi, mighty damn close. What's your name?"

"Chevette," she said. "I know you must be from somewhere close, 'cause you play the music like the old men used to when I was a baby."

"Well, you know when I play I always kinda direct my music t'somebody out in the crowd. I musta known you was from down home because'a how you looked."

"You was playin' for me?"

"Prettiest thing out here."

Chevette didn't smile, didn't show pleasure at this compliment. The closest thing to an emotion on her face was hunger. The little yellow girl she had by the hand could feel it. She stared up at Chevette and then she smiled at Soupspoon.

"You gonna play some more?"

"Uh-huh."

Sono came up then with the baby on her hip. Soupspoon could tell that it was Sono who was the children's mother.

"Sono, this is, is . . . What's your name, uncle?" Chevette asked.

"I know who he is, Chevette. I'm the one brought us here. But you know it's gettin' too hot for George and Hamela. We got to get outta this sun," she said. "Hi, Mr. Wise. You played real nice. I knew you would."

"Yeah," Chevette said. "Real good."

"Could we go now?" Sono said. "I'm hungry." The baby was struggling in her arms and crying on and off.

"You gonna be here awhile?" Chevette asked.

"Prob'ly till they break down. I'm here with my friends."

"We come back when they eat."

Soupspoon was sure that the girls would be back. He'd been a musician long enough to tell. He nodded at them as Rudy and his entourage came up from behind.

"Hey, Soup," he said, putting an arm around each of the two young women. "You know you never played for me before."

"You didn't like my music when you used t'come visit, Rudy. You just liked ice cream and the Lone Ranger."

"Then call me a fool." Rudy was grinning. "What you think, Chevette? You think Atwater here should come play at my club?"

"Uh-huh," she said. Soupspoon could see much more than that in her eyes.

"What you think, Sono?" Rudy asked his waitress. "Do we need some blues down there?"

"I guess that be okay," sour-mouthed Sono said. "Least we have somethin' good for you old folks."

"You wanna pay'im?" Kiki's voice came from behind. Her gaunt face, that had never been pretty, was now sick with alcohol. Soupspoon had seen that bony-eyed look many times before. *On their way to the grave.* Her eyes drooped and her smile made him want to cry.

"That'd be great," she said, looking into Billy Slick's face. "You could help us make some money while I find a new job."

"Yeah," Billy Slick said under the pressure of her gaze.

"What's your name?" Kiki asked.

"Come on, Billy," Rudy said. "Put your eyes back in your head. We gotta go."

"What? What I did?" he asked, but his eyes were locked with Kiki's.

"You wanna help me stack shirts, Kiki?" Randy asked.

"Not right now." There was a big smile for Billy on her face.

"So, Soup, you still wanna play for me?" Rudy asked.

"Yeah. Damn right." He saw Chevette smiling at him and Kiki leaning toward Billy Slick. He could smell the Delta on the sweat of his friends.

"You get Randy here's number. He gonna be my business agent. Right, Randy?"

"Sure thing, Mr. Wise."

"All right." Rudy was looking at the boy, at his hair actually.

"Give Billy here how he could get in touch wit' you and he'll tell you what we could do tomorrow."

Randy scribbled his phone number on a brown paper bag. He handed the bag to Billy but the big man hardly noticed. He was talking to Kiki while she studied his face.

"Come on, Billy," Rudy said again.

Rudy left with Billy and Cholo. Sono and Chevette hung around with the kids nearby. But before Soup could talk to them he turned to Kiki again.

"What's the matter wit' you, girl? Why you drinkin' like that?" Soupspoon was really worried.

"It's okay, honey. I can take it. I can take it."

Her arms felt cool around Soupspoon's neck as she whispered, "That was beautiful, honey. I knew you were something. I knew it."

They walked together, Kiki draped over him, to Randy. He was sulking and counting the money from Soupspoon's bucket.

"Forty-two dollars not counting the twenty-dollar bill somebody put in. Sixty-two in all."

"Man, if I made money like that back in the old days in the Delta I might coulda retired."

"It's all yours, Mr. Wise."

"Uh-uh, Randy. We partners, so we split it."

"But I got the shirts."

"Don't matter. Don't matter at all. You got me here and I'ma pay ya for it."

Kiki slid from Soupspoon to the ground next to Randy's feet. She put her head on his lap and he moved his dusky fingers in her hair.

The afternoon set was more popular than the morning. Sono and Chevette came back. The little girl liked dancing with Chevette. The baby boy was asleep most of the time in Sono's arms.

Music came back to Soupspoon from a time so long ago that it didn't even seem real anymore. He felt like he was making up the music. There wasn't a thing he had to worry about. He didn't even mind the pain.

Don't have no baby
no one t'call me dear.
I don't have no baby
don't have no one to care.

I got pocket fulla money
shoes been a thousand miles.
But I ain't found me no baby
walkin' till the sun go down.

They made eighty-three dollars in the afternoon. Randy gave Soup-spoon ninety-seven dollars in bills and kept the change for his "bank." Kiki sobered a little but was hungover. She went with Randy to take his shirts to the station wagon while Soupspoon looked after the door and cinder blocks.

Sono and Chevette came up with the children and a big bulky-looking young man. They came over to Soupspoon while he was packing away his guitar. The little girl Hamela was crying and Sono tried to calm her down. Soupspoon liked Sono more then, because she wasn't yelling at the child. But he really liked Chevette. There was something about a woman-child with a baby in her arms that made him feel good.

"What's the matter with your leg, uncle?" Chevette asked.

"Musta been sittin' funny. You know you had me workin' hard out there."

Chevette showed him her teeth. "You was workin' fo'you. I ain't done nuthin'."

Soupspoon held out his hand to the big young man and said, "Atwater Wise, but my friends call me Soupspoon."

"Gerald Pickford, but call me Gerry." The young man's voice was high and crackly but Soupspoon had heard worse in men. It's better to be a big man, he always said, if you got a girl's voice.

And Gerry was big. He was barrel-chested and long-armed. His face was all pushed together and sharp like a wedge. He wasn't a pretty man by any means.

"I'm hungry," Chevette said. "Why'ont we go get sumpin' t'eat."

"I cain't go with you guys," Sono said. "I got the kids here."

"We could take them to Swenson's," Gerry offered. "They could have some ice cream."

"Ice cream," Hamela said.

"I got money from my guitar right chere in my pocket. The sundaes is on me." Soupspoon looked straight into Chevette's eyes.

Randy drove up and looked around for any extra shirts he might have left. Then he flipped down the back door of the station wagon and started to load in cinder blocks. Without a word Gerry lent a hand.

"Where's Kiki?" Soupspoon asked.

"She's asleep in the backseat."

"You need help, Randy?" Soupspoon picked up his guitar case.

"No, sir. We got this. Jump in."

"Naw, uh-uh, don't worry 'bout me. We goin' out. Tell Kiki that I'll be back later on."

Randy looked at the girls and gave a quick smirk. "You got it, Mr. Wise. You want me to take your guitar?"

"No, no. I got it."

TWENTY-ONE

ig lumbering Gerry and Soupspoon went with Chevelle,
Sono, Hamela, and baby
George to the ice cream parlor on Mercer. The adults had hamburgers. Hamela had chocolate ice cream with strawberry syrup
and George had his mother's milk. When everybody was through,
George started whimpering and Gerry picked him up in his big
hands. After a while George stopped crying and even smiled for his
big playmate. Soon the baby was sleeping in the crook of Gerry's
arm. His tiny lips pushed in and out and his little chest pumped like
a bird's.

"That music was really good, Mr., um, Mr. Wise," Gerry said.
He was whispering.

Soupspoon smiled at the gentleness of this awkward, high-
voiced man.

"Call me Soup. And thank ye for the compliment."

"I mean it. It was real good." Without looking he stroked
George's forehead with his finger. Sono smiled in spite of her taci-
turn nature.

"You two married?" Soupspoon asked.

The question brought a sad frown to Gerry's face. He looked
over at Sono with dread.

"I'm only ever gonna get married once in this life," Sono said
with the solemn voice of a preacher. She reached out to touch

Gerry's arm, and in doing so, George's little hand. "I mean I love Gerry but I was married to Tony and when he died I promised God that I'd never marry another man."

"What he die of?"

The three young people, even child Hamela, went quiet. Soupspoon understood that something was wrong about the death. Sono and Gerry glanced away, but Chevette didn't avoid his eyes.

"They thought he was a drug dealer, uncle," she said.

"Who did?"

Chevette hunched her shoulders. "Nobody knows. But the cops said that Tony was wearin' the same kinda purple runnin' suit that somebody who stole from some uptown dope dealers was wearin'. They said that the guys prob'ly shot'im without makin' sure who it was."

Hamela put her hand up on her mother's elbow; her big brown eyes, in the fluorescent light, were like moons.

"That was five years ago," Sono said. "But if it was ninety-five Tony'd still be my only huzbun. Ain't no other man gonna take his place."

"Oh come on, Sono. You know you love Gerry," Chevette said.

"I ain't never said I cain't have no boyfriend," Sono told Soupspoon as if he were a judge reviewing her case. "Pinklon come an' told me that he loved me. He come up here an' spend my money an' get me pregnant. And then when they cut me open for George he off wit' his bitches an' leave Hamela in the 'partment fot three days by herself. If it wasn't for Chevette, Hamela woulda died."

"Hamela was scared of the dark," Chevette said. "And her momma told her that she couldn't play with matches, so she couldn't light the candles."

"Yeah," Hamela agreed.

"Why didn't she just turn on the lights?" Soupspoon asked.

"They done turnt off the phone, gas, and electric while I was pregnant. Said I owed them twelve hundred dollars includin' deposits, an' that I cain't get it turned on till I pay'em. So I said fuck'em," Sono said. "Only reason we got heat is that it's steam an' everybody gets it. Everybody should get they lights too."

"So Chevy turned on the candles," Hamela said. "And she stayed with me in my bed."

"How come you didn't take her up to your house?" Soupspoon asked.

" 'Cause my a'nt is a bitch, that's why. If you don't give her no money she ain't gonna spit."

"Where she live?"

"Upstairs. My momma send me up here from Shreveport 'cause she got nerves. She kept Buster but I come up here, an' momma send part of her welfare to A'nt Vella. Only A'nt Vella don't care nuthin' 'bout nobody 'cept for how much money they got.

"When Hamela needed me I come on down to Sono's an' stayed."

Soupspoon was listening but he was also watching. Watching Sono watch Gerry. Whenever baby George would begin to frown and move around, Gerry rubbed his forehead with his finger. Then George's face smoothed out and Sono glowed.

Sono was all smiles for Gerry.

"Why don't we take the babies home to bed and get some wine?" she asked.

Soupspoon got two bottles of good red wine in one of the liquor stores on Broadway and then treated for the taxi down to the girls' building, not far from Rudy's nameless club.

Getting a cab wasn't easy for a gang of black folks and their babies. Every time they'd hold up their hands for a cab the driver sped up or turned on his OFF DUTY lights. Finally Sono stood out alone. She was the lightest-skinned one of them. The first cab she hailed stopped. The Pakistani driver was upset at first. But he liked Hamela, who sat on Soupspoon's lap in the front seat. He drove them the crooked road to their big apartment building and Soupspoon gave him a two-dollar tip.

"Black people could treat you right too," he said while handing the man the money.

"Thank you, sir!" The cabbie nodded and grinned.

Soupspoon wondered if the young foreigner understood.

Sono's apartment was large enough for the family and Chevette. Hamela had her own room and George had a crib next to Sono's bed. Chevette stayed on the couch in the family living room. Everything was nice except that there was no electricity and no phone. The youngsters went around lighting candles when they got home. There were candles all over the house; in the living room, kitchen, and toilet.

The first thing they did was to put George in his crib. Hamela was crying and didn't want to be left alone. So they all went in with her to put her to bed.

Soupspoon sat in the corner and played soft chords while Gerry told the story of the Lion Who Thought He Was a Man. It was a long rambling tale that was funny in places; all about a lonely lion who wanted friends so he pretended that he was something else. Sono and Chevette, only girls themselves really, sat beside the bed listening intently. Hamela was a little queen with her big teeth and drowsy eyes. She was asleep for five minutes before the adults could tear themselves away.

By the end of the first bottle of wine, Gerry had told of his whole dream to write a history of black people. He was a student at Hunter College and still lived with his mother in a big house in Queens. He was going to get his Ph.D. in history because "black people's history isn't all that dry stuff that white people have. Black people's history is stories and words and music. Black people have built the culture of America with their play, and nobody knows it really because it's not written down in books. You see, books make things seem real, and even if you've got something else just as real, if it's not in a book then nobody cares. . . ." He went on like that for a while. Sono beamed at him while he talked, moving his big hands in the air and looking into her Asian eyes.

They were sitting in Sono's small kitchen; Sono and Gerry across from Soupspoon and Chevette. When Soupspoon pulled the cork out of the second bottle, Sono said, "I bet you never heard the music they play 'round here."

"What music?" Soupspoon wanted to know.

"Down Charlton. Chili Morton and them."

"Who's that?"

"It's a band like, play at this restaurant on Charlton."

"What kind of music is it?"

"I don't know all that stuff. It's just that they play good and maybe you'd like it." Sono turned to Chevette. "Why don't we go down there?"

"Why'ont you an' Gerry go on," Chevette said. "Me an' uncle stay here with the kids."

Sono raised her eyebrows and caught Gerry by one of his big fingers. "Com'on," she said. "Let's get outside."

Sono's couch was just large enough to serve as Chevette's bed. "I don't mind sleepin' in it," she told Soupspoon. "I ain't all that big, and at least I don't got no big nigger runnin' 'round tryin' t'look in my drawers."

"What you mean?" Soupspoon felt comfortable in the young woman's company. Candles flickered around the room and the muted sound of salsa music came in through the walls.

Chevette was beautiful and knew it; but she didn't care about it. She was open and friendly and sure enough in herself that she didn't mind if somebody might not like her. Soupspoon saw home in that girl; life so hard that it made you good.

"When I used to live upstairs my a'ntee had this goofy old man named Willy up there. He always comin' in on me when I'as on the toilet or in the bathtub. I had t'stop takin' baths a'cause'a him. I had to come down here even if I had to pee."

"So that's why you come down here to live?"

"Uh-huh. Sono's nice. She mad all the time but that's 'cause she got these babies and a lotta bills from when she lived wit' Pinklon and then when she was in the hospital. She work now, but a good girl cain't make no money at Rudy's."

"You're a good girl," Soupspoon declared.

Chevette smiled. She moved three inches closer, put her hands together as in prayer, and clamped them tightly between her knees.

"I like you, uncle," she said.

"Yeah?"

"Yeah," she said. She reached out and ran her small finger around his thumb. Then she brought her hand back between her knees.

"Shoo'," Soupspoon snorted. "I'm old enough t'be yo' daddy or, what was that you said, huh, yeah, uncle."

"You ain't old." Chevette brought her shoulders forward and looked slantwise at Soupspoon. "Old is in your head. Old is when you cain't laugh no more."

"Who told you that?"

"Nobody need t'tell me what I could see, uncle." She touched his thumb again. His hand jumped, and she smiled. "When Hamela an' me be playin' it's not like I'm old and she's a baby. We like each other an' we like to laugh. There's all these young men walkin' around cussin' an' talkin' mean. They say all kindsa nasty things when you be walkin' down the street. An' even if they talkin' nice it's just 'cause they want sumpin'."

Chevette put her hand next to his, comparing their sizes.

"They don't never laugh an' sing, buy a girl her dinner and her taxi ride just 'cause it's nice. They don't just be nice to be nice."

"Somebody should be nice to you." Soupspoon's heart took shape in his mind. The blood was singing ahead of the beat.

"You see?" she said. "Between you an' me an' Hamela we all the same age."

"You could have anything you want, girl." Soupspoon didn't think about putting his hand on Chevette's thigh. It was just that he was sitting there next to her and she was turned toward him with her leg up on the couch. "It ain't like the old days when a black man or a black woman had to look at the ground when a white walked by," he said. "If you got dreams today you could have'em. Ain't nobody could stop you from that."

"I want it too, uncle. You know I want me some money and nice clothes. And I wanna good man who looks good too. You know, like a real black man. Like coal but fine too. An' you know I love Hamela and little George but I don't want no babies, not right now I don't. You see, I wanna get some money on my own with a good job and then I want a man who could work too. And mosta the time we be up here workin' in the days an' goin' out to some clubs on the weekend. An' then we have us a house down in New Orleans, up near the lake. They got some nice houses up on the river up there. And we could go down there 'round Christmastime up until Mardi Gras. And then my momma an' them could stay there the rest'a the time so we don't have ta waste the rent when we up here . . ."

"But what would you do?"

"Huh?"

"What kinda job would you get?"

Chevette sucked her tooth and licked the last bit of orange lipstick from her lips. "Oh," she sang and leaned forward to hold Soupspoon's hand to her leg. "I don't know. I could be a nurse, because I really like to help people. Or I could be a computer operator. You know Sono got a girlfriend works for the city in computers. She's only trainin' but they pay good for that and they pay for your doctors too. But really I'd like to make clothes. Or maybe I could go to FIT and work my way through bein' a model and then when I get too old for that I could design things. You know, kinda like get the experience first and then go out on my own. They got a lotta pretty black models now, just like you said. You don't have to be white no more."

"You sure pretty enough to do it," Soupspoon said. He moved his finger along with hers. The pain in his hip, just under being sharp, moved somewhere in his chest. It was cancer or sex, he didn't care which. He felt the beginnings of an erection with surprise.

"I better be gettin' outta here. I mean gettin' home," he said.

Chevette didn't let go of the fingers on her leg. "What do you dream about, uncle?"

Soupspoon tried to remember the last time he actually heard his heart beating.

"I don't know. I'm too old to be dreamin' 'bout what's gonna happen. When I dream it's about what was."

Chevette moved a little closer. She picked up his hand and held it in his lap.

"Um," he said.

"What do you dream about the past?"

"I don't know really. It's like everything I did seems to be happenin' all the time. Like things that was over start up again."

"Like what do you mean? Like old friends?"

"I knowed a man name of Robert Johnson," he said, and he felt that he'd said that same thing over and over, day and night, for his whole life. He said it to the crowds of people in smoky clubs all around the blues circuit in Chicago, Cleveland, Pittsburgh, Miami, Los Angeles, Seattle, and a hundred other places that all looked the same. He said it in the morning when he watched himself in the mirror; and on the toilet when he grunted and strained and needed something in his mind to hold on to. He said it to himself when walking down some familiar street in a strange town. He'd said it to Mavis Spivey when she was talking about the loss of her only son.

"What, uncle?" Chevette said. Her face was closer to his now. The back of her hand rested on his half-hard thing. He put his hand to the back of her neck.

"I wanna cry," he said.

"How come?"

"You got a nice face, Chevette. Big ole eyes and kissy lips. . . ."

Chevette leaned forward to kiss him lightly. He felt the pressure of her hand and sat there for the longest single moment he ever felt in his long life. He didn't even want to breathe because breathing distracted him from this beautiful girl.

"Tell 'bout your friend," she whispered.

"Just a lazy nigger is all. Lazy nigger could play music that was brand new."

"Did you like him?"

"I loved him, Chevette. And when he died it broke my heart to know that he was gone. 'Cause you know livin' weren't the thing when I was young man comin' up. Livin' was bein' a slave. An' all you could really do was lose yo'self in whiskey, women, and the blues. An' when you got tired'a that it was time to die. An' the onliest man I ever met who could face that truth and still be a man was Robert Johnson."

"He was brave, your friend?"

"It wasn't that so much but he never let himself know that he was scared. He had somethin' t'hold on to."

"What was that?" She turned her hand around to hold on to him. When his eyes got big she grinned.

"I don't know."

"How long ago did he die?"

"Fifty years this year."

"Fifty? Damn, that's how old my grandmother is."

Their hands began moving together. A girl of eighteen and a man who could have sired her grandmother. They kissed and she wasn't sad. He moved his soft leathery hands on her young skin and she trembled for him.

"You a virgin, girl?"

Chevette shook her head to say that she was not. She didn't like to stick her tongue in his mouth but she took his thing out of his pants and stroked it.

"Go over and get that bottle'a wine," he said.

She did as she was told but first she took off the torn shirt top and cutoff jeans. Then she poured out a glass of wine and blew out all of the candles except for one. She brought the wine and the candle back to him.

She dipped her right hand into the glass and then let the liquor dribble from her fingers into Soupspoon's open mouth. With her left hand she guided his only half-solid cock up and down until she finally got it in.

Between the tastes of wine from her hand Soupspoon told the girl how pretty she was and how wonderful she was. He told her that she was young and beautiful and generous and he meant every word that he said.

He felt the pain when she got excited and rode him hard. But she seemed to get more pleasure from his hands moving over her body as she moved slowly like waves over his chest.

Much later on the door came open. Chevette was still riding the old man. His cock was now limp and lolling between his legs. But his hands still moved slowly on her and his whispers still thrilled her.

Sono and Gerry watched for a while and then they moved into her room, closing the door behind them.

TWENTY-TWO

ll Kiki saw was a crazy-quilt pattern of bright lights and hard things. Asphalt, concrete, dried vomit in the street, hydrants, lampposts, and droves of wild honking cars. Randy supported her on the way up the stairs. She knew she shouldn't have been yelling, that he wouldn't have dropped her. But she couldn't help it. It didn't matter, because nobody came to her aid; nobody called the police.

"What the fuck is wrong with you, Randy?" she shouted when he sat her down on the bed. She tried to get up to go at him but her right leg slid out to the side and she went to the ground. "Get the fuck away!"

Randy backed away toward the door. Kiki's rage was so strong that there was foam at the corners of her mouth. Her yelling and screaming sounded more like a dog barking than a human being. Randy was all the more scared because of her lack of control over her legs. She'd try to get up and then fall back to the floor, all the time yelling and coughing and spitting foam.

She watched him back out of the door and shut it against her pleas. He didn't want to get near her. The fool! Didn't he understand how bad she felt? How hard things were? Didn't he know that she needed, needed . . . needed him to push her arms down and hold her so down.

Fez picked up the turquoise receiver on the first ring. "Yeah."

"Fez?"

"You got it?"

"Hey, man. I don't want you tellin' anybody where you got this," Roger said.

"I need that address, Roger."

"Don't you have the call sheet?"

"They don't have her address on the call sheet."

There was a long pause on the line. Fez held the receiver close to his mouth so Roger could hear the angry breath.

Roger gave him the address of the Beldin Arms. He said, "Don't tell anybody that I . . ." and Fez hung up the phone.

Fez snorted once and turned off the lamp by smashing it with the back of his hand.

Soupspoon woke up to an exquisite pang that moved in a circle around his hip. He raised his head with a sudden jerk, eyes wide, mouth open to answer a call. Chevette slept snuggled in the crack where the cushions met the back of their makeshift bed. He got to his feet in agony, the smell of burnt wax and fresh baby in the air. Light from a faraway sun found its way to windows buried down the ventilation shaft, barely illuminated the empty wine bottles on the table. The hazy gray floor spread before him like a vast morning swamp to an old brown god.

His throat was dry. So dry that it felt as if no amount of water could quench it. Like he had died and awakened, a corpse on judgment day. Fear prickled his forehead and shoulders. He hobbled to the sink, where he guzzled water, like when he was a boy and again like the last time he was dying.

He blundered by Hamela's bed to the bathroom that connected the child's room to her mother's. While he stood there staring down into the toilet he heard a high-pitched but masculine "Unghh!" from Sono's bedroom. A little later a baby cried. Sono laughed and then said something that he couldn't make out.

When Soupspoon got back to the kitchen he took his guitar

from its case and sat down at the table to practice chords along the frets.

"Uncle?"

"Yeah?"

Chevette had a blanket wrapped around her. She kissed Soup-spoon on the cheek before sitting down in the chair next to him.

"Cain't sleep?" she asked.

"I get up early."

Chevette crossed her long thin legs so they stuck out between the fold in the blanket.

Soupspoon lit a candle and watched it flicker until it became sure. Chevette watched the little fire too. Soon they were looking at each other over the flame.

"You hate me, uncle?"

"Hate you? Why I'ma hate you?"

"I'ont know," she said. "It just might be that you think that it was wrong for me to be wit' you last night. You might think that I was like a whore or sumpin'."

"Is that what *you* think?" Soupspoon asked.

"No."

"So why would I?"

"I got to go to the bathroom," she answered.

She got up and walked away quickly, making the sound of marsh breezes with the blanket trailing along the floor.

When she came back she was wearing a plaid skirt and a green sweater. Her face was set hard but he could see the same friendly girl inside the scowl.

"I just liked you because you was nice an' you had on nice clothes," she said. " 'Cause you was playin' good music but you was still friendly wit' my friends. It's just that you was nice an' I was drinkin'. You know I don't usually drink—an' I never take drugs."

"But you sorry 'bout you'n me last night?" he asked.

"It's just that I don't hardly know you, uncle. I mean there you are . . ." She stopped herself from calling him old. "An' here I am. I don't want you to think bad about me."

Soupspoon waited a long minute in the candlelight. Then he said, "Can we start over?"

"What you mean?"

"I mean that we just forget about yesterday. Yesterday never happened."

"You mean like you don't even know me?"

"Almost. I mean that you know me but that you don't owe me nuthin'. Maybe you might like me if I'm nice but nuthin' says that you got to care."

"An' you gonna be nice?"

"I'd like to buy you lunch this afternoon at Ayer's American Café. You know, over near St. Mark's Place."

"I know where it is."

T W E N T Y - T H R E E

Late in the morning Kiki found herself lying on the floor. A blade of sunlight speared her brain through the left eye. Her right hand and arm were swollen, numb things that had lost circulation under her head. She remembered throwing up twice; the smell was all around her but she couldn't get up.

She was stuck to the floor, plastered down as if by a bucket of thick glue. The sun jabbed into her. Her stomach was dry leather. Her bowels grumbled and threatened. But motion was what she most feared: getting up, getting up and walking across the room.

A shudder went through her and then a dry heave. Her eyes closed but the left eyelid was bright red and throbbing from the sun. Even when she was asleep the hurt was wide awake.

When she opened her eyes again, Soupspoon was coming through the door. He had on the same clothes as at the street fair. His tie was loose but everything else was the same.

"Kiki! What happened to you?"

"Hi, daddy," a very young girl answered. "Where you been?"

It took a long time to get Kiki off the floor and out of her clothes. While she ran a hot tub he mopped up. After that he made old-fashioned grits swimming with butter and topped with fried onions.

He brought a bowl to her bath.

"Not right now, Soup. But could you get me a beer out the re-frigerator?"

"You don't need that, honey."

"Please get it. It'll settle my stomach."

"Kiki, it's booze done turned your stomach upside down."

"I want a beer."

"But, honey . . ."

"Will you please get me a beer right now, Atwater?" Kiki ordered.

When the beer was finished she was in a better mood.

"Where were you last night?" she asked in a friendly tone.

"I went out wit' some friends."

"You get some pussy out there?" She sounded sober but Soupspoon could tell by her language that she was leaning toward drunk.

"Kiki, we gotta talk."

"About what?"

"Bout this thing wit' yo' job an' the money we stole."

"Don't worry about that, Soupspoon. They can't prove I did it."

"But they could find me. I mean, I signed them forms. All they gotta do is ask around and they could find where I am."

"But not for a while, honey. Insurance companies have to do an investigation first. They have to prove that it was a forgery or fraud or whatever first and then they have to prove who did it. We still have time."

"But time for what? What could we do?"

"Go somewhere."

"Where?"

"I don't know . . . down south."

"What?"

"I been thinkin' about goin' back down home anyway, daddy. You know, to Arkansas."

"How a black man and white woman gonna hide down there? Are you crazy?"

"Crazy enough to help you, Mr. Wise," she said.

And Soupspoon knew it was true. As true as the music playing even then in his mind.

He wasn't worried about the law. He was way past the law now. It was time again to move on, but he couldn't do that until he made sure that Kiki was safe. But that was like trying to carry a frightened cat from a burning house. All she knew how to do was hack and scratch. It came naturally, like breathing and death.

In the early afternoon Kiki was only on her third beer. Soupspoon was playing chords out of the broken window. A knock came at the door and she went to answer it. Randy and a black man with a battered face and dressed in a pink suit stood at the door.

"Hi?" she said with the question in her eye for the stranger.

"I'm Billy. Remember? We met yesterday—at the street fair."

"Yeah." Kiki smiled. "It was about some kind of job, right?"

Billy smiled back. Kiki's hand moved to her purse before she realized that she wasn't carrying it.

"Hey, Kiki," Randy interrupted. "Spoon here?"

"Huh? What? Randy, did you bring me home last night?"

"Uh-huh. Don't you remember?"

"Why'd you leave me on the floor?" The question was sweet, like the smell of bug spray.

"You told me to go home. Don't you remember?"

Kiki remembered wanting something, needing something—her desires slipping away. She felt as if she were falling sideways. All she could see was objects and people against a pitch-black background. The gun she got from Hattie; Soupspoon; the pitiful brown flowers her father bought leftover to put on Katherine's grave; and this black brute who smiled and smelled like the devil. Everything she saw was in bold detail against the night, as if they generated their own light. And there was that smell, a smell like her father that still turned her stomach even after all these years.

"Billy got an offer for Soup," Randy said when Kiki didn't answer.

"How much?" Soupspoon asked.

Randy led Billy into the room around Kiki. She watched them go over to the window.

"Rudy says one hundred dollars plus tips," Billy said. He kept turning his head to regard Kiki as she came over to them.

"A hundred dollars a night?" Kiki put her hand on Billy's shoulder to punctuate the question.

"Well, at least tomorrow night," Billy said.

Kiki squeezed his arm.

"Uh," Billy continued. "We have to see how he do after that."

Kiki's heart skipped. She couldn't inhale. In her mind she traveled back to the woods where Hector was holding her down, keeping her from even a wrong breath. She smiled and could see that same smile come into Billy's face.

"Tomorrow night?" Kiki asked.

"Yeah."

Kiki forgot about Randy and Soupspoon. Every particle of her mind was on Hector or Billy or whatever he was called. Her hand clutched his arm, the fingernails would have drawn blood if not for his jacket.

"That's good," she said.

"What time?" Soupspoon asked.

Kiki was surprised to hear his voice. She turned toward the window; he was still there, still holding his guitar.

"Eight o'clock, Spoon." Billy pulled away from Kiki's grasp but then he touched her chin with his knuckle. "Later if you want it. But not after nine."

"I'll be there," Soupspoon said.

"Me too." Kiki was looking at Billy's profile. She started to laugh.

"What's funny?" Randy wanted to know.

"Nuthin'." Kiki shrugged. "You all boys want some whiskey?"

They drank a celebratory toast to their new business. Then they drank to Soupspoon. Kiki took a drink all on her own. Billy toasted her full glass with his empty one.

"I got to go out," Soupspoon said to Kiki after he'd downed the drink.

"Out where?"

"Just t'see some friends. Might be pretty late. But I want you t'take care'a yourself. Okay?"

The redhead poured herself another drink and toasted Billy's empty glass.

"Okay, hon," she said to Soupspoon while gazing into Billy's eyes. "I'll be here all night. I need the rest."

"We could have dinner, babe," Randy said. He went up close to her, touched her arm lightly.

"No, Randy. I got to rest. You know I had too much to drink last night. Mm. I'm gonna be all right. Buck naked in the bed."

"I could come over . . ."

"Tomorrow, baby. We'll go over to this man's club and hear Soup."

The men left after a while. Each of them went his own separate way. Randy went to his tiny room of old magazines and T-shirts. Billy went to the bar. And Soupspoon went to a little café near St. Mark's to meet Chevette.

"Bye," Kiki said to Billy at the door. She pinched his forearm hard and showed him her teeth in what might have been a grin.

She was napping in her chair, with a half-full glass of sour mash in her hand, when her eyes snapped open. She didn't know what happened so she took a sip. The tapping, which she remembered now, came again at the front door.

"Yeah?" Kiki called out.

The tapping came again. Suddenly Kiki was completely sober and straight. She stepped out of her shoes and went lightly toward her purse. She removed the revolver, threw the safety, and went to the door.

"Who is it?" she asked in a hoarse alcoholic voice.

Tapping again.

It was a light sound, quick and feminine. But it still could have been Fez. He could have gotten her address from the company database before they suspended him.

"Who is it?" she asked again. She leveled the barrel at the height of a big man's chest and held her breath.

The hammer made very little noise as she cocked it into place. One, two, thr—

"Does a Mr. Atwater Wise live here?" A woman's voice. A black woman. A southern black woman.

Kiki ran to put the pistol on the top shelf in the closet. "Just a minute!" she shouted. Then she ran back to the door and opened it, fixing her hair and shaking from the desire to kill somebody.

Mavis wore a plain blue dress with dark seams and a white collar. The dress was in an old style, maybe as far back as the sixties, and a little too short, Kiki thought, for an older woman. She was hatless. Her hair was straightened and tied back into two interwoven braids. She held a blue pocketbook before her like a Roman shield.

"Does Atwater Wise live here?" she asked again.

"Who's askin'?" Kiki said back. She didn't feel angry but she said it just the same.

"I was told that he lived here by Rudy Peckell. He called me just a little while ago and happened to mention it. You see, I'm Atwater's wife, Mavis Spivey. At least . . ." Mavis seemed confused for a moment. "At least I was his wife a long time ago. I got a divorce but he was the only one that I ever actually married."

"Come in," Kiki said. She led Mavis to the table that served as the dinette inside the studio.

Mavis looked around at the bad plaster near the ceiling, at the men's socks and pants on the floor.

Kiki felt embarrassed under the scrutiny. "You want something to drink?"

"No thank you." Mavis sat in the chair holding the pocketbook tight against her knees.

Kiki poured a little extra whiskey in her glass. "Soupspoon's been staying here with me for a few months now."

"Is he your man?"

"No, I think he's scared'a girls. Did you want to see Atwater?" Kiki asked after taking a sip.

"No. I already seen 'im. Now I wanted to see where he was livin'. And, and if he needed anything."

"He doesn't need anything here," Kiki said. "We got food and we're gonna get a sofa bed so he could sleep better." She kicked the pants so that they slid under the couch. "I told him that I'd take the couch and that he could have the bed, but you know Soup—he's a real gentleman."

"An' you know how t'take care of a sick man with cancer?"

"He *was* sick, ma'am. He *had* cancer. But we took him to the doctor in time and that's all cleared up now. He's all better now."

"Hm! Well. I'm glad to hear that. I guess these doctors nowadays can do things that we couldn't even think of when I was comin' up."

"Soupspoon, I mean Atwater, just went out," Kiki said. "I don't know when he's gonna be comin' back."

"That's okay," Mavis said. "I don't need to see him. You could tell'im that I was here."

"You want to leave a number or something?"

"He know how to get me . . . if he want." Mavis leaned forward in her chair as if she were about to stand up. "I'll be goin' now. But lemme tell you somethin' before I do that."

"Yes?" Kiki found that she had to hold her head sideways in order to see straight.

"You in the wrong business here."

"What?"

"Livin' wit' a bluesman is bad business no matter who you are or who he is. It don't even matter that he's old an' maybe gonna die soon. An' ain't no young white girl gonna bear up under that," Mavis said. "I'm just sayin' it. I don't expect you to hear it."

"I don't know what you mean, Miss Spivey. Soupspoon hardly even plays now. And he's just a man anyway. It doesn't matter what he does with his time."

"You could think that if you wanna, honey. But a man like that only know how to be sorry. They broke him down and killed him fifty years ago but it just ain't caught up wit' him yet."

"Atwater's a good man. He's better than mosta the trash you find in these streets." Kiki was trying to be strong against Mavis's will.

"Yeah, he's good, like an angel is good," Mavis agreed. "But we ain't made t'mess wit' angels, girl. Angels draw up to all the evil and all the hurt in the world. They watch babies dyin', that's what they do. They take all the pain and shout it out. Angels livin' with evil and with death. That's their stock in trade. Murderers and thieves and times so hard that you could cry blood. That's where you find angels. I'd no sooner spend a evenin' with an angel than I'd whore out here in these streets. I'd kill myself before I'd break bread with a angel."

Kiki was under the spell of the older woman's words. She felt as if Mavis had something special just for her. And that something was beautiful and hard like diamonds. The only thing in Kiki's mind was to keep Mavis there in front of her, to keep her talking.

"Why don't you stay with me and have a drink, ma'am? Nobody's coming back for a while yet."

Mavis got comfortable but she didn't drink. Kiki asked her about where she was raised and where she first met Soupspoon. Soon came the story of how Mavis had left her common-law husband Rafael and gone out to Texas where she and her son Cortland lived in a house near a levee. She grew red roses all around the house and sold them to white people in Houston on Friday and Saturday nights. Blood-red roses that were sleek and handsome with tight petals and a rich dark scent. She'd sell half a dozen for a dollar and could make up to twenty dollars in a week. Cort was five and spent all of his days like a river rat; out of the trees and into the water. He had friends everywhere and he loved everybody as much as they loved him.

". . . he cried when the sun went down and he laughed at the moon," she claimed. But then one day he was in the storm ditch dug out at the side of the road and there was a cloudburst coming. Mavis saw it moving like a slate wall toward their house. She called out to

Cort and then ran. She got there before the rains but the water was already crashing down the deep ditch. Cort was gone. She was going to jump in after her missing son but a neighbor grabbed her and then the deluge hit.

"He's gone out to sea," Mavis said as if it had happened yesterday and they might still reclaim his body on the shore.

Kiki went through all of her cigarettes and started on Mavis's during their talk. She had two full glasses of whiskey and a hard time to keep from crying.

"That's why I had to leave Atwater," Mavis said simply. "That's why he had to go."

"Why?" Kiki could hear an echo in the room, an echo she'd never heard before.

"Atwater married me, but it wasn't 'cause'a me. Even when he was lovin' me it was really Robert Johnson he was lovin'."

"That man he keeps talkin' about?"

"Yeah. I met him once and kissed him twice but when Atwater hears that I met Bob Johnson he all over me like white on rice. He'd do anything to feel what Robert Johnson felt."

"Why'd you marry him then? If you knew that he was bad for you why didn't you just leave?"

"I didn't care, not at first. He wanna marry me that was okay. Maybe somethin' good wanna come from that. It was like I didn't have no mind'a my own."

"You just did it? You didn't even care?"

"That's how most people live, honey. It's just your white people got a li'l money think they could plan out a life. Ain't no plan gonna save them. What do they know? It don't matter what they say or how beautiful they is. And even if you really love someone, when things get hard everything goes. Everything."

Kiki sipped her drink. She noticed that there was a small shiver running through the older woman. She wanted to say something, to ask why Mavis was so bitter, but she felt too weak.

"That's why Atwater here wit' you," Mavis said. "He drawn to all that liquor you suckin'."

"I brought him here. He didn't come to me."

Mavis nodded wisely.

Kiki wanted to rip her eyes out. "I did!" she yelled.

"Go back home, girl," Mavis said.

"Is that why you left?' Because he was a bluesman?"

The sneer on Mavis's face showed like a bad taste in her mouth.

"I wasn't that smart," she said. "But I knew that somethin' was wrong. Atwater was out playin' his guitar all over the place. He was in them foul-smellin' bars an' then come home with that stink in his clothes an' hair an' skin. He come home smellin' like whores an' gunfights and blood.

"That was the first time Cort come to me."

"Who?" Kiki asked, thinking that she had somehow missed part of the story.

"My boy."

"But . . . he died, right?"

"Yeah. He did. At least he prob'ly did. But I wasn't talkin' to him really. It's just that I was sittin' 'round the house so much all alone, except when li'l Rudy come over, and I was always, always thinkin' about Cort. I started talkin' to'im an' thinkin' 'bout what he would say back." Mavis looked up at Kiki and smiled a child's smile. "You know he loved me an' forgived me for lettin' him drown.

"I was happy then to be alone and talkin' to him. He came mostly when I was cleanin'. An' if the house was all clean an' bright, an' if everything was calm an' quiet, then I could sit for hours an' talk to him."

Mavis smiled in her memories but then she got serious. "I ain't crazy, you know," she went on. "Atwater went outta town to play. He be out in the road for weeks at a time an' then he'd just be back for a coupla days. I liked it—for a while. It'd take me a whole mont' just to get ready t'be in the same house wit' him for a few days.

"You see, I wanted t'be clean. I wanted t'be pure. My life was always filthy an' that's why my baby died. I know it's true. That's why . . ."

Those were the last words Kiki remembered before she passed out.

An hour later Kiki realized that she was staring at an empty chair. Mavis was gone. Or, maybe, she'd never been there. But it didn't matter much. Kiki had another idea.

TWENTY-FOUR

A s the hours go by Kiki stays where she is—settling into her chair. Settling into her new life. Into the whiskey and through the dread.

Home. That's what Mavis had said. Angels and home. The room is chill and silent. The bills just two weeks past due. They sit in a corner of her mind gathered with the stone boy and her father's hand soaked in her blood and feces. With big-bellied white men and all those years on the twenty-seventh floor. Sitting and answering phones and smiling.

All gone.

There's nothing she wants and nobody can hurt her.

"I got an angel for a good-luck charm," she says out loud. The studio is dark except for the light on the broken windowpane.

The knock comes just when she thinks it should. She rises up smiling at how light she is, at the ease of standing, at her hand brushing against the light switch. The room comes as no surprise. Her heart thrills—one hand on the pistol and the other on the doorknob.

Her finger is on the trigger in her purse but she knows she won't be shooting.

"Hi," Billy says. He's got on a raspberry-colored suit.

She feels a grin and says with her eyes, "Come in."

She throws Soupspoon's blankets on the floor and they sit.

"Whiskey?"

"Naw, uh-uh, thanks anyway."

"What do you want then?" She's talking like Hattie, feeling Hattie's big black body filling hers. Her skin tight and full with a black goddess.

"Soupspoon sleep here?" Billy slaps the cushions and she just has to kiss him. Her tongue pushing against his teeth for a moment and then past, inside his mouth. She licks the stale smoke from his last cigarette.

"Yeah," she answers.

"Where is he?" He's not afraid of her. He's not full of sad love and kisses like Randy. Billy is a meat eater. He's cold-blooded and fine. If he wanted to he could fly.

"Out," Kiki says, and then, "Talk to me."

"What you want me to say?"

"I don't care, just talk. Tell me something real, something about you."

"You nuts, girl?"

"Where you from?"

"I don't know. All over I guess."

She takes his hand and splays it against her chest.

"Come on, talk to me," she says.

For hours they say very little. Make hardly any noise at all. Billy moves like a snake; he's burrowing down, hugging her closer and closer still. She comes in pictures tinted in red. Her gun in Hattie's hand is fired and a horse falls dead to the ground. A thousand pounds of dead horseflesh falling hard. Sometimes he falls on top of her and sometimes she's thrown. Then she's riding again. First at a canter, then a gallup. At a full run she holds the gun to his ear. . . .

"What you thinkin' 'bout?" Billy asks.

"Have you ever killed anything big?"

"Caught a catfish weighed twenty-two pounds once."

"You got a pistol in your drawers."

She laughs when he reaches for the pants next to the bed.

"You ever kill anything big?" she asks again.

"With this gun?"

"Yes," she says clearly.

"How come?"

"I want to know what it feels like. What it feels like on the inside. Like when you fuck me like you do. Can you feel it like that? Does it hug you from the inside? Suck something out that you didn't even know was in there?"

"What's wrong with you, girl?"

Instead of answering, Kiki grabs for the pistol in Billy's hand. He jumps backward, away from her, and she laughs. A bright pain comes into the middle of her forehead and she laughs again.

"You scared I'ma take your gun, Billy?"

He doesn't answer, just sits there leaning back on the bed.

"I got my own gun, hon," she says softly, moving her hand down over his belly. "I don't need yours." Her hand goes all the way down to his balls. She squeezes, gets a rise. "You can keep your gun. Lie back now." Kiki's breath comes as clean and deep as it did in the woods with Hector. "I'm gonna get on top now, Billy. But you don't have to be scared because you got the gun."

"You are crazy," he says, but he doesn't fight her.

He doesn't let go of the gun either.

At Ayer's American Café, Soupspoon and Chevette sat across from each other at a rust-spotted chrome and torn red Naugahyde booth. Soupspoon had on another of his old suits. It was crayon-blue with navy lapels and buttons. Chevette wore a fake leopard leotard and purple velour hot pants with flat-soled shoes of matching material.

"You got a girlfriend, uncle?" Chevette had a chocolate milk shake. Soupspoon played with his oatmeal.

His chest ached and he could feel the outline of that blood-black splinter in his hip. He took two Percocets from his pocket and used the ice water to down them.

"You sick?"

"Naw. Ain't a thing wrong wit' me. Not a thing."

Chevette smiled. "I like you."

"I love you," Soupspoon said.

"So?" she asked.

"So what?"

Chevette's hand slid across the table right under his. "You got a girlfriend?"

"I got you."

"You wanna go up to Sono's? Her an' Gerry took the kids to the Bronx."

"She like Gerry?"

"I'ont know. I mean she think he kinda retarded-like but at least he like her kids an' stuff. You know the kinda mens Sono usually be wit' wanna lock the kids in the bathroom until he done his business."

"She gonna marry him?"

"I'ont know—they just gone to the zoo."

"But I mean is she gonna play like his girlfriend or she gonna be serious?"

Chevette smiled. "When the last time you been wit' a girl, uncle?"

"Last night."

"I mean before that."

Soupspoon thought of Mavis. He had a few women after her but she was the last one that he cared about.

"I don't know, baby. It's been so long I can't remember."

"You let Gerry get his own girl then," she said in a woman's voice.

Later that night, while Kiki lay in her bed begging Billy to fire his pistol, Soupspoon and Chevette reclined on her sofa fully clad. The babies were asleep and Sono and Gerry were in their own bed.

"Sumpin' wrong, uncle?" she whispered in his ear.

"Uh-uh." He'd just been half asleep dreaming about running fast down a creek bed. His heart had picked up its pace and he had the notion that if Chevette hadn't spoken it would have stopped from the exertion of the race.

"How come you don't wanna kiss me then?"

"You too young for me, girl." He put his arm around the back of her neck and she raised up to look down on him.

"I'm eighteen. I'm old enough."

"You need a young man to make you feel good. Shoo', I can hardly keep my attention."

She let her hand trail down along his chest.

"You do just fine," she said. "You know I don't like to do it all that much anyway. I just like to hug mostly. An' I like how you talk t'me."

"You like my sweet talk, huh? I guess I got a lotta practice at that."

"It's not what you say, uncle. Not all of it. But I could tell by the way you sound that you like me an' you need me t'feel sumpin'. I mean you like *me*. It's not like how I dress or if they's sumpin' special I gotta do. You like me like I am."

Soupspoon didn't have an answer to that. It was true. Chevette was the last woman in his life. He cried inside even at the thought of her.

"I need somebody t'be nice t'me, uncle," she said. "I don't need no boyfriend an' no babies. I just wanna start livin'. An' I been lonely up here in New York."

"I'll be your friend, Chevette. I don't have to kiss you to be here."

"You don't think I'm pretty no mo'?"

He kissed her in answer. She smiled and pulled on his ear.

T W E N T Y - F I V E

illy and Kiki went to Randy's table at about eleven the next morning. The long-haired boy was unpacking his magazines and comic books.

"Randy." Kiki took Billy by the hand and pulled him over to the table. "Billy wants to talk to you about something."

"Yeah?" Randy was looking at their hands.

"This gonna be somethin', brother." Billy disengaged from Kiki and offered the hand to Randy. "It's just a hunnert dollars at first but that's just the start."

"I don't know why you're talking to me. I don't have anything to do with it."

"But you see." Billy never lost his broken smile. "I'ma be like a agent. I'ma have me a lotta guys gettin' gigs an' like that. But Soupspoon gonna need a manager. Thatta be you. You see that way we got a business. What they call a network. We brothers be helpin' each other."

"I don't see it," Randy said.

"Oh come on, Randy," Kiki said, moving from Billy to him.

"It's a black thing, brother," Billy said. "We gots to get the money and the business on our side."

"I don't know what the hell you think, man!" Randy shouted. "But I'm not even a Negro. I'm Arab and South American."

"What?" Billy looked confused.

"You go on," Kiki said to Billy. "I'll talk to Randy."

"You like him?" Randy was sitting at the table in Kiki's apartment. She sat on the sink with her mane of red hair thrown back.

"What's wrong with you, Randy?"

"I asked you if you liked him."

"You don't own me, baby. I never said that to you. If I like somebody then that's my business. And the same goes for you."

"Well, then that's okay. I mean, I don't care what you do either." The tears in his eyes didn't sound in his words.

Kiki fought the urge to laugh.

"But I'm not gonna help him," Randy said.

"Why not? He hasn't done anything to you. All he is is a black man trying to make his way in this world. He wants to help all of us."

"What's he gonna do for you?"

"I just like to talk with him, that's all."

"About what?"

"Just talk, that's all. And I got fired and so Soupspoon gotta make some money till I get something else."

"Why'd they fire you?"

"I got mad at them. I got in late and they wanted to make a big deal out of it and so I got mad and they fired me."

Randy lowered his voice and asked, "Is it because of you drinking?"

"*No!* And you should mind your own fuckin' business, Randy!" Kiki flung herself off the sink. "What I do and don't do don't have a thing to do with you! If I wanna talk to somebody or if I want a drink it don't have a goddamned thing to do with you!" Kiki went up to him so that she was looking down over his head. "Do you understand that?"

"I gotta go," the boy whispered.

"You gotta help me, Randy."

"Help you what?"

"Soupspoon has to have some money."

"I could lend you the rent."

"Not for me, honey. I got five hundred and some dollars in the bank right now." Her voice softened then. "Soup's better now but I can't leave him until I know that he's gonna be okay."

"Leave where?"

Kiki sat down in Randy's lap and put her arm around his neck. "I've got to get out of here, honey. I've got to get out of New York."

"Why?"

"I'm finished with all of this now. I'm going back home. And I need you and Billy to make sure Soup's gonna be okay."

"I just can't see why you gotta leave. I thought you didn't even like your family."

"Will you help me?"

"What do you want me to do?"

"Just help me out. Help me. Go with me tonight and be there for Soup. He's better from the cancer now but he's still tired. He needs us to be there for him."

"Can I come back home with you after that?"

"I don't know," Kiki said, looking straight into his eyes, begging him silently not to ask again.

"Why not?"

"I don't know. You don't always come home with me."

"But I'm asking you. I want to come home with you."

"I told you I don't know, Randy."

He took her hands in his. "Please."

"Look. I'll tell you. Billy's probably gonna come home with me after. I mean it's no big thing, I just, I just want to spend a little time with him. That's all. But I could come over to your place tomorrow morning after he leaves—or after I leave him."

Randy didn't speak.

After three minutes had gone by, Kiki pulled her hands from his.

"Well?" she asked.

"I want you, Kiki."

"I'm not up for sale, Randy. I never promised you anything. I like you. I like Billy too. And right now I want to be with him." In-

side Kiki was laughing and ashamed. "But when I leave here it's
going to be alone."

"Can't I come with you?"

"No."

"Why not? I could transfer my credits. I could get a job."

"If I went with anybody it would be with Soup. And I can't go
with him because he's colored. And down where I'm going they
wouldn't stand for that."

"So?" The tears were coming down Randy's eggshell-brown
cheeks.

"You're black too, Randy."

"No. I'm . . ."

"Yes you are, honey. You're a Negro. Maybe not in your mind.
Maybe in your mind you're John Wayne. But back here in America
you're just another black man."

The tears were gone. When Randy stood up, Kiki almost fell
from his lap. When she moved to touch him he pushed her away.

"Don't you see how stupid this is, Randy? How somebody
white has to tell you what you are?"

"I've got to get back down to my store, Kiki. I've got to go."

"Don't be like that, honey. I'm your friend. I've always been
your friend."

"Uh-huh, I know. Listen, I'll try to get things together and get
down to the club tonight. But I just remembered that I got a test in
the morning. So I'll have to leave early and I won't be home in the
morning anyway."

Kiki leaned back against the sink.

Randy studied the floor.

"Okay," she said. "Whatever you say. If you could come for a
while that would be nice."

"I'll try."

Kiki didn't watch him leave. She was already thinking about
the night.

TWENTY-SIX

oupspoon didn't want to start
playing until after ten, but a
fight was close to breaking out
and he started early to keep the peace.

Life is pain say the great man.
Lord, the blues knows it's true.

Life is hard says the good man.
Ha! Bad man say it too.

If it wasn't for my good girl
I'd die from these ole breathin' blues.

Soupspoon and Chevette had made it to Rudy's place by eight-fif-
teen. Chevette wore a simple black dress with a string of plastic
pearls. Gerry was right behind them. He had on what was probably
his high school graduation suit. Sono poured them all drinks.

"Billy ain't around yet," she said with a sour twist to her
mouth.

"You like it?" Gerry asked.

"It's all right. I mean, it's fine," Soupspoon said.

Soupspoon looked around. Black men populated the stale
room. They smoked and drank and listened to the radio. Everybody
was waiting. Waiting, Soupspoon knew, for the big man to come

and the gambling to begin. But they were waiting for him too. They didn't know it but they were waiting for him to play his blues.

I had a six-shooter and a big black horse
posse close behind.

I had a pocket fulla gold
my best friend's girl beside.

You know they gonna catch up to me someday.
Baby, I really don't mind.

Sono had a beautiful face and what they used to call a generous figure. She put Gerry's arm around her waist and kissed his big neck.

Kiki came in with Billy Slick an hour later. She had her right arm around his waist and her left hand deep down in his front pocket. Her lipstick was askew, as was the hem of her short red dress.

Her eyes glittered with the spectacle of the room. Her mouth was moving but the words were silent. Her lipstick-smeared teeth formed a vengeful smile.

Soupspoon was tuning his guitar when Billy Slick, Kiki glued to his side, strutted up to the bar. He bumped into a short man who had broad shoulders. The short man dropped his drink.

"What's wit' you?" the powerful little man said.

"Forget it," was Billy's answer, his voice filled with swagger.

"What?" The shorter man shoved his hand into his pocket. With the other hand he grabbed Billy's arm. Billy tried to tug his way free but couldn't.

Men from both sides of the bar ran over to pull them apart. The smaller man was jumping and stamping to get free. Billy didn't do much but he had his hand in his pocket now too.

That's when Soupspoon began strumming and blowing on his harp. It was the musician's job to keep things happening and keep violence down to a minimum. The men slowly turned their attention to the music.

By the time Rudolph came in, the bar was in full party swing.

The big Hawaiian and Rudy hardly even got the attention of the crowd.

You know I seen the Lord an' he seen me.
Say, Soup, have you lost your mind?

He had twenty angels and a big white car
table set with crawfish pie.

He say this here could all be yours
just kiss these breathin' blues goodbye.

The liquor ran and the dice flew. Everybody who ever came to Rudy's nameless bar was there that night. Even Rudy couldn't help but grin. Money was passing from hand to hand and Soupspoon played his fingers ragged.

Whenever the music stopped the men drifted back over to the craps. But soon Soupspoon was playing again. His hip and breast ached with cancer. He felt light-headed with the pain of every human being who had ever died. There was more in his heart than he could sing. He could imagine words and notes that he couldn't reach. He wanted to play with Robert Johnson again.

Chevette stared at her boyfriend with fierce childish pride. Whenever he looked at her he smiled.

It was the music that filled her heart. Music that scurried like a scared dog cowering and dashing underfoot. It was a towering world of heavy blows that brought a song of yelps and cries; of a hard pounding heart.

"What am I doin' here?" the music whines.

"Nowhere, baby. I'm comin' home," the same song replies.

If you heard the words they made no sense. But if you felt the music it could make you cry.

There was no shame in that bastard cur, running between those legs with fear and desire. There were no words about how he got there; like a baby who tastes the cold air—he dances to the pain and howls.

By late evening Soupspoon felt as if he could fly. His fingers remembered the notes and chords on their own and nothing could bring him down. He filled four glass mugs with tips. His head was fevered and his feet were cold. Hardheaded gambling men had gone home to bring out their women so they could dance to celebrate their winnings or drink to forget their loss.

There was dancing and gambling and Soupspoon singing the blues. Billy sat with Kiki and Randy sat nearby.

When it got late, Kiki got rowdy and sick. Billy said that he'd take her home while Randy looked after Soupspoon.

"I'm gonna kill him," Kiki said over and over. She said it to the taxi driver and to half the people in the bar. In the hall of her floor she pulled out the .32 Hattie had given her.

"Put that thing away!" Billy wrenched the gun from her hand.

"Ow!" she cried. "You hurt!"

"I'm going to kill him," Kiki said. Billy had her shoes off. She was a wreck at the edge of the bed.

"You better wait till tomorrow."

"Where's my gun?"

"It's over on the table, but I got the bullets though."

"That's okay. I got more. I got more than enough."

TWENTY-SEVEN

I t was late in the morning and Soupspoon was asleep on Sono's couch. He could hear Hamela playing and Georgie's scream. If he didn't move, nothing hurt, and so he lay there, not awake, breathing fast like a kitten because he couldn't seem to take a deep breath.

Then there was a loud noise and a man shouting, "You ain't gonna shame me, you little whore!"

Soupspoon opened his eyes to see a huge man batter through the door. Chevette tried to run from the man but he caught her by the arm and slapped her one, two, three times.

Soupspoon jumped up off the couch but fell to the floor. "Leggo her!" he shouted.

Right then Gerry ran in from the bedroom, naked and holding a pair of pants over his crotch.

"Get out!" Sono cried, coming in fast behind Gerry. Gerry ran ahead, swinging his fist, but missed. The man caught Gerry by the wrist, releasing Chevette. Gerry had one more punch in him, though. He swung his left arm upward, pulling the man down with his weight, and connected with a shocking blow to Willy's face.

"Fuckin' shit!" Willy pulled Gerry up by the arm and gave the boy a savage uppercut to the gut.

Gerry vomited on Willy's legs.

"Goddamn shit!" Willy pushed Gerry back two steps and hit

the doddering naked boy twice in the head. Gerry didn't seem bothered by the blows. He kept holding his stomach, white liquid dribbling out between his lips.

Soupspoon was trying to get up but his hip wouldn't release. He looked for something to throw at Willy's head but all he could reach was cushions.

Willy reared back to throw another blow but stopped suddenly and brought his hands to his head. "Oh!" he moaned and went down on both knees.

Gerry was down on his knees by then too, blood and vomit dripping from his face. They faced each other like exotic priests in the middle of a desperate ritual.

Sono came up then and started hitting Willy again with the heavy saucepan.

"Mothahfuckah! Mothahfuckah!" the wild girl screamed. When she hit Willy in the head he bellowed like bull at the slaughter. Soupspoon saw Hamela take little George and hug him to her bird chest. Her eyes were big but she wasn't crying.

"Mothahfuckah!" Sono yelled again. Chevette was holding Gerry. Willy crawled from the room trying to ward off the saucepan.

Sono slammed the broken door behind him and turned to see her home.

Soupspoon saw what her mad eye saw. All the furniture turned over, the baby crying. Gerry was on his back with one hand trying to cover his little bell-shaped cock.

Chevette took Sono and the kids into the other room. Then she came back for Gerry. At last she helped her boyfriend back up on the couch.

"You okay, uncle?"

"My legs wouldn't take me there."

By afternoon they had the house back together. The story in the building was that Chevette's aunt had kicked Willy out because that way she figured Chevette would come back. What she was really afraid of, Chevette said, was that her sister would find out and stop sending money to take care of her. Willy had come to get his revenge and to drag Chevette back so that Vella would take him back.

He got his wish. Vella wound up taking Willy to the emergency room for a broken jaw.

"His jaw was broke in three places," Chevette said.

Gerry decided to take the whole family out to his mother's home in Flatbush. "We got a lotta room out there," he said. Both of his eyes were swollen and his stomach still hurt.

"What your momma gonna say 'bout me'n these kids?" Sono asked. Gerry was only twenty and hadn't told his mother about his Manhattan girlfriend.

"What she gonna say?" he declared. "I pay for everything with my loans and my library job—and you need the help."

Sono showed a smile that let you know what she was like when her load was lightened. She went right to work packing.

Soupspoon gave all of his salary and tip money to Chevette.

"You go on with'em," he said. "Use that money to buy food."

"Cain't I come home wichyou, Uncle?"

"I gotta have my own place 'fore you could do that. You go on an' help Sono and them. I'ma stay here an' try t'play at Rudy's again."

He took Gerry to the side while Sono and Chevette got the kids ready.

"Take these for me, Gerry," Soupspoon said. He handed Gerry four cassette tapes that he'd been carrying around in his guitar case.

"What's this?" Gerry asked.

"It's everything I remember. It's some songs and a lotta stories about the days when I'as comin' up. I got a man's address written down right here. He writes about the blues. You call'im an' tell'im you wanna write down what I said. You tell'im you wanna write a history article about me."

"Wow. Absolutely, Mr. Wise."

It took Soupspoon half an hour to walk back to Kiki's and another half an hour to make it up the stairs. When he got there he found Kiki and Billy together. They were making out on his couch.

"We wondered when you was gonna come, man," Billy said.

Kiki came up to him with a worried look in her bloodshot eyes. "You okay, Soup?"

"Yeah, 'course I am. It's you that's three shades'a pale."

"You sure?"

"I'm fine, fine. Just a little tired is all."

Billy plugged in the phone and called Rudy, who was happy to hear that Soupspoon wanted to play again.

"I need some sleep if I'm gonna play, though," the old man said. He laid down on Kiki's bed, no pillow at his head and his hands stretched out straight at his side. His fingers picked and jumped on the blankets and his eyeballs rolled behind the lids.

He imagined what being dead would be like. The cool tickle of stale coffin air and darkness so deep that even the sun couldn't reach it. All around the murmur of the dead. Young people and old remembering their lives just the way they happened.

"I stoled Mr. Onceit's chickens an' lawd was he mad! Man like to busta gut over three scrawny chickens. You know life mean more than some scrawny chickens."

"Will you marry me, Elsie B.?"

"Nigger! Strip down an' prove it that you ain't got my nickel!"

Then a scatter of baby talk and the sound of worms. Colors don't mean a damn thing if you're dead. No blue, no red. You remember what people were; not what they looked like exactly but if they were big then you remember big and if they were loving and sexy you remember holding them, rolling with them.

Evil brings about hot spots and prickles.

But it's all just a dream. Day in and day out all the things that ever happened, just like they happened. Never the littlest change. Because when you die everything is sealed. It's like you're asleep and can't wake up. Because if you could wake up you would change it. Not go down that road or maybe call up Ruby and Inez and tell them how much you loved them. If you could wake up.

". . . wake him up. We gotta get down there soon."

"But he looks sick." Kiki's talking. "Look how he's moving."

"He looks sick."

But not dead. Not yet.

Robert Johnson with his evil eye looking around the crowd for a woman. His fingers so tight that they could make music without strings. Music in his shoulders and down in his feet. Words that rhyme with the ache in your bones and music so right that it's more like rain than notes; more like a woman's call than need. Not that pretty even stuff that they box in radios and stereos. Not even something that you can catch in a beat. It's the earth moving and babies looking from side to side.

"Soupspoon?"

The people all broke out talking after Bobby Grand died. He wanted to hear them because death and music are the same things. Hot baby with his heart thumping starts it all out. Hollering rhythm.

"Soupspoon? Are you awake, honey?"

"Look at how he's jerkin' around."

The walking and running and praying for rain. And all it does is wash away your feet in the mud.

"They all gone soon enough. You didn't have to worry."

"What, honey?" Kiki asks.

"Blues is the fish and the fisherman is what plays'em."

"What, man?" Billy asks.

"I got a rowboat fulla blues." Soupspoon opened his eyes then. He saw his friends and thought that they were the most beautiful sight in the world. His heart was running fast.

"If the blues was fish and I was on the blue sea. I'd have a rowboat fulla blues wish they could swim away from me."

"You gonna sing that tonight?" Billy asked. He gave Soupspoon his hand and helped him upright.

"If I live that long."

Billy and Soupspoon went together down to the club. Billy was full of blustery con man chatter, the kind of talk men use to fool themselves.

Soupspoon limped and ached, hot and ragged embers embed-
ded in his body. He needed to clear his throat but waited until he
was on his stool at Rudy's to do it.

He didn't play dance tunes or love songs that night. He played
"A Long Time Down the Line, "Satan Gave Me Back My Soul,"
"One Last Bullet," and "Shine Whiskey Mind."

Nobody danced, but they did laugh. Soupspoon didn't even get
up to go to the toilet. He was working like a sharecropper; every
step he took put him another step behind. But he was playing the
music right for one time in his life. He ordered straight whiskey and
told Sono to keep it topped off.

"My ribs," he hollered, "is the jailhouse. The blues is my heart."

Kiki came late with Randy. She was drunk to begin with. As the
night wore on she turned mean. If a man looked at her she'd call
him out for his disrespect. And if Randy tried to stop her she'd turn
on him with vicious anger. But it wasn't until she grabbed a jolly
girl named Tiffany by the hair for laughing that Rudolph said she
had to go.

Billy and Randy grabbed Kiki from either side and dragged her
from the nameless bar.

"I'll come back to get you," Randy whispered to Soupspoon.

"I'll be waitin'," the guitar man replied.

"Motherfuckin' cocksuckin' bastards!" she yelled.

"Hey!" the cab driver, a small-framed mustachioed man, said.
"Keep the cursing down."

"Just drive, man," Billy said.

"Does she wanna go with you?" the cab driver asked.

"Motherfucker." Kiki pronounced the words perfectly.

"She drunk, man. All we wanna do is take her home."

"I'll kick your fuckin' ass! I'll bite off your goddamned dick!"

The three of them sat on the curb in front of the Beldin Arms. Kiki
started crying when she realized that the men weren't going to let
her go.

"Please," she sobbed. "Please let me go."

A car full of three burly white youths stopped at one point. "What the fuck you guys doin' to her?" the front passenger said.

"What fuckin' difference it make to you, paddy-boy?" Kiki yelled back.

"I'm sorry, Randy," Kiki said as they went up the stairs. Billy was with them.

When they reached Kiki's floor, Randy asked, "You got your keys, Kiki?"

He remembered that days later in the hospital room. The last words he said to Kiki: "You got your keys, Kiki?" And then a sound something like wind but really the shuffle of rubber soles on the granite flooring. A big man with oily hair. Kiki's last words to him—"Oh no!"—sounding completely sober, and then the knife.

He did right to rush the big white man with the knife in his hand. Randy pushed Kiki back. The knife didn't feel like anything going in but then there was pain in a place that Randy wanted to tear out of his body. "Nigger!" the white man muttered. Their bodies came together except where the knife was. Their lips touched, men's kiss. And the knife came out and went in again.

"In and out," the ambulance driver had said. "He's lucky JD didn't twist it."

JD. John Doe at Mercy. The bright red lights and the lifejacket that they inflated around him. Remembering Kiki's scream and weakness in his knees that he tried to fight. He saw the big man catch Kiki by the throat and lift her. He saw the knife come up and then Billy from behind the red hair. But all Billy got for his trouble was an elbow in the throat. He went down gagging and coughing. Then a bright star blossomed from Kiki's handbag. Randy remembered going down sideways and the white man saying "Huh?" before dropping Kiki and running down the stairs.

Kiki didn't think at all. She saw the knife and went straight for her gun. He grabbed her just as her hand closed on the butt. Then he slowed down for a moment to hit Billy—that was his downfall. Without taking the pistol out of the purse Kiki shot Fez in the neck.

He put his hand somewhere below his left ear and turned to run. He pushed Billy down over Randy and took the stairs five at a time.

It was the running that made Kiki act. She followed after Fez, shooting. The first shot caught him in the leg. It didn't stop him from running, though. The next shot missed. Kiki stopped at the third floor and shot over the banister, hitting Fez in the arm.

Maybe Fez thought it was a four-shooter. He made his stand on the second floor. He held the knife high above his head and lurched forward on his wounded leg.

"If a wild animal charge you," Hester Grule, the crazy cousin in Hollywood, had always said, "don't lose your head. Take time and hit'em in the big part'a their body. Aim! Don't shoot wild, 'cause then he get ya. Wild animal want blood." And the wildest animal, Kiki knew, was man.

She went down on one knee again and shot Fez right in the center of his blue shirt. She went up high for the last shot and made a spot slightly darker than the white man's skin just above his left eye. Fez fell on top of Kiki. The knife skittered on the stairs.

Kiki rolled the dead man over and went through his pockets as fast as she could. There was a stack of new bills, probably from a cash machine, and a wallet. Kiki took everything and jumped up over the body and down the remaining stairs. Most of the blood was on her purple jacket, so she dropped that into a city trash can on the corner. But then she remembered Randy and Billy in a heap at the top of the stairs. From a pay phone she called 911 but from the sounds of sirens everywhere she knew that they were already on their way.

She couldn't remember if there had been anybody in the hallway or on the street when she'd come out with the pistol showing through her ruined handbag.

She dropped the pistol and empty purse down a sewage drain and made for the subway.

She took a subway to the Port Authority and an early bus to Hoboken.

The morning paper said that Randall Chesterton was in stable condition and that, after being held overnight, William Hurdy had been released as a suspect.

That was the last she ever heard about either of them. And, though she still thinks about Soupspoon from time to time, she never found out about him after that last night either.

She fled to Atlanta and then to Chattanooga. She lived for three years in New Orleans with a gambler named Arcady. She stole his pistol one night and boarded a Greyhound to Hogston, Arkansas.

She came to the house in the early morning. There was dew on the magnolias and the bees were still asleep

Charla Wilson, a straw-headed old white woman who was a stranger to Kiki, answered the door. Kiki took her hand out of her purse and asked about her parents.

"Waters? Child," she said sadly. "They been gone for six years now. First him of cancer in the liver and then her one month later— weak heart, they said. I'm so sorry."

There wasn't a will. Waters Photographic Inc. had twenty-seven stores that the family lawyer had run while waiting for Kiki's return. Everything was hers. The house that Charla Wilson rented, a Jaguar car, and a chest full of silver coins impressed with the image of her father's profile.

Everybody remembered her family. Complete strangers told her stories about her childhood that she had no memory of.

She went to Hattie's house and found her old nursemaid still there. She didn't even look much older, but Kiki knew that she had to be over seventy.

"Hector?" Hattie said. "He died twelve years ago last March. Heart just stopped one day while he was restin' under that ole avocado tree'a his."

It nearly broke Kiki's heart when the old woman refused to come live in the big house with her.

"I like my own rooms, child," she said. "But you could come on out an' visit whenever you want."

She ran into Brewster Collins in town the first Saturday she was back. He had put on a big belly and worked for an oil delivery company that was based in Little Rock. They went out that night. Before sunup Kiki was asking him to bite her thigh.

They were married two weeks later.

Kiki Collins bought her husband the woodmill he'd always wanted, had four kids, and moved into an even bigger house surrounded by magnolia trees. She kept bees out behind the garage and gave up liquor.

Her only vice was speeding on the interstate in the afternoons. When the policemen took her license and went back to call it in there was a wild glee alive in her. Every time they checked her name she wondered if the warrant had made its way down south.

TWENTY-EIGHT

At two a.m. Soupspoon finished his last set. Neither Billy nor Randy had come back so Rudy gave Soup the hundred dollars for that night's work.

"You're worth every goddamned dime," the big gambler said as he shook Atwater's hand. "You maybe could come twice a week."

"Yeah. I'd like that." Soupspoon's head felt light and hot. He was worried about Kiki and there was a swarm of fire ants crawling in his chest.

There was a full moon out and lots of people in their cars. The ache in his chest went up into his shoulder and down into his back.

He made it three blocks before he had to stop. He grabbed onto the side of a building. Suddenly the pain was gone. There was a feeling of warmth all around his head and the sound of all the guitar music he'd played that night. The notes were too long and ill-fitted. It wasn't the neat little tunes he played so well. It was dark and deep music—like the ocean. It was so beautiful but it wasn't his.

He was sprawled out on his back in the early morning before the police came. They put him in a ward full of men in hospital beds. He was thirsty but he couldn't talk.

Nurses came and doctors too. But nobody Soupspoon recognized found him in his deathbed. They put needles in his arm and smiled at or ignored him. He was mute again. The infection back in his throat from hours on cold stone.

"Heart attack," some woman's voice said. Through the dark Soupspoon imagined that she was talking about him. Two wards down, Randy lay with stab wounds to his stomach. At Fourteenth Street and Avenue A, Mavis Spivey was changing a 100-watt bulb.

Heart attack. Something white people died of when he was a boy. Negroes died from gunshot and knife wounds, pneumonia and fever. Negroes died from broken hearts and alcohol but not from no weak heart. Negroes had strong hearts and stronger backs. They carried the whole world on their shoulders and when they sighed it came out blues.

In the late night, in the dark room where red and blue lights winked and old men smelled and died. In the late night Soupspoon saw a dark shadow of a man cross the room and pull a chair up beside him.

"Randy?"

But when the young man lit his cigarette Soupspoon could see RL's evil, handsome face in the flame. Even after he blew out the match his face stayed alight. He smiled but his cold eyes told Atwater that he was finally going to die.

RL didn't say anything, but that didn't surprise Soupspoon. He knew that ghosts couldn't talk like men anymore. All they do is to haunt you with what they once looked like.

The tobacco smelled good. Really good. He felt a chill pass through his body and thought, *Chilly death pass through me like a rill through the woods, like maybe I'ma wake up and all this I been goin' through is just a dream. The kinda dream that somebody like RL would have. A evil long-lastin' dream about all the bad things could happen here.*

"Is that what you tellin' me?" Soupspoon asked. He didn't believe that he could think up such thing. Life was all he knew. RL was the one knew what came after. He could see it with his dead eye. The eye looking at Soupspoon right then.

Then pain sang through the old man's bones. It was loud and

pure. Soupspoon felt himself open wide. He could see everything, even in the dark. He could hear the soft humming of hospital machines and the hushed conversation of the two nurses in the hall, he could hear the roaches scuttling under his bed and the earth settling underground. His hands opened wide and his toes splayed out. He shit and pissed in a hard stream. He opened his mouth wide and stuck out his tongue. The bright pain turned into a light that burned through everything. He could see things but he didn't understand what they were. He didn't care though. The pain was gone and all he had left was the light. He raised up from the bed a few inches and then suddenly fell back. The light flicked on and off. *I'm dead,* went through Soupspoon's mind. The light went down and down. He marked the darkness, an old fisherman now well past sunset at the edge of the sea.

When the room was black he remembered who he was in a spiraling echo that played itself out.